T0162576

THE DAWN
OF TIME TRAVEL

THE DAWN
OF TIME TRAVEL

Authored by Richard Tiernan

iUniverse, Inc.
Bloomington

THE DAWN OF TIME TRAVEL

Copyright © 2011 by Richard Tiernan

All rights reserved. No part of this book may be used or reproduced by any means, graphic, electronic, or mechanical, including photocopying, recording, taping or by any information storage retrieval system without the written permission of the publisher except in the case of brief quotations embodied in critical articles and reviews.

iUniverse books may be ordered through booksellers or by contacting:

iUniverse
1663 Liberty Drive
Bloomington, IN 47403
www.iuniverse.com
1-800-Authors (1-800-288-4677)

Because of the dynamic nature of the Internet, any web addresses or links contained in this book may have changed since publication and may no longer be valid. The views expressed in this work are solely those of the author and do not necessarily reflect the views of the publisher, and the publisher hereby disclaims any responsibility for them.

Any people depicted in stock imagery provided by Thinkstock are models, and such images are being used for illustrative purposes only.

Certain stock imagery © Thinkstock.

ISBN: 978-1-4620-2990-7 (sc)
ISBN: 978-1-4620-2991-4 (e)

Printed in the United States of America

iUniverse rev. date: 07/21/2011

This book is dedicated to my uncle, Jack Spencer, who was a pilot in World War II; to my parents; my wife, Mary; and to the McDermott Family of Rochester, N.Y.

CHAPTER 1

In a blink of an eye, Jack Spencer found himself outside, in a cold wilderness, not at all where he had expected to be. Something must have gone drastically wrong.

Spencer arrived in the river valley in the winter. He used all his army survival skills just to stay alive. His Army Rangers training had taught him to come prepared for anything. He had brought along a small first aid kit, a Swiss Army knife, a lighter, some fishing line, two hooks, and his Browning automatic with several clips of extra ammunition.

But when Jack arrived in his Armani suit, white shirt, tie, and leather shoes, he was far from being dressed for the elements. He pulled up the collar of his suit coat and used his tie as a headband to keep his forehead and ears warm. This made the cold air almost bearable in the afternoon sun, but Jack knew he would need to do more than this to survive the possibly freezing night.

His first priority would be to keep warm. So Jack searched the area until he found a rock overhang surrounded by pine trees at the base of the mountain. The site was sheltered from the wind and snow, making it seem at least ten degrees warmer. He gathered up some dry branches and made a large fire against the rock wall base of the mountain. The radiation from the rock wall created a wave of heat about ten feet from the fire. Jack slept on the ground by the fire his first night, spending a good part of the night keeping the fire going to stay warm.

While awake during the night, he planned what he would do the next day. Food and a better shelter would be his next priority.

The warmth of the sun brought Jack awake. Already ten o'clock by his watch, not that time mattered very much in his new surroundings, he wondered how close he had come to freezing to death before the sun warmed his body after the fire burned out in the early morning hours.

Jack's stomach growled. He thought to himself, 'Do I hunt or fish'? Remembering how long it sometimes takes to catch a fish, he decided to hunt. Walking through the trees, Jack saw rabbit tracks in the snow. He followed the tracks for some distance until he saw a rabbit. Although an ex-Army Ranger who seldom missed at close range, his stomach told him not to miss. His shot found its target and Jack carried his meal back to the camp. He skinned the rabbit, cooked the meat on a sharpened stick over fire, and filled his empty stomach. The rabbit's skin was staked out in the sun to later be made into a winter hat.

After his meal, Jack gathered rocks, and logs from fallen trees, and made a lean-to fort at the base of the mountain. He positioned the fort so the open side faced the rock wall and the fire. This effort consumed the remainder of the daylight, but Jack was rewarded with a warmer night's sleep his second night in the river valley.

Jack spent the next seven days hunting and fishing. The river, only about a quarter mile away, providing most of his nourishment. He shot a deer by the river's edge during the early morning hours of the third day. The deer provided meat and some new clothing. Jack wrapped deerskin around his shoes and pant legs, up to his knees. This made walking through the snow and ice more bearable.

Jack had not seen any sign of another human being and wondered just where the heck he was. Then late one afternoon, as he cooked a fish over his campfire, Jack thought he felt the presence of someone watching him. He saw shadows moving through the trees. The shadows seemed to shift and then stop. He wondered if his eyes were playing tricks on him until he heard a dry tree branch crack. He hollered, "Who's there?" The shadows vanished. That night, Jack kept the fire going and didn't sleep. He kept his automatic by his side all night, thinking, 'I'm not alone'.

CHAPTER 2

Tommy had been Ricky's friend since he could remember. The two boys had just finished the sixth grade and were off for the summer. It was July 15, 2000, a Saturday morning, and they were on their way to the river to fish and enjoy the beautiful day.

Ricky said, "I've got peanut butter and jelly sandwiches. What'd you bring?"

"Ham and cheese."

"Have you got enough worms this time?"

"Of course. Do you think I am stupid or something? Look at the fishing knife my dad gave me for getting a good report card."

Ricky looked at the knife, handed it back to Tommy, and said, "That's a cool knife."

The two boys reached the river and fished for an hour or so in their favorite spot. Not getting any bites, They decided to move farther down the river. The boys walked for about ten minutes along the river's edge until they came upon a location where the river was about two hundred feet wide. They had never fished in this area before and had hopes of catching a big one here.

After getting his bait set up, Tommy cast out into the water and let his red and white bobber float down stream a bit. Ricky soon did the same. The boys stood on the bank of the river about twenty feet apart so they wouldn't be hitting each other. Tommy caught the first fish, a small one that he threw back. Tommy was half Native American and his father had taught him from an early age to respect the earth and everything on it. Ricky had picked up on this good attitude towards nature through his friendship with Tommy.

Ricky soon hooked into a big fish and was struggling to land it. Tommy put down his rod and came over to lend a hand if needed. Ricky waded out into the shallow water to grab his fish and fell over something in the water. He dropped his pole and the fish got away. Tommy looked at Ricky covered with water and sand and started laughing. Ricky, angry at first, smiled and picked up the object that caused him to trip. He put it over his head and was about to throw it at Tommy when he saw the expression on Tommy's face turn from a smile to a gasp. Ricky looked at the object in his hands and let it fall back into the shallow water. It was a skull.

Both boys looked at each other for a brief moment and shrieked, "Let's get the hell out of here!" They hastily picked up their gear and high-tailed it, running until out of breath.

When they stopped to gain their breath, Tommy asked, "What are we gonna do?"

"I don't know," Ricky said, "but I think we better tell somebody."

"What if that person was murdered and the body thrown in the river to hide it?"

"Yeah, and what if the killer is still around here?"

"Yeah, we better tell somebody."

They went straight to Ricky's house where they found his mom in the kitchen. They both started talking at once.

"Okay," his mother said, "one at a time. What happened?"

Ricky took a breath of air and said, "We were fishing along the river, except this time we went farther downstream than we usually do. I was pulling in a really big fish, when I fell over a human skull in the shallow water."

"How do you know it was a human skull?" his mother asked.

"Because it looked like a human skull. I know a human skull when I see one, but I've never held one in my hands. It scared the piss out of me."

"Don't use that kind of language in this house young man. I'd better call the Sheriff."

She picked up her phone and punched 911.

"Sheriff's office, Deputy Packard, what can I do to help you?"

"This is Mrs. Johnson, at 121 Blueberry Street. My son and his friend were fishing along the Black River today and say they found a human skull."

"We did, Mom."

"Be quiet!" she said.

Deputy Packard said, "I'll send a car to your home right away. Have the boys stay there to talk to the deputies."

"Thank you," she said, and hung up.

"A sheriff's car will be coming over soon. You better call your mom, Tommy, and let her know what's going on."

"Okay."

"And you better change into some dry clothes, Ricky, before the Sheriff gets here."

"Okay, but please call me Rick in front of my friends and the Sheriff."

About ten minutes later, the Sheriff's car turned into their driveway. Deputies Ryan and Brown came to the front door and introduced themselves. "What's this about finding a human skull along the Black River?"

"Yeah. We found a skull."

"And what's your name?"

"Rick Johnson, and my friend's name is Tommy Littlefield."

"Just where did you find this skull?"

"We were fishing on the other side of the river."

"You mean on the Indian reservation side of the river? Only Indians and people with special permission are allowed to fish there."

"We know. Tommy's mom and dad live on the reservation and I am his friend, aren't I, Tommy?"

"Sure. We fish there all the time, but we never fished that far down stream before."

"Can you take us to the exact spot where you found the skull?"

"Sure. It's all right, isn't it, Mom?"

"Yeah, sure, Ricky; I mean Rick. I think I'll call your father and your family too, Tommy, and let 'em know what's going on."

"Okay," said Rick. "Well, let's go!"

It took the deputies and the boys only five minutes in the sheriff's car to get to the point where they needed to go on foot. It then took another twenty-five minutes to reach the place where the boys found the skull. When they arrived, Deputy Ryan had the boys repeat, for the sake of clarity, exactly what happened that morning.

After telling his story to the deputies, Ricky pointed to the skull in the water. Only a small portion of the skull was visible. Deputy Ryan took off his shoes, socks, and rolled up his pants. He waded out into the water and carefully picked up the skull.

"It sure looks like a human skull to me. There's a large crack in the back of the skull. This person might have been murdered." Deputy Ryan replaced the skull in the water as he found it. Then feeling the sandy river bottom with his feet, Ryan said, "I think there are more bones here."

Brown helped Ryan look for more bones in the soft sand of the shallow water. As the two boys looked on, more bones were found. They decided to leave the bones as they were in the water. They then staked off the site for about ten yards in all directions with traditional yellow tape.

By late afternoon, there were two more deputies, Joe Bianco from the coroner's office, and detective Frank McDermott from the sheriff's office. The boy's fathers were also present at what had become a possible crime scene.

CHAPTER 3

Frank McDermott and Joe Bianco had been friends for years. Joe, the coroner for the town of Black River, while good at his job, did not have as many opportunities to use his talents as a big city coroner would. He was of moderate build, in his mid forties, and had thinning black hair with a circular bald spot at the back of his head.

Frank had worked his way up from deputy to detective after twenty years with the sheriff's office and night school studying criminology. He had wanted to be a detective from the time he read his first Sherlock Holmes novel. Even now, he read everything he could get his hands on about the latest police techniques and the science of criminology.

When Frank arrived at the site, he questioned Ricky and Tommy until satisfied they could tell him no more about what they had found. He had the deputies expand the original marked-off area and then enlisted everyone to begin an inch-by-inch search of the area noting where all objects were found.

Joe Bianco took pictures of the bones and the area in the water relative to the land where the bones were found. Several more bones turned up.

Frank went over to Joe Bianco who was looking at the skull, and asked him what he thought.

"I'm not sure, Frank. This one has been in the water for some time. It's too early for me to make any judgments. There's a large crack in the back of the skull. I want to take the bones back to the lab and study them a bit."

"Okay, Joe, but let me know as soon as you have something. I'll send Harry Packard over to work with you to make an artist's drawing of the person from the skull. We can run it through missing persons to try and get a match. If there's a murderer running around our little corner of the earth, I want to get him off the streets as soon as possible."

"Sure, Frank, but an artist's sketch of this one will take a while to come up with."

"Packard is one of the best, Joe."

"I know, Frank. I can't believe he hasn't been snatched up by one of the big cities by now."

"He probably will be some day. But until he is we're lucky to have him working for us."

"I'll get right on it."

"Thanks, Joe."

Frank then talked to Tommy's father, the son of the chief of the Indian reservation. They had grown up together and had played football on their high school team. George Littlefield was five-foot-ten and about two hundred and twenty five pounds.

"You still look like a running back, George."

"How've you been, Frank?"

"Just fine. Your boy and the Johnson kid sure stumbled over one this time."

"Literally."

"He's a good boy, George. You can be proud of him."

"You bet I am. That boy is going to college if I can swing it."

"Is he good in school?"

"He gets all As. He's only ten, but he can throw a football farther than I could at his age."

"That's great, George."

George called the boys over to meet Frank. "Boys, I'd like you to meet an old friend of mine, Frank McDermott."

Tommy smiled and said, "I've heard my dad talk about how you and he played football together."

"Yeah. Your dad was better than I was, though. He was the real team hero. I'm sorry I put you boys through so many questions."

"Oh, that's okay, Mr. McDermott," Tommy said. "Do you think this person could have been murdered?"

"Well, it could be a murder or just a simple drowning of a fisherman. We probably won't know for some time, but we wouldn't even have a case to investigate if it wasn't for the smart reactions of you boys to tell someone what you found. It'll be getting dark in about a half-hour. We better get back to the road."

As they walked, George and Frank continued their conversation. "You know, Frank, this is reservation land. I'll need to talk to my father and the tribal elders to let 'em know what's going on."

"Sure, George. I expected you'd want to do that. I know your roots are deeply tied to this area."

"As I've mentioned to you before, Frank, my people have been here for thousands of years. Their spirits guide us in this life. My father believes he's given the power to guide our people through these spirits. I'll talk to him tonight."

"George, when it comes to a possible murder investigation, I'll take all the help I can get. I'll keep in touch with you and let you know what we find out. In the mean time I gotta have the coroner's office examine the bones."

"Okay, Frank. Good to see you again."

As Frank drove back to the office, he remembered how much he enjoyed playing on the reservation with George as a boy. He remembered sleeping in a tepee just like the Indians did. They would hunt rabbits with bows and arrows. Frank remembered actually killing his first rabbit and learning how to skin and cook it. George had learned the Indian skills from boyhood and taught Frank many of them.

When they later played football in high school, Frank, the quarterback and George, the halfback made many a touchdown together simply because they intuitively knew each other's moves.

Back at headquarters, Frank stopped into Sheriff Dave Tucker's office. Tucker, a good administrator, was tall and lean, in his mid fifties, with gray hair. The two men had worked closely together for many years and were good friends. Frank filled Dave in on what had transpired and what he planned to do next. Dave nodded his head in agreement, smiled and said, "Come with me. I want to introduce you to the new girl we've been expecting." Frank followed Dave to another office where a young woman in a tan, pants suit was busy at a desk unpacking her things. Dave introduced Frank to Mary Webber.

Mary, a black haired beauty of medium height, was in her late thirties.

"Miss Mary Webber, this is detective Frank McDermott."

"Nice to meet you, Mr. McDermott."

"Call me Frank."

"You can call me Miss Webber if you please."

Dave said, "Miss Webber graduated top of her class from Georgetown University, and has been working with the FBI ever since. She's got a lot of expertise in the area of computers. I hope to bring this office into the twenty-first century."

"Well, I'll look forward to that, Miss Webber," Frank said. "What brings a FBI specialist to a small town like Black River?"

"I was raised here, actually. My father passed away recently, and my mom, being alone, suggested I live here with her for a while. The FBI gave me a leave of absence, rather than releasing me, so that I might decide within a year what I want to do. This way I get to stay with my mom and visit with my old friends."

"I take it you're not married then."

"That's right. Is there any other personal information you want to ask me, Mr. McDermott?"

"I'm sorry, Miss Webber. It isn't every day we get a FBI computer specialist to work with, and especially one as good looking as you are."

Mary blushed, turned to Dave Tucker and asked when she could expect the special computer she requested the first hour she was in the sheriff's office.

"We'll get it as soon as we are able, Miss Webber," was Dave's reply. "I think we can get it for you in a day or two."

"And I need unlimited Internet access."

"We'll get whatever you require. I meant what I said about giving you a free reign to bring this department into the next century."

"I'm on my way home, Miss Webber," Frank said. "Can I give you a lift home?"

"No thank you. I have my own car, Mr. McDermott."

"Well, then see you tomorrow."

Frank had not met any girl that had stirred him like Mary Webber since he lost his wife. The last girl he called "good looking" was his wife. He wondered what got into him to say that to another woman at this point in his life. When his wife died of cancer a year and a half ago, he had planned to stay a bachelor. As Frank drove home, he thought of his wife and their wonderful twenty years together. As he walked through the front door and was greeted by the silence of an empty house, he thought to himself: 'I'm only forty-two. I still have my life ahead of me. Maybe I'll consider dating again.'

CHAPTER 4

The next day, Frank was at work before seven thirty, eager to get to work on his possible murder case. He also wanted to be there when Mary came to work to talk to her. Frank met with Harry Packard soon after Harry came in.

Harry, now twenty-five, had worked for the department since high school. He was the kind of kid who drew the faces of the teacher or his classmates while only half listening to his teacher. He had a natural talent for drawing people and things, especially faces.

When Harry first came into the sheriff's office looking for a job, Dave Tucker asked Harry what he felt he could do for the office. Harry said he wanted to be a sheriff's deputy and to aid the office somehow with his drawing skills. To demonstrate his drawing skills, Harry then asked Dave to bring someone into the office for one minute, no longer. So Dave brought Frank McDermott into the office and introduced him. He abruptly asked Frank to leave the office after only a minute. Harry spent the next five minutes sketching Frank's face.

When Dave and Frank saw the results, Frank said, "I think you had better hire 'em, Dave."

Dave hired Harry and sent him to cadet school. When Harry started with the sheriff's office, Frank mentored him, teaching him everything he knew about being a good deputy and about criminology in general. They became close friends. He was now a deputy sheriff and sketch artist for the sheriff's office.

Frank filled in Harry about the skull and the possible murder investigation, and asked him to go over to the coroner's office with his sketchpad and work with Joe Bianco.

When Mary Webber came into work at eight o'clock, Frank was quick to say, "Good morning Miss Webber. This is Deputy Harry Packard."

"It's nice to meet you, Miss Webber. That's what I've heard you want to be called."

"Yeah, I guess I got that from working a lot of years with the FBI. They believe in keeping relationships at work more formal."

"Well, we want you to feel at home here, Miss Webber," Frank said, with a big smile, "so we will certainly honor your wishes."

Mary smiled back and asked, "What can I do to help while I'm waiting for the new computer equipment?"

Frank told Mary the story of how two boys found a human skull the day before and he wanted to identify the person as soon as possible. "Maybe you can help us by looking through missing persons on the computer."

"Sure. That's easy once I'm up and running. I'll be glad to help find out whose skull it is, but I'll need at least an artist sketch to start an investigation."

Mary had only remotely noticed Harry drawing while they were talking. He handed her a perfect sketch of herself and said, "I'll call you later, Frank," as he started for the door.

Mary looked at the sketch and said to Frank, "He's very good, but how can he make a sketch from a skull?"

"From what Harry has told me, he envisions in his mind what the person would look like if they had the standard amount of skin over each area of the face and head. He has studied the human skeleton, especially the head, like a surgeon. He probably knows more about the human head than most doctors do. Harry has made it his specialty."

"But how will He know if it is a man or a woman?"

"You'll have to ask Harry that. I think they need more of the skeleton to determine if it is a man or a woman. That reminds me. I need to get the river lowered in the area where they found the skull so we can examine the site in more detail."

"How do you do that?"

"I just call the Army Corps of Engineers and ask them to lower the river behind dam number twenty-three. That is, after I explain why I need to do it, and provide 'em with the proper paperwork from our local judge. Would you be interested in coming with me today while I start my investigation, Miss Webber?"

"Sounds like it could be more interesting than waiting around here for my computer equipment."

"Let's clear it with the sheriff."

They went over to Tucker's office. Frank asked Dave if it was all right with him for Miss Webber to follow him around for a day and he said, "Sure, it will be good for both of you."

Mary asked Dave if she could add a scanner to the list of computer equipment she wanted, and Dave said, "Sure, Miss Webber."

As Mary turned to leave, Dave whispered to Frank, "What's a scanner?"

Frank smiled and shrugged his shoulders as he followed Mary out.

Frank then called Judge Marks and explained why he was calling. The judge always seemed to be a busy man and usually asked Frank to be as brief as possible. Judge Marks had already heard most of the story on the local news. The local TV station had picked up the story and had interviewed the two boys on TV the night before.

The judge said he would have the paperwork ready by ten o'clock at the Town Clerk's office.

Frank thanked him and then called Lloyd Kramer at the Army Corps of Engineer's office. When he put down the phone, he told

Mary, "The wheels are in motion to lower the river at the site." As they left the sheriff's office together around quarter to ten, Frank noticed the Sheriff smile at them on the way out.

Frank and Mary's first stop was to pickup the paperwork from the Town Clerk's office. After introducing Mary to everyone in the office, they then drove to the Army Corps of Engineer's office. Once there, Frank introduced Mary to Lloyd Kramer.

Lloyd Kramer had been with the Army Corps of Engineers over thirty years and knew the local Black River dams project like the back of his hand. Lloyd was a good friend of the local Indians who had been his neighbors for many years.

Lloyd told them, "I'll call Chief Joseph Littlefield and let him know I'm going to lower the river at the court's request so that officials can farther investigate the site where the skull was found. You can have your people at the site tomorrow morning, Frank. The river will be lowered enough by then."

Frank and Mary stopped for lunch at Frank's favorite restaurant. The Black River Restaurant overlooked the river from the top of a scenic hill. When Mary told Frank that she remembered her parents bringing her to this restaurant when she was younger, he knew he had made a good choice for their first meal together. Frank's friend seated them at good table by the windows overlooking the river.

Frank thought their conversation was a bit awkward at first, but soon found they had both attended the local high school and knew many of the same teachers.

Mary said, "Could you possibly be the same Frank McDermott who took the football team to an undefeated season as quarterback?"

"The same, Miss Webber."

"I remember seeing your picture along with George Littlefield's in the school trophy case. You were somewhat of a legend to my boyfriend at the time."

"And whatever happened to him, Miss Webber?"

"Do you think you might call me Mary while we're not in the office?"

"It sure sounds better to me," was Frank's reply.

"Oh, my old boyfriend went off to college and married a girl he met there. The last I've heard of him, they have four kids. What about you, you haven't told me if you're married?"

"Well, I was until my wife died of cancer about a year and a half ago. We were married twenty years."

"Do you have children?"

"Just one son, James. He's grown now with a family of his own. I see him from time to time, usually during the holidays."

Frank enjoyed the remainder of their luncheon conversation and hoped Mary enjoyed it, also. He wondered if Mary might like to go out on a date with him sometime, but felt it too soon to ask her.

After lunch, they drove to the coroner's office.

The coroner's office was an imposing building on Main Street of the little town of Black River, West Virginia. The three-story brick building was set back from the sidewalk by a green lawn, sidewalk, and oak trees that lined Main Street. The town of Black River was located in a beautiful river valley surrounded by some of the most beautiful mountains one could only imagine unless seen through their own eyes.

Frank parked, and they entered through the front door. Joe Bianco's secretary recognized Frank and led them to a basement room where they found Joe and Harry studying the skull.

Frank introduced Mary and asked, "Can you tell us anything new yet, Joe?"

"No, not much yet. I have some suspicions, but I'd rather keep them to myself until I have a friend of mine look at the skull."

"The river will be lowered today by the Corps. Lloyd Kramer said we could expect the river to be low enough by tomorrow morning."

"Okay, Frank. I'll have my crew there at eight o'clock."

"Good. We'll meet you there. Any progress yet, Harry?"

"Any progress? You know, Frank, if this were being done in a forensic lab, they would take weeks to apply the correct thickness of clay to the skull to recreate the likeness of its owner. Then they would make a plaster mold of the head and color in the facial features. They would add hair to bring the person to life again. You're asking me to simply sit here, and figure all that out in my mind, and come up with a sketch of the person."

"Well, how long do you think it will take you?"

"Oh, give me until at least tomorrow, Frank."

"You're the best, Harry. Joe, I'll see you in the morning at the site at eight o'clock."

"Okay, Frank. See you tomorrow. Nice to meet you, Miss Webber."

Frank and Mary went back to the sheriff's office where they found some of the computer equipment already had arrived.

Mary thanked Frank for lunch and told him she enjoyed the day. Frank remarked that he also enjoyed the day and looked forward to working with her. She went to the office Sheriff Tucker had assigned her, and started to set up the computer hardware.

The following day, Frank and the others combed the muddy site that had been mostly under water the day the boys found the skull. The searchers turned up what appeared to be the entire skeleton of the person. They also recorded finding bones of fish, pieces of plastic, and bits of wood. Frank and Deputy Ryan carefully recorded where everything was found with photographs and measurements. They put all the items into plastic bags and turned the items over to the coroner's office for examination. Mary stayed back at the office hooking up her computer hardware and loading software.

CHAPTER 5

When dawn came, the next day, Jack Spencer, having slept very little, climbed up the mountain above the treetops so he could get a better view of his surroundings. He saw the smoke of another campfire in the distance and was overjoyed to think there might be another human being in this seemingly deserted area. Looking toward the smoke in the distance, the river was on his right, cutting through the thick forest. The trees were lightly covered with snow making a beautiful, panoramic scene of winter in a river valley. While returning to his camp, Jack thought, 'I'm sure I saw the shadows of someone last night. Whoever created the smoke must know I'm here. If they had wanted to kill me in the night, they probably could have; yet they left me alone. I'm going to follow the river in the general direction of the smoke and investigate.'

He gathered up some of his things including his fishing line, hooks and Browning automatic, and started walking along the river in the general direction of the smoke. About an hour later, he came upon a trail he guessed might lead to the source of the smoke. He took this trail, off to the left, until he came to a clearing not far from the river and saw the Indian encampment.

There were seven Indian tepees and three times as many people covered in buckskin and animal furs. A child of about ten saw Jack and wildly hollered for the rest to look in his direction. He politely waved to them as if these people were long lost relatives. The Indians looked at this pale-faced stranger dressed in his dark blue Armani suit and gave him a bewildered look.

When Jack started to approach the Indians, the men brought out their bows, arrows, and spears. He put his hands up and retreated, walking backward and making no aggressive moves until he was sure the Indian men were not going to pursue him. He followed the river back to his camp looking over his shoulder. While walking, he thought about this encounter and decided, 'these people didn't try to kill me. Maybe I can make friends. I will make a concerted effort to win their friendship. My survival might depend on it.'

Jack went fishing the next day and was lucky enough to catch half a dozen fish. After cooking and eating one fish, he walked back to the edge of the Indian encampment and made his presence known. He walked forward holding up the other five fish and laid them on the damp snow in front of the Indians. Jack stepped back from the fish and opened his arms in the customary gesture of an offering. One Indian walked over to the fish, and raised his arms in a gesture of thanks. Jack returned to his camp happy to have made this gesture, but knowing full well this was only a start at friendship.

It took Jack more than a simple offering of fish to win their trust. Each day he would spend a little time on the outskirts of the Indian encampment looking for an opportunity to be helpful.

One morning, Jack followed the Indian men as they left the encampment on a hunt. He stayed a short distance behind and tried to stay out of sight. The hunters surrounded a small cave in the mountainside. Two young men ventured into the cave, each with a spear in one hand and a torch in the other. Soon they came running out of the cave with a black bear in full pursuit. The other hunters were at the ready with their spears, bows, and arrows. The bear tripped the second man coming out of the cave and was just about on top of him when Jack stepped out from behind a tree and put one bullet from his Browning automatic between the bear's eyes to bring down the beast.

The Indians just stood there stunned, looking at the bear and the stranger, not understanding what had just happened. They had heard a sound like thunder, witnessed the dead bear, and then the stranger. After a few awkward moments of silence, Jack smiled at them. Gradually the young man, who was almost killed by the bear, smiled and slowly walked up to Jack. He put his hand on Jack's shoulder and looked at the other hunters for some sign of approval. Several more men came up to the stranger and grunted sounds of acceptance as they slapped him on the back. Jack smiled, walked over to the bear, and put his foot on the bear's head, letting them know that he, indeed, killed the bear.

Jack helped the Indian hunters lash the legs of the bear to a long spear. He then followed the Indians as they carried the bear to their encampment.

When the hunting party reached the encampment, the women and children greeted them, but acted surprised to see the stranger. The young man who was saved from the bear pointed to Jack and seemed to act out the story of how Jack killed the bear and saved his life. Jack didn't know how much of the story was actually comprehended by the women and children, but he watched, as gradually everyone seemed to be looking and smiling at him. Jack smiled in return and raised his right hand in acknowledgement. One by one, the Indians raised their right hands in response.

The young man spoke to a woman who was with two of the children. Jack assumed this was probably the young man's family. The man spoke to the children and each child took one of his hands and led him to a tepee, followed by the young man and the woman.

Once inside the tepee, Jack was led to a bearskin rug. The two children reclined on the rug and pretended to be asleep. The children then got up, smiled, and pointed to the bearskin, indicating this was Jack's place to sleep. That night, Jack discovered the young man and woman and the two children also slept in this tepee.

He found sleeping in the tepee with his new friends was more comfortable than his lean-to fort at the base of the mountain. The tepee had a fire in the center that kept them warm all night. He got his first full night of sleep since his arrival in the river valley.

Jack felt like a visitor for several days. However, as time passed, he pitched in with the chores and came to feel more at home living with the Indians. He was somewhat of an oddity to these simple people with his white skin, strange clothes and speech. His teeth were intact and white, which seemed to be a marvel to the Indian people. But his special briefcase lap-top computer, not to mention his lighter, Swiss Army knife, and Browning automatic, were magic to these people. In time, he demonstrated all of his magic.

While most of the newcomer's modern devices had obvious advantages in his new circumstances, Jack's computer became completely useless after the batteries ran out. So Jack decided to give himself a little extra protection for hunting wild animals. He made his Samsonite briefcase into body armor. He took out the special computer and cut out the top and bottom sides of the case to make a chest and back protector with leather straps over the shoulders and at the sides. This gave Jack lightweight body protection that was superior to anything the other Indian hunters had.

The Indians communicated in a kind of homemade sign language and words. Jack found, after a few weeks with these people, he had mastered the two dozen words which made up their language. He got to know each Indian by name.

Eventually, Jack's new living conditions took a toll on his wardrobe. His suit, white shirt, and leather shoes soon looked like they had been through a war. His tie was used as a headband, to bundle firewood, and, lastly, as a tourniquet to stop the bleeding of a fellow hunter's forearm that was badly cut by another black bear during Jack's second hunt. His basic first aid knowledge kept the younger hunter from bleeding to death.

Jack wished he had learned more about animals and nature while he was in school. Thank God for his army survival training. He never expected to need it as much as he had in the last two months living in the river valley.

Some weeks later, while hunting with the Indians, Jack and the other men came upon a herd of deer, or it came upon them. They were about to cross a shallow spot in the river when behind them came the thundering roar of the herd. Jack's group turned too late to save one young man who had already been trampled. Jack pulled out his Browning and got off just one shot before he was stepped on and pushed by the herd as it ran forward. As the deer crossed the river, the herd carried Jack into the water and fatally trampled him under them.

When Harry Packard arrived at the coroner's office the next day, Joe Bianco introduced Harry to John Post, a forensics analysis friend who Joe had asked for help. John had traveled to Black River from Charlottesville, Virginia where he was head of forensics for their coroner's office.

They were examining the skull and skeleton, which they had meticulously laid out and assembled.

After introducing Harry to John Post, Joe explained to Harry, "This person was a man of medium height, probably about five foot nine or ten. We've asked an archeologist friend of ours to join us because we think this isn't a recent death. We suspect the bones could be very old. Our friend should be here in a little while."

A half-hour later, they were joined by Richard Farley who was an archeologist of some notoriety. He had written books on the subject and taught at several universities during his twenty-some years in his field. Richard was five foot eleven with gray hair and beard. In his coat and tie, he looked every bit like the university professor that he was.

When Richard looked at the bones, laid out on the table, he said, "I'm glad you called me, Joe. This could be a rare find. I'd like very much to study the bones with you guys, if it is all right with you."

"Sure, Richard. That's why we called you."

The four men worked together all day, until Harry reminded them it was getting close to midnight and he wanted to get some sleep.

Joe glanced at his watch and said, "Oh, sorry. I had no idea it was that late. Let's break for tonight and start again in the morning."

The next day also seemed to fly by for this team. By early afternoon, Harry had discarded a dozen sketches, but he had one that was his best guess of what the man must have looked like. Harry called Frank and asked him to come over and see what he had come up with.

When Frank arrived, he was amazed at their progress. Joe introduced Frank to John Post and Richard Farley.

Harry showed Frank the sketch and said, "There is just one catch, Frank. These guys think this guy died hundreds, maybe thousands of years ago."

"What makes you think that?"

"We've never seen bones of this color from a recent death."

"Well, so much for the murder investigation."

Harry smiled and said, "Hey, Frank, why don't we give my sketch to Miss Webber and ask her to do a missing persons check for us?" The other men smiled.

Frank hesitated and said, "Okay, but you guys will need to keep quiet about the age of the skeleton until she finishes her search, if you want to have some fun."

"We can give her a couple of days, Frank," was Joe's reply. "I want to send a piece of bone to be carbon-dated. That will take a couple of days at least. We shouldn't release anything to the press until we get this report, anyway. We could be wrong about the age of the bones, and wouldn't want our eminent friend Richard Farley to lose face."

"Okay, guys. Let's have some fun with Miss Webber."

Frank left for the sheriff's office with the sketch.

Once at the office, Frank showed the sketch to Mary and asked her to run it through missing persons for him. She told Frank that she would get right on it. Frank felt a little guilty, but not much, and enjoyed it anyway. He hoped Mary would take it in good humor when she found out it was a practical joke.

Joe Bianco left Richard Farley and John Post examining the skeleton, to personally deliver a piece of bone to a materials lab in the town of Beckley where radio carbon dating would determine the age of the bones.

After an hours drive, Joe gave the specimen to his friend Brian Phillips, who said, "Give me your fax number, Joe, and I'll send you the results as soon as I have 'em."

Joe wrote down his name and fax number, thanked Brian for his help, and started back to the office.

When Joe arrived at the coroner's office, he found Richard Farley was the only member of the team still working. John Post had returned home to his regular job and Harry had returned to the sheriff's office.

Richard said, "Come over here for a minute, Joe. How would you characterize this skull relative to the modern day skulls of people you have examined before?"

"Well, except for the color of the skull, it doesn't look all that different to me."

"That's exactly what I was thinking, too. The Indians have inhabited this land for thousands of years. If this guy was an Indian, who died hundreds or thousands of years ago, his skull would likely be flat at the back from the custom of being carried strapped to a board on his mother's back. This guy was also taller and thinner than most of the Indian skeletons that I've examined previously."

"What are you saying, this guy was a white man?"

"More precisely, I would say this guy was a Caucasian. That usually embraces the peoples of Europe, southwestern Asia, and northern Africa. It surely wouldn't classify him as an Indian."

"This guy is probably an early white settler in this area some two hundred years ago."

"I don't know, Joe. I think this guy is older than that based on the color of the bones. I recently reviewed Indian bones, which were about eight thousand years old, and they had the same color as these."

"We'd better document everything and talk to Frank about it tomorrow."

"Okay, Joe, but we better not let this out to the public until we have some more answers, including the carbon dating."

The next morning, Joe and Richard called Frank at the sheriff's office and asked him to stop over. When Frank arrived, they began telling him of their findings.

"When do you expect to get the carbon dating results, Joe?"

"Maybe today, Frank."

"Well, let's see what that tells us. Give me a call when you get the results."

Later that day, Joe got a call from Brian Phillips. Brian was very excited.

"Hey, Joe, where did you get that piece of bone you gave me to carbon date for you?"

"Why, how old is it?"

"The results indicate it's nine thousand years old. So where did you get it, from some museum?"

"I think I'd better get back to you later on that, Brian. Can you fax me the official results?"

Joe called Frank and said, "You better come over here again."

"Did you get the carbon dating results?"

"That's why we need to talk to you."

"Can you tell me over the phone?"

"I think we better tell you in person."

"I'll be right over."

When Frank heard the results and looked at the official report, he said, "Wow! You guys said old, but I had no idea you meant that old."

"Neither did we."

"The press is going to have a field day with this news," said Richard. "Why don't we have a specimen from the skull carbon-dated?"

"Good idea," said Joe, "and how about taking another bone specimen, also."

"Sounds like we should do both," said Frank.

Frank headed back to his office.

Richard and Joe carefully prepared the specimens, labeling the bone specimen with a "B", and the skull specimen with a "S." They then left for the carbon dating lab.

When Frank got back to the sheriff's office, both Harry and Miss Webber wanted to know if he had any results yet. Frank just said, "They're still working on it."

When they arrived at the lab in Beckley, Joe Bianco introduced Richard Farley to Brian Phillips. Joe and Richard had decided, on the way to the lab, not to tell Brian any more than he needed to know at this point. They told Brian that they were surprised at the age of the specimen and wanted him to analyze two more specimens to be sure of his findings.

Brian said, "These specimens wouldn't be from the skeleton the two boys found in the riverbank, would they?"

"Well, officially, we'd rather not say at this point; but unofficially, they just might be. By the way, we don't want this to get out to the press until I release the official coroner's report."

"I understand, Joe, but to the archeologists and paleontologists of the world, this is hot stuff."

"Yes, well, just keep it under your hat for right now, if you please."

CHAPTER 6

After Richard and Joe left the carbon dating lab, Brian ran into another worker in the lab who said, "I heard you turned up results of nine thousand years on that specimen you did for the Black River Coroner's Office."

"Yes, they gave me two more specimens to run as a check. It's that skeleton those two boys found in the riverbank, but don't say anything to anyone yet."

By the next day, the press was waiting for Joe as he arrived at the coroner's office.

"Hey, Joe. Is it true the skeleton the boys found by the riverbank is nine thousand years old?"

Joe just said, "No comment," as he pushed through two rows of reporters.

When Richard arrived, a half-hour later, he found the same scene. They blocked his way and started asking who he was.

When he gave his name, one reporter said, "Aren't you, Farley, the archeologist who has written books on the subject?"

"Yes, I am," Richard replied.

"Then there must be some truth about this skeleton being thousands of years old, or otherwise, why are you here?"

"The coroner's office asked me to help with the case. That's all I care to say at this time."

As Richard pushed his way past the crowd to the door, another reporter hollered, "What's the big secret, anyway?"

Richard hollered back as he opened the door, "We want to be sure of our findings."

All day long, the coroner's office received calls wanting more information about the skeleton. The sheriff's office was also hounded with calls. Frank instructed everyone to give a "no comment" response.

Frank was sitting at his desk thinking about the two things that caused him to lose sleep the night before. He was contemplating the reaction people might have if the bones really turned out to be nine thousand years old. Putting this thought aside, he went back to the subject that really kept him awake, Mary. He enjoyed her company the day they spent together and wanted to develop their relationship. He was leaning back in his chair wondering if it was too soon to ask Mary to go out with him, when Mary rushed in. "Frank, I've got a match for your missing person."

"What did you say?" He was completely stunned, but managed to keep his cool, and waited for Mary to tell him more.

"I said, I got a perfect match from the sketch Harry gave me. I had to expand my search around the country until I got a match. Look at this picture of a Jack Spencer, from Warrenton, Virginia. He's been missing for about six months. His picture is a close match to Harry's sketch."

Frank looked at the picture and said, "Wow! Sure is." He thought to himself, 'It's got to be a coincidence,' but added, "What can you tell me about this Spencer?"

"Well, I just got the match. I'll go back and find out more from the computer."

"Thanks, Miss Webber. Good job!"

Frank walked her to the door and watched, bewildered, as Mary returned to her office. Frank looked at the missing person report and decided to head back to the coroner's office to make sure his friends were not playing an elaborate hoax on him. Frank found two reporters still outside the coroner's office. He got past them without answering any questions and went in. As Frank approached, both Joe and Richard started to tell Frank the news they had just received from Brian Phillips.

"One at a time," Frank said.

"Frank, all the specimens were found to be nine thousand years old. I've had reporters and archeologists from all over the world calling here all day asking if we have a nine-thousand year-old skeleton."

"How did they find out, Joe?"

"I don't know, but you know how news travels in our little world. We'll have to confirm the information that the skeleton is nine thousand years old. The whole world seems to already know that."

"You're right, Joe. Go ahead. I need to get back to the office. I'll see you later."

Frank headed back to the office, convinced his friends were not playing a hoax on him. What Frank kept to himself was that he wanted to get back to the office before Miss Webber told anyone else about finding a missing person. Frank thought to himself as he was driving back, 'Coincidence or not, I'm curious why she found such a close match to Harry's sketch. I think I'll follow up on her report. Besides, I'll need her help to find out more about the missing person. It'll give us something to do together.'

Frank went straight to Mary's office where he found her busy at work on the computer.

Mary stopped what she was doing, smiled and said, "Hi, Frank."

"Hi, Mary. Did you tell anyone else yet about finding a match?"

"No, Harry is out of the office and Sheriff Tucker has been very busy."

"Good. I'd hoped you hadn't."

"Why?"

"Because the skeleton has been carbon-dated to be nine thousand years old."

"That's impossible, I've got a current match!"

"I know. I don't understand it either. You can see why I don't want it to get around that you found a match to a nine-thousand-year-old skeleton."

"Sure, Frank, but I don't understand why I did find a match. The computer is usually right."

"Neither do I. Can you tell me anything more about this Jack Spencer person?"

"I found out quite a bit. He worked for Uncle Sam most of his adult life in one way or another. He was in the Army Rangers and had quite a military record. At the time of his disappearance, he was working for some special group of the NSA."

"Did he have any relatives?"

"Yes, a wife in Virginia. She filed the missing persons report."

"How old was he at the time he disappeared?"

"I think I read forty-five."

"Can you get me the phone number and address of his wife?"

"Sure, Frank."

"I think I would like to drive to Virginia and pay her a visit. Oh, under the circumstances, let's just keep this between you and me."

"Okay, Frank. I understand."

Frank looked at Mary, smiled, hesitated and said, "Mary, would you like to go out for dinner with me tonight?"

"You mean on a date?"

"Sure, if you want to call it that."

"Mary hesitated, smiled back and said, That sounds nice. What should I wear?"

"Oh, I was thinking of going to the Black River Restaurant again. I guess I'm a creature of habit."

"That's fine with me, Frank."

"Is seven o'clock okay with you?"

"I'll be ready at seven. Here, I'll give you my mother's address."

As she handed him the address, Frank said with a smile, "I'll look forward to seeing you at seven."

CHAPTER 7

Frank went back to his desk and called the Black River Restaurant. He asked his friend for a quiet table in the far corner for seven thirty. Frank knew his friend would be glad to comply because he always left good tips.

Frank left for home at five o'clock. In between shaving and showering, he switched channels on the TV. He found both local and national TV channels were covering the nine-thousand-year-old skeleton story.

When Frank stopped to get Mary at her mother's home, he felt like a kid again. Mary looked beautiful in her light blue, summer dress. He wore tan slacks, a white sports shirt, and a blue blazer.

When Frank and Mary reached the restaurant, they were escorted to the best table in the corner as Frank had requested.

As they sat down, Mary said, "Did you see all the news stories about our skeleton? I saw one story that said the local Indian Federation has already filed a claim with the local courts for custody of the bones. They want to rebury them."

"I'm not surprised. My friend, George Littlefield, has told me the Indians believe it's important for the spirit to remain in the place where the person dies. They feel very deeply about this."

"That's interesting. I heard that the Archeological Society is taking the other side of the coin. They're requesting access to the site where the bones were found on the reservation to perform an archeological dig."

"Is that right?" said Frank. "That'll sure stir up things around here for a while."

Just then, Frank's waiter friend stopped at their table and took their drink order. As he walked away, Frank pointed out the window to the Black River and said, "I've always enjoyed the way the sun sparkles on the water at this time of night."

"It's beautiful. How did you get such a good table? The view from here is spectacular."

"The waiter is a friend of mine." Frank smiled at Mary and asked, "How are you enjoying being back home so far?"

"I've always liked this town, and I kind of enjoy being a computer expert for the sheriff's office. When I worked for the FBI, I was just one of many computer specialists."

"Are you what I think they call a hacker?"

"Well, that's sometimes required at the FBI. After all, for the FBI to keep up with all the smart young people today, they need to be up to date on all the latest hardware, software, and what's going on the Internet. That's a constant job in itself, and getting harder all the time as the computer industry and Internet continue to expand."

Frank's friend returned with their drinks and Frank introduced him to Mary. As the waiter walked away, Frank said, "How did you ever get so interested in computers, anyway?"

"Why do you ask, Frank? Do you see it only as a man's game?"

"No, no, I didn't mean it that way. Oh, I guess I put my foot into it this time."

"Not really. I was just putting you on guard. I guess that's a bad habit of mine. Actually, if you really want to know, my father got me interested in computers. He wrote computer software for a lot of companies as an independent agent. He made quite a good living at it, too. He worked at home. As an only child, I would watch him, sometimes for hours. He was always very willing to explain everything to me unless he had one of those deadlines. By the time I was ten, I had my own computer, which was unusual for a young girl at that time. By the time I was fifteen, I would help my dad write programs when he felt I could contribute. By the time I was eighteen, I could hack my way into just about any computer in the world. When the FBI found out about me, they decided to offer me an education at Georgetown University, provided I spend at least three years working for them after I graduated. It was too good an opportunity not to accept. And here I am today."

"And glad I am that you are, Mary."

"Thanks, Frank. So how did you get into police work?"

"I loved mysteries from the time I was a kid. My parents got me started on the Hardy Boys and Tom Swift novels. I couldn't get enough of those. Then I started reading Sherlock Holmes. Sometimes, when there was a nationally publicized crime, I would read all I could about it, and try and solve it for the police. One time, when I was about seventeen, I was trying to solve a case where several women were found strangled over a period of about six months. I picked up on a clue and called the police in LA. I told the policeman the murderer must be left-handed because the scarf found around each woman's neck had a left-handed twist. The officer wondered who the heck I was. When I told him I was a teenager, the guy asked if I had ever been to LA. When I explained I had never been to California, he just hung up. I guess that taught me a little about human nature. But when they finally caught the murderer, sure enough, he was left-handed.

"I started working for the sheriff's office right out of high school. I studied the science of criminology in night school. I try to keep up on all the latest techniques by reading a lot. I made detective in five years."

Frank's friend returned and took their dinner order. As the waiter left, Mary said, "Have you had many big cases to crack?"

"Oh, we've had a few cases of domestic shootings, kids running away from home, robberies, and occasionally a murder; but over all, not nearly as many as a big city. I'll bet you had some interesting cases with the FBI, Mary."

"Yeah, I did at that, but none that I'm at liberty to talk in specifics about. Mostly drug, organized crime, counterfeiting, and terrorist activity."

"Wow! That sounds interesting. This small town stuff will seem tame to you."

"I need a breather from the FBI. I find it quite nice being back in the small town atmosphere, where life seems a bit simpler. Let me change the subject to your case, Frank."

"You mean our case."

"Yeah, thanks. Oh, I was able to get the name, address and phone number of Mrs. Jack Spencer for you. I'll give it to you at work tomorrow."

"Good. I'll give her a call in the morning and ask if I can visit with her. I think it might be worth a drive to Virginia to find out more about this missing person. It'll probably turn out to be just a coincidence that Harry's sketch looks like this guy, but it's the closest thing to a mystery I've had in some time."

"Would it be all right for me to go with you?"

"Sure, that's a great idea. I'll clear it with Dave Tucker in the morning. We'll probably stay over night and return the day after tomorrow. Is that all right with you?"

"Sure. I've done a lot of traveling for the Bureau, and I can help you find your way around the Washington area."

Their dinners arrived and the food was wonderful. Frank found Mary easy to talk to. She seemed to be enjoying their time together. About nine o'clock, Frank noticed the time and suggested he take her home. Neither could understand where the time had gone, and commented on how they had enjoyed the evening.

When Frank walked Mary to her front door, she said, "Thank you for a wonderful meal. Maybe you will let me make dinner for you some time."

Frank said, with a big smile, "I'll have to check my busy calendar."

Mary smiled, leaned into Frank's arms, gave him a good night kiss on the lips, and went into the house. Frank felt like he was sixteen again as he returned to his car and drove off.

The next morning, Frank got a call from George Littlefield. "Frank, I just wanted to let you know the Indian Federation has officially asked to have the bones returned to the reservation for reburial."

"I heard that. I also heard that Richard Farley has requested to study the bones and the site in more detail on behalf of the Archeological Society. I hope there isn't going to be a fight over these bones."

"Frank, if somebody dug up the bones of someone from your family, just how would you react?"

"I understand. Obviously I would react the same way under those circumstances, but if I was told it was an ancestor nine thousand years old, I might consider letting the experts look at the bones for a period of time before reburial."

"Frank, you've been my friend too long for us to argue over this, but you must know how strongly my people feel about not disturbing the sprits of our ancestors."

"You're right. We've been friends for a long time, so what I'm going to tell you now is based on our friendship."

"What's that?"

"Well, I've been working with Joe Bianco from the coroner's office, and this Richard Farley, who is a well known archeologist. After reviewing the skeleton, Farley thinks it is Caucasian. He said this means the peoples of Europe, southwestern Asia, and northern African ancestry. He wouldn't classify the skeleton as Indian."

"How sure is he?"

"He seems reasonably sure. I don't know how this will affect the request your Federation made to rebury the bones, but as your friend, I wanted to keep you up to date."

"Thanks. Let me know if there are any other developments, will you?"

"Sure, George."

Mary knocked on Frank's office door as he put down the phone.

"Good morning, Mary," he said with a smile.

"Good morning, Frank," she replied, also, with a smile. "Thanks again for dinner last night."

"I enjoyed it, Mary."

"Here's the address and phone number I promised you."

"Thanks. I'll call Mrs. Spencer and ask her if it would be all right to visit her later today. I'll clear our trip with Dave, and get back to you after I make the call."

Frank called Mrs. Jack Spencer. He told her who he was and that he had a potential lead in the disappearance of her husband. Frank then asked her if it would be all right if he and Mary could visit with her later in the day. She said it would be fine with her.

Frank went into Dave Tucker's office. He filled in the Sheriff about how Harry's sketch came up as a missing person, even though the skeleton turned out to be nine thousand years old. And that he and Mary were going to Warrenton, Virginia to visit with the wife of the missing man.

The Sheriff laughed and said, "I think you're on a wild goose chase, Frank."

"Yes. I guess you could say that, but look at this picture of the missing person, and look at the sketch that Harry made."

"Wow! That is uncanny. I know how much you like a good mystery, Frank, but down deep, you must know this is just a coincidence."

"You're probably right, but I don't like to leave stones unturned. And besides, it will give me a chance to get to know Mary a little better."

Dave smiled. "Okay, Frank. It's probably about three hours over to Warrenton, so you both better pack an overnight bag and return in the daylight."

"Thanks. That's a good idea."

CHAPTER 8

Frank and Mary stopped for overnight bags at their homes. Frank picked up Mary, and they were off to Warrenton. It was a pleasant summer day, a little overcast, but a good day to travel by car.

Frank said, "Did I see you put a laptop computer into the back seat?"

"Sure did. That's my office while away from the office and my window to the world."

"Might come in handy at that."

After a little while, Frank said, "You know, when I told the Sheriff what we wanted to do, he thought we were going on a wild goose chase. Dave was surprised Harry's sketch was a close match to the missing person, but he thought it was just a coincidence. I told Dave I wanted to check it out just the same, and that it would give you and me a chance to work together. If nothing else is accomplished by this trip than you and I becoming better friends, it will be a success."

"Thanks. That's a nice thing to say."

Their conversation flowed easily with some laughter, as they spent the time getting better acquainted.

They reached Warrenton in about three hours. They stopped at a Hampton Inn, checked into two adjoining rooms for the night, and called Mrs. Spencer for directions. They were at her home about five minutes later.

"Mrs. Spencer, this is Mary Webber, and my name is Frank McDermott."

She invited them in and said, "Please sit down and tell me all about the possible lead you mentioned in my husband's disappearance."

Frank said, "Well, Mrs. Spencer, have you heard on TV or read anything about the nine-thousand-year-old skeleton found along the Black River?"

"Yes, I believe I did see that on TV."

"Please look at this sketch."

"Why, that looks just like my husband."

"Mrs. Spencer, a man from our office who has a knack for drawing faces made this sketch. He made this sketch from the skull of the nine-thousand-year-old man found along the Black River."

"Really! Please tell me more, Mr. McDermott."

"Well, I really can't explain why the sketch looks like your husband. It must be just a complete coincidence. Could you tell us a few things about your husband?"

"Why sure. What would you like to know?"

"For a start, how tall is he?"

"Oh, he's five foot nine and a half. He always says five foot ten."

"Am I correct that he's been missing for about six months?"

"Yes, that's correct. He disappeared the day after our wedding anniversary." A few tears ran down her cheeks, and Mary moved over next to her to comfort her.

"Can you tell us what he did for a living?"

"He worked for the government."

"In what capacity?"

"I couldn't say, actually, because he worked for the National Security Agency, and you know how they are about keeping quiet about their work." She said the last few words of her sentence slowly and looked off into space.

"Can you tell us who his immediate supervisor is? We'd like to talk with him if he'll see us."

Mrs. Spencer continued looking off into space and didn't seem to hear Frank's question.

Frank said, "Mrs. Spencer, are you all right?"

She snapped out of her trance and said, "What did you say?"

He repeated, "are you all right, Mrs. Spencer?"

"Yes, yes, what was your question?"

Her sad composure seemed, to Frank, to have been lifted from her and replaced by a more optimistic look.

"Can you tell us who your husband's immediate supervisor is? We'd like to talk with him."

"Yes, just a minute. I'll write down his name and phone number for you, if you think it will help find my Jack."

While Mrs. Spencer was out of the room, Frank said to Mary, "Do you think it odd that she found it interesting that the sketch of a nine-thousand-year-old man looked like her husband?"

"Yes, I think I would have asked us to leave, thinking we were a couple of crackpots."

"That's kind of what I was expecting her to do the whole while we were driving here. Did you see the way her expression changed?"

"Yeah. One minute she had tears running down her cheeks, she goes into a trance, and comes out of it like it's a new day."

When Mrs. Spencer returned with the name and phone number, her friendly attitude had changed. She said, "I called my husband's boss to let him know you would be getting in touch with him."

Frank started to ask another question, when Mrs. Spencer said, "That's really all I can tell you about my husband's disappearance. Thank you for coming by to visit with me."

Frank and Mary stood up at the obvious request for them to leave, thanked Mrs. Spencer for being kind enough to see them, and left.

As soon as they got in the car, Mary said, "That sure was a quick change in personality. One moment she was answering all our questions and the next she couldn't get rid of us quickly enough."

"Yes, I wonder what Jack Spencer's boss said to her?"

"What's his name, Frank?"

"She wrote down Mark Denver and only provided a phone number. Let's go back to the motel and plug in your computer. Maybe you can find out something about Spencer's boss."

"Okay. My curiosity is working overtime, too."

They drove back to the Hampton Inn, and met in Mary's room. Mary hooked up her computer to the nearest phone line and began typing in commands, while Frank sat next to her looking on. In just a few minutes, Mary was into one of the nation's main computers looking up records on Denver.

"Look at this guy, Frank. Denver has degrees in engineering, math, and a doctorate in physics from MIT. He's fifty-three years old and has worked for the NSA since 1973. Denver has written several papers on quantum physics. It also looks like he has headed up several projects because it specifies his title as a project leader."

"Can you find out what his current project is?"

"I'll try."

After several attempts, she said, "I can't seem to find out what he's currently doing."

"Well, that's a start. Let's call Denver at the phone number Mrs. Spencer gave us and see what he has to say."

Frank dialed the number, and after talking with Denver's secretary, got him on the phone.

"Hello, Mr. Denver. My name is Frank McDermott. I'm investigating the disappearance of Jack Spencer. Mrs. Spencer gave me your name as his immediate supervisor. Can you tell me anything that would help find him?"

"Mr. McDermott, for the record, who do you work for?"

When Frank told him who he was, Denver said, "I don't understand why a detective from your area would be looking for a missing person in this area." He went on to say, "Mrs. Spencer mentioned something about a nine-thousand-year-old skeleton."

Frank said, "It's rather complicated. Is it possible for me to meet with you to discuss this in person?"

Denver hesitated for a moment, and suggested they meet at a restaurant in Washington at seven that evening.

Frank said, "Just a minute," and asked Mary if she was familiar with the restaurant.

She said, "Yes."

Frank then told Denver, "Miss Webber, my associate, will be coming, also. We'll meet you at the restaurant at seven."

Denver asked where they were staying, and Frank told him. Denver told Frank he would reserve a table in his name at the restaurant.

Frank said, "See you at seven," and hung up.

"I'm a little surprised this guy is willing to meet us for dinner, aren't you, Mary?"

"Yeah, if it were me, I probably would have referred us to the local police and tried to stay out of it."

"That's what I was thinking, too. Maybe we're getting the wrong idea, but at least we'll have an interesting dinner with a scientist."

"Actually, I was looking forward to an interesting dinner with a detective, Frank."

He blushed. Mary smiled and said, "How about getting out of here so a lady can prepare herself for a night out."

He smiled, went into the adjoining room, and closed the door behind him.

At five to seven, Frank and Mary arrived at the restaurant. They went in and gave Denver's name. They were promptly seated at a table in the far corner, seemingly reserved for special people who frequented the place. The restaurant was furnished with mahogany walls, with tables and chairs to match.

A few minutes later, Mark Denver walked over and introduced himself.

Denver was dressed in gray slacks, blue blazer, white shirt, and red tie. He was about six feet tall, thin, and looked distinguished with gray hair.

As they made introductions, Frank and Mary did not mention Mary's affiliation with the FBI as Frank thought it might tend to keep Denver from opening up about his work.

After the introductions and compliments over the choice of restaurant, they ordered drinks.

Denver said, "I agreed to meet you here tonight because I'm curious why detectives from your area are looking for Jack Spencer. Have you found any clues to his disappearance?"

Frank pulled out the drawing, which Harry had made, and explained to Denver at length how they came to have this picture.

Denver looked at the picture while Frank was explaining how it was made, and said, "Now I understand why you are on this mistaken adventure. I think this picture is similar to Jack Spencer, but certainly not a close enough resemblance to Jack to warrant your trip to Washington. How did you happen to match this picture with Spencer?"

Mary started to speak, and Frank broke in and said, "Just a lucky chance match with missing persons reports that get circulated through our office."

Denver said, "I read about this nine-thousand-year-old-skeleton found in your area. Just exactly where did they find it?"

Frank answered Denver's question.

Denver said, "According to the report I saw on the early news, the archeologists think the skeleton is a white man. Why do they think this instead of an ancient Indian man?"

"Some experts who have examined it claim it's a skeleton of a Caucasian based on the shape of the skull. The bones, as I mentioned, were found on an Indian reservation."

"That's interesting, but what possible connection could a nine-thousand-year-old- skeleton have with my friend who has been missing for six months?"

"Probably none."

"So why did you really come all the way to Washington to pursue this case?"

"Well, you've got me there, Mr. Denver. I guess it's been too long since I've had a case to investigate."

"Well, frankly, Mr. McDermott, I thought you might have a lead in my friend's disappearance or I wouldn't have suggested this meeting for dinner tonight."

"I'm sorry, Mr. Denver. Please allow me to pick up the tab for dinner as some compensation. And please call me Frank."

Denver smiled and said, "Well, shall we order? They have really good food here. And please call me Mark."

They ordered dinner and Frank changed the subject by asking, "What kind of work do you do for the government?"

"Well, mostly rather boring mathematical projections. The purpose of my group is to project the possible future by mathematically extrapolating past and current events."

"Just how do you do that?" Mary asked.

"We plug great amounts of information into a computer and use algorithms to have the computer extrapolate the data and make projections of what might happen. We then pass this information to another group whose job it is to prepare for the possible events, to maintain the national security of our country, and for the world, for that matter."

Frank said, "You lost me at 'algorithms.' Could you explain that once again in laymen's terms?"

"Sure. Take the issue of global warming for example. For years we've been monitoring the temperature rise in the oceans and around the earth. We've been gathering data on the gradual depletion of the ozone layer. We plug this data into our computer and have it plot two curves on a graph. The two curves show the relationship between the depletion of the ozone layer with the temperature rise of the earth. The curves are plotted over time showing just how fast conditions are changing. We also record how fast the earth's oceans are rising due to the melting of ice at the earth's polar caps. We plot a lot of additional information along with the data I just mentioned and create a formula, or algorithm, with the greatest common divisor. This formula records the overall changes on the earth versus time giving my group a method of determining how long man has to reverse the situation."

"Wow! That sounds like a very important responsibility."

"We take it very seriously, Miss Webber."

"If you don't mind my asking," Frank said, "just how did Jack Spencer help your group?"

Denver hesitated a bit, and said, "Jack was one of the people who helped gather information for us."

"And just how do you gather information?"

"There are several primary ways, but I'm not at liberty to define them for you. Trust me, we know what we're doing."

"What an interesting job," Mary said.

"It can be at times, Miss Webber, but usually it's just a routine like many other jobs."

Their dinners arrived, and the conversation turned to how good the food was, and other polite conversation. At the end of the meal, Frank picked up the check. He thanked Denver for joining them for dinner and selecting such a good restaurant. Frank and Mary said good-by to Denver in the parking lot and headed back to Warrenton.

Mark Denver took out his cell phone and made a call. "This is Denver, do you have them in sight?"

"Yes, Mark. We'll keep an eye on them."

"Did you bug their car and motel rooms?"

"Yes."

"Good. Stay on them, keep in touch, and most importantly, don't let them know you're watching them."

CHAPTER 9

On the way back to Warrenton, Frank and Mary talked about the dinner they had with Mark Denver.

"Mary, what did you think of Denver?"

"It seemed strange to me that his reaction to Harry's drawing was different than Mrs. Spencer's."

"That's exactly what I thought, too. Mrs. Spencer thought the drawing looked like her husband. Denver's reaction was that we didn't have a good enough match. By the way, thanks for not telling him how we got the information. If he knew you are affiliated with the FBI, he probably would have clammed up in a hurry."

"He might have walked out of the restaurant and left us there, Frank."

"Do you believe his story on what he does for the government?"

"It sounded plausible."

"That's what I thought, also. Do you think you could get any more information from your computer on what his current project is?"

"Then you don't believe what Denver told us?"

"Well, he left me wanting to know more about what he does."

"I'll see what I can find out, but hacking into the NSA computers could get us a lot of attention in a big hurry."

"Can you get in without being detected?"

"Maybe, but one of my jobs with the FBI was to fix the Bureau's system to keep other hackers out. If the NSA has my fixes, I doubt I can get in without being detected. Are you sure we have enough to go on to pursue this further?"

"Maybe not. Let's sleep on it tonight and talk about it more tomorrow.

"Mary, from the background you found about Spencer, do you think he would be the type of person who would collect information for a computer?"

"Lots of ex-military people wind up working for the government in some capacity."

"Yes, but didn't Spencer's profile make him sound more like an action type of person than a data gatherer?"

"Yeah. I guess I would agree with that, but we don't know how Spencer gathered information. Maybe his role was an active one and not one of a person who simply does research."

"You're probably right. Denver wouldn't say much about their methods of gathering information, so who knows what Spencer's role might have been."

"You surely seem to want this to be some kind of mystery, Frank. Are you always this suspicious about other people's motives?"

"Maybe I've read too many detective novels in my day. This whole thing has had me in a quandary ever since you found a really good match to Harry's drawing. Over the years I've learned to trust Harry's ability to draw faces."

"Harry really is remarkable. Has he ever made a face from a skeleton before?"

"Yes. Back about two years ago, there was a skeleton found on a local farm. Harry made a drawing from the skull just as he did this time. The skeleton turned out to be one of the farmer's relatives who had died about eighty years ago and was buried on the farm. The farmer found an old family picture from which we were able to enlarge the women's face. It was a direct match with Harry's drawing."

"That's amazing."

"The farmer later found a small headstone with the woman's name on it. The headstone had apparently been accidentally plowed underground over the years. The farmer didn't know there was a burial site on the farm."

"I'd say that puts Harry in a class by himself."

"Yes, I've been wondering for years when he'll leave us for big city detective work."

As Frank and Mary pulled into the parking lot of the Hampton Inn, Frank started to say something about a car he had seen following them all the way from Washington. He decided not to say anything to Mary, thinking she might really think him overly suspicious. So he let it slide as just a coincidence.

Frank walked Mary to her door and said, "Thanks for all your help today. Traveling with you has been a real pleasure."

"I enjoyed it, too."

"How about if I pick you up for breakfast at nine. By the time we start back, the local traffic will have diminished."

"Sounds good to me, Frank. See you in the morning."

Mary smiled and gave Frank a kiss good night and went into her room. He paused outside the door for a moment, thinking life is good.

When Mary entered her room, she noticed the phone and phone jack she had connected her computer into had been moved to the table beside the bed. She could have sworn she left them on the bed. She put the phone and connector back on the bed and hooked up her laptop.

She wasn't tired and thought it might be a good time of night to try and hack into the NSA's computer. After just a few minutes, Mary found the firewalls she had put into the FBI's computers hadn't been programmed into the NSA system as yet.

Mary did a search using the name Mark Denver. After finding some general information about him, she decided to try and get a list of projects he was connected with. The computer indicated Denver had only been associated with one project over the past ten years. The project code name was "REPEAT." She worked for another twenty minutes, breaking the security code, and found that REPEAT stood for Respect Environment, Preserve Earth for All Time. Mary copied down enough information so she could accurately tell Frank about it in the morning.

She tried to get more information about the project and couldn't get past another security gate. She then decided to try and get the names of the people who worked for Denver. Mary found a list of sixty-four people and made a copy. Then she searched for the chain of command, and determined there were ten people on Denver's immediate staff who were direct reports. The remaining people reported to these ten people. Mary started to profile the ten people. She got the profiles for the first five and decided to quit for the night. At about twelve thirty, she closed her eyes and went to sleep.

A little after 1:00 A.M., Mark Denver was awakened by a call.

"Mark, sorry to wake you, but I thought you would want to be brought up to date."

The person who was calling Denver worked for the security branch of the NSA and was a long time friend of Mark's.

"You aren't going to believe this. The women with Frank McDermott is none other than Mary Webber."

"Yes, I know her name," Mark said with a little frustration. "Am I supposed to know who she is?"

"Mary Webber is one of the foremost computer hackers in the country. She works for the FBI."

"The FBI! What have they got to do with Frank McDermott and the Black River Sheriff's Office?"

"I don't know, Mark. I'll have to talk to somebody in the FBI to find out."

"You could have told me this in the morning, couldn't you?"

Ray Blackwell said, "I'm just beginning. This Webber woman has already found out the name of your organization and identified your workers. She copied the profiles of five of your direct reports."

Denver started to say something, but Ray interrupted, "There's more. This McDermott is a real bloodhound, suspicious as hell. I think he may have spotted us on the trip to Warrenton."

"That's not good. Why do you say McDermott is suspicious?"

"At the restaurant, you told McDermott that the drawing he had didn't closely resemble Jack."

"Yeah. So?"

"Well, Mrs. Spencer evidently told them it was a good match."

"Oh, shit! Anything else?"

"Yes. McDermott talked about how you said Jack was some kind of a data gatherer for your group and McDermott didn't think Jack's profile fit that type of job. But I think McDermott and Webber bought your cover of being people who predict the future by extrapolating computer data. They figured maybe Jack gathered information in some other way than just doing research."

"That's good. What else?"

"Apparently Mary Webber provided the FBI with some kind of new programming to keep out would-be hackers. Webber mentioned to McDermott that if the NSA had the Bureau's programming, she probably wouldn't be able to get into our computers without our knowing it."

"I'll have our computer group discretely contact the FBI tomorrow and ask their people if they have anything new we could benefit from."

"I hope that's soon enough. Webber may have a lot more information by the time our computer group installs the update."

"I know. We just can't afford to make any more mistakes that might add fuel to their desire to know more. I probably shouldn't have even met with them."

"Well, what's done is done."

"Yeah. Thanks for that. You better get some sleep. No sense in following them back to Black River. You might draw more suspicion."

"Okay, Mark, but if we did follow McDermott and Webber, we could pick up their conversation, and learn more about what they are thinking."

"You might at that. Do you think you can keep your people out of sight?"

"I'll have them use a repair van, instead of a car, in the morning."

"Okay, Ray. Thanks, and get some rest."

"I'll call you at your office tomorrow."

The next morning, Frank knocked on Mary's door at 9:00 A.M.

"Just a minute, Frank," and she opened the door.

"Mary, do you want to put our things in the trunk of the car now, and check out after breakfast?"

"Sure, Frank, everything but my toothbrush so I can make a last minute stop before we leave."

They put their bags into the trunk of Frank's Mercury Marquis and put Mary's computer in the back seat.

When Frank and Mary entered the breakfast area of the Hampton Inn, they found there was the typical help-yourself format that was popular with many business people on the run. They got what they wanted and sat down in the corner of the small clean room that was empty except for one man reading a newspaper in another corner.

Mary was anxious to tell Frank what she found out. "Last night I did a little hacking before going to bed."

"That's great. Did you find anything startling?"

"I believe I was able to get in without being detected. I'll give you the details during the trip back. I think you'll find them interesting."

"With that news, I think I'll pass up a second cup of coffee."

"You can take one with you, if you like."

"Good idea."

They finished their breakfast, checked out, and went back to their rooms for a last minute stop.

As Frank and Mary left the parking lot, the man, who had been reading the newspaper at breakfast, came out and got into a white van with another man. Both were dressed in repairmen outfits. They pulled out of the parking lot and stayed a good distance behind Frank. One man reached into the back, turned on the recording equipment, and put on an earphone set.

CHAPTER 10

"So, Mary, what did you find out about Denver?"

"For the last ten years, Mark Denver has headed up a project called, REPEAT. It's an acronym for Respect Environment, Preserve Earth for All Time. Does that sound like an organization that feeds computers to extrapolate future events?"

"I don't know. I think they could come up with a better name than that if their job is to extrapolate data and predict the future."

"Mark has sixty-four people currently working for him, ten of whom make up his immediate staff. The others report to the ten senior staff members. I profiled five of Mark's senior staff before I turned in for the night."

"How late did you stay up?"

"Oh, until about twelve-thirty I guess. When I was younger, I would stay up all hours of the night."

"You still look pretty young to me, Mary."

"Frank, I've been meaning to ask you a question. When we first met, you made a comment about me."

"What was that?"

"You called me good looking. Are you normally quick to make comments like that to women you don't know?"

"Only when they're as good looking as you are. Actually, I remember thinking later that day, what made me say that. The last person I called good looking was my wife."

"Then why did you make that comment to me?"

"I really do think you're beautiful, Mary. I'm sorry if I made you feel uneasy."

"Actually, Frank, I think you are good looking, too."

"Oh, yeah?"

"Yeah. I do."

Mary moved over next to Frank and put her arm around his shoulder, while he was driving.

"Mary, if we had had this conversation last night, I don't think you would have had time to hack into the NSA computer."

Frank and Mary spent the next hour of the trip exchanging pleasantries typical of a budding relationship. After a while they got back on the subject of Mark Denver.

Mary said, "Do you want to hear the profiles of the five people?"

"Sure."

Mary reached into the back seat and got out her lap top computer. She turned it on and retrieved the profile information.

"The first one is Jason Bedford. He has several degrees including a doctorate in physics from MIT. Bedford has written a book called 'Magnetism and Its Uses in Modern Society'. He was recruited by Mark Denver nine years ago to work on the project.

"The second person is Samuel Magnum. He was also recruited nine years ago from MIT. Magnum has a doctorate in electrical engineering and seems to be a specialist in the area of electronic controls because he wrote several papers on how to use electronic controls to manage magnetic resonance.

"The third person is Sally Stevens. She has a doctorate in history and was a professor at the University of Virginia until three years ago when Mark recruited her.

"The fourth person is Dylan O'Grady. He has a master's degree in mechanical engineering from Ohio State University. He wrote a book ten years ago called 'How to Manage Complicated Designs.' It looks like O'Grady has been on the project from the start.

"The fifth person I profiled last night is Captain Paul Andrews. He's had quite a military career including the Army Rangers, West Point, and strategist assigned to General Schwarzkopf during the Gulf War in 1991. There's a lot more in their profiles, but that's a quick summary."

"That's quite an impressive list of people, Mary. I guess if you were priming a computer with information and trying to make it extrapolate the future, you would need brilliant people like these."

"You're probably right. Do you want me to pursue this any further?"

"What if you got the remaining five profiles and we'll see what other people make up Denver's senior staff."

"Okay. It's kind of fun hacking into the NSA, anyway."

"Can I watch you do it the next time?"

"Sure. Why don't you stop over to my home tonight for dinner? I'd like you to meet my mother. We can do some hacking after dinner."

Frank smiled, and Mary said, "Just computer hacking, Frank."

When Frank and Mary stopped off for lunch, Frank noticed a white van pull into the parking lot after them, but he didn't think anything of it. When they came out of the restaurant after lunch, he noticed the two men eating in their van. He wondered why they didn't go into the restaurant to eat since it was a nice local restaurant, but not exactly a scenic picnic area place to stop for lunch. Twenty minutes later down the road, he noticed the white van turn in the same direction they did after passing an intersection.

A few miles down the road, Frank made a sharp turn to the right after going around a long curve in the road. He pulled over and watched the road he had just left.

Mary said, "What are you doing, Frank?"

"Well, I don't want to get you upset, but I want to check out a hunch that a white van might be following us."

As Mary turned to look out the back window as Frank was doing, the white van passed the turn off. After a minute, Frank turned around and started back onto the road. After another couple of minutes, the white van passed them going the other way.

"Looks like you might be right, Frank."

The men in the van stopped and put in a call to Ray Blackwell. Ray wasn't too happy when he learned they blew their cover. Ray told them to return to base and forget about following McDermott and Webber anymore. They gave Ray a summary of what they had heard including the developing relationship between Mary and Frank. Ray told them he would get back to them and hung up.

"Do you think they really were following us, Frank?"

"I think so, but it could have been a coincidence."

"You know last night when I came back to my room, I could've sworn I left the phone on the center of the bed. It was on the night table," she said.

"I could've sworn we were followed to the motel last night, also. I didn't say anything to you because I wasn't sure I was right."

"This isn't adding up, Frank. When we started out on this trip, I thought it was going to be just a boondoggle. "

"I know what you mean. I wonder what we've stumbled onto?"

Frank and Mary both were quiet thinking to themselves for the next several miles. Frank was first to speak.

"I've been thinking about all this. I'd like to have more information before we tell Tucker about you hacking into the NSA computer and about our suspicions of being followed. Dave might think we are paranoid about being followed, and I'm sure he would raise an eyebrow about you hacking into the NSA computer."

"You're probably right. What should we tell him?"

"Let's tell him everything except the things you found out on the computer and our suspicions of being followed."

"Okay, Frank."

They arrived back in Black River at two-thirty. After checking in at the sheriff's office, Frank took Mary to her home, and helped her with her bag. Mary's mother greeted them at the door and asked them if they had a good trip.

"Just fine, Mom. Do you have enough food for Frank to come to dinner tonight?"

"Sure. Is six-thirty okay with you, Mr. McDermott?"

"That would be great, Mrs. Webber. Please call me Frank."

At six-thirty that night, Frank arrived back at the Webber home, clean-shaven and casual in his khakis and polo shirt. Mary greeted him at the door with a kiss.

They paused, holding each other in their arms for a few moments until Frank said, "What smells so good?"

"That's my mom's Spanish rice. Nobody in the world makes it like she does. It takes her hours to make it, and lucky for you, my mom made up a batch of it yesterday for my arrival back home. Mom's Spanish rice always seems to taste better the second day."

They had a delightful dinner. Mrs. Webber told Frank she knew his parents and had baby-sat him when he was a baby. When she started telling how she had changed his diapers, Mary said, "Really mother, you're embarrassing us."

Frank laughed and told Mrs. Webber how wonderful her Spanish rice was.

Mary said, "I guess there are advantages and disadvantages to living in a small town."

She then explained to her mother that she and Frank needed to do some work on the computer after dinner, and hoped she didn't mind letting them work by themselves.

"Oh, I know you young people want to be alone. You know I was young once myself."

Mary and Frank adjourned to the living room where she had already set up her lap top computer. They sat next to each other on the sofa with the computer open in front of them on Mary's lap. She quickly repeated the steps she had used the night before to get into the NSA computer.

Frank was completely amazed. "I've never seen anybody do that before. I don't understand how you got past the password screen."

Mary explained, "Every computer programmer needs to put a back door into their own program, that allows them to gain entrance, in case something has gone wrong. That way, if the programmer is called upon to fix it, even if someone else has protected the program with a password, the programmer can still get in. Having written many programs in my day, I know how most programmers do this, and I simply use their back door. You have to know a lot about programming codes to be able to do this. That's why most people aren't able to get past the password."

A few keystrokes later, she found the profile of the sixth person on Mark Denver's senior staff.

Mary paraphrased: "His name is David Owen, an environmentalist. Looks like he's an expert in computers, statistics, and history. Owen has degrees from several universities. He wrote several papers on how to get computer languages to talk to one another.

"The seventh person is Jane Kirkpatrick. She's a mathematician and quantum physicist who has written a book called 'The Many Frequencies of Magnetism'."

"Another expert in magnetism," Frank commented.

"The eighth person is Steven Harrington, a computer graphics and simulation expert. He wrote a book fifteen years ago called 'CAD-CAM for Modern Design and Manufacturing'."

"Doesn't CAD-CAM stand for computer aided design and manufacturing, Mary?"

"Sure does. With experts in design, drafting, and other areas, you might expect Denver's team was creating a product."

"What about the last two people?"

"The ninth person is Michael Walker, a computer expert and head of security for Mark Denver."

As Mary pulled up the tenth staff leader, Frank read out loud, "Jack Spencer, so he was one of Denver's ten senior staff leaders on the project."

"Looks that way. I wonder why Spencer hasn't been replaced after being missing for six months. It says he was in the Army Rangers and went to West Point, just like Paul Andrews. It lists Spencer as a logistics expert."

Mary made a copy of the profiles and turned off her computer just as her mother came in and said, "Good night."

"Thanks, again for the great dinner, Mrs. Webber. Your Spanish rice was terrific."

As Mary and Frank sat there alone in the quiet living room pondering the events of the past twenty-four hours, they felt closer to each other than they had to anyone in quite some time. Without really thinking about it, there had been a natural attraction for one another from the day they met. Working and traveling together had sparked something missing in both of them. After talking for a while, they put their arms around each other and kissed passionately.

CHAPTER 11

At an underground facility set deep in the Virginia hills, Mark Denver assembled his senior staff.

"Where's Sam?" Mark asked. Then as Sam entered the conference room. "Oh, there you are, Sam. Close the door. Okay, the reason I got you together today is to let you know how important it is to step up the production of Sam's new control.

"In the last couple of days, there's been a leak. This is not a security breach or anything like that. It seems to be a simple case of coincidences in which some people, outside our agency, have stumbled on facts, which could lead them to what we're doing. I don't have to remind you how important it is for national security to keep our project secret. Without going into the details at this time, just let me say, Mike Walker and I are working with NSA Security to monitor the situation. But because of the possibility of more information coming out, we need to step up our team's efforts on the new control. How's the control coming, Sam?"

Sam Magnum was thirty-five, with a little gray at the temples of his black hair. He looked out through his titanium-framed glasses and said, "We're working on the prototype day and night in the model shop."

"How long, Sam?"

"I figure as least another three weeks."

"Can you make it in two?"

"We can try."

"Good. Make it two. How much time will it take to get the control up and running?"

"About a week, and then we need another week to complete the trials."

"A month may be too long, Sam. Does anyone have any ideas of how we can cut down the trial time?"

Jane Kirkpatrick spoke up and said, "Don't forget, Mark, not spending enough time on control trials is what got us in this situation in the first place."

"How could I forget," Mark said sarcastically. "Any other comments?"

Mark waited a few seconds and said, "Jane, you and Jason know the most about controlling the resonance frequencies of magnetism. How about brainstorming ideas with your groups to limit the number of trials required to prove out Sam's control."

"Sure. We'll get right on it."

"Jason, is that okay with you?"

"Yes. I'll set up a meeting for one o'clock this afternoon with our combined groups."

"Paul, what's the status of our retrieval strategy?"

Paul Andrews spoke up in his deep voice. "We already have two or three ideas we've been working on."

"Good. As you know, we may only get one chance at this, so we need to make it good. Any other comments?" After a pause, Mark said, "Okay. Let's plan on getting together for quick updates every morning at eight, right here. Let me know if there's anything else you need to make this happen."

As they were leaving the room, Mark asked Mike Walker, head of security, to stay.

When the others had left the room, Mark closed the door and said, "You're pretty much up to date, except for Ray's report this morning. Ray called off his guys when they were spotted shortly after lunch yesterday. I think we need a better way of keeping up to date on what Frank McDermott and Mary Webber are doing. Got any ideas?"

"I've thought of one. What if I insert myself into their sheriff's department? I'll try to gain their confidence and work with them every day. I can keep you up to date on what they know."

"That's not bad, but just how would you insert yourself and expect to get their confidence overnight?"

"Let me develop a plan and get back to you on that. I've got some ideas, but I need to think them out a bit further."

"Get back to me as soon as you can, Mike."

"Okay. Oh, by the way, Mark, I checked on this Mary Webber with my counterpart in the FBI. She's on a leave of absence from the FBI for one year. When her father died, she elected to go live with her mother for a time, to try to decide what she wants to do next. She would have resigned, but the FBI didn't want to lose her. So she agreed to the one-year leave, and easily got a job with the local sheriff's office in Black River where she grew up. So it's just a coincidence Mary Webber is working with Frank McDermott at this time."

"Well, lucky me!" Mark said in disgust. "What did you tell your counterpart in the FBI when you inquired about Mary Webber?"

"Oh, I told him I had heard through the grapevine that Mary worked for the FBI, and we wanted to get her to add some security protocol to our computer system."

"Good thinking, Mike. I don't want the Bureau on our case as well as the Black River Sheriff's Office."

Back at the sheriff's office, Frank was just arriving for work. Dave Tucker greeted him as he walked in.

"How was your trip to Virginia?"

"It was a good trip. We wound up having dinner in Washington with Mark Denver, the supervisor of the missing man we were asking about."

"How did that go?"

"Well, do you have some time to talk about it?"

"Sure. Come into my office."

"Let me get Mary, and we'll meet you in your office in a few minutes."

"By the way, how did you and Miss Webber hit it off?"

"I really like her, Dave. She's great to work with."

Frank knocked on Mary's open door and said, "Good morning, Mary. Did you sleep well?"

"Yeah, Frank, how about you?"

"Very well. Your mother's meal was great and the company after dinner was even better," he said with a big smile. Mary smiled back.

"Can you come with me to Dave's office so we can bring him up to date on what happened on our trip?"

"Sure."

Mary got up and started for the door. Before going out of her office, she paused, closed the door over half way, and with a sly smile on her face, gave Frank a hug and a kiss.

Frank shut the door all the way and took Mary in his arms and kissed her.

After a few moments, Frank said, "We better get to Dave's office before I have an embarrassing bulge in my pants."

They both smiled. Mary turned and led the way out as Frank opened the door.

It took them about half an hour to bring Dave up to date, leaving out the parts about Mary hacking into the NSA computer and their suspicions of being followed. They did tell Dave how Denver's reaction to Harry's drawing was different from Mrs. Spencer's reaction.

Dave raised an eyebrow and said, "That does seem strange. What are you going to do now?"

Frank looked at Mary to see if she was going to say anything, and said, "I thought I'd go back to the coroner's office and see if anything new is known about the bones."

"I guess you missed the morning news," said Dave.

"What news?"

"It's been on all the local news and some national news coverage that the local Indians have taken over the front lawn of the coroner's office. The Indians have pitched two tepees, and are camping out there until the bones are released to them for reburial on Indian land. It's been a mess with the local and national media people on the scene. The National Archeological Society has sent in their heavy hitters to get in their two cents as well. Richard Farley seems to be the spokesman for the Archeological Society since he was in on it from the start."

"Who's leading the Indian group?"

"None other than the chief of the reservation, Joseph Littlefield, himself. He's been sleeping in one of the tepees."

"I know Joseph and his son, George, very well. I'd better get over there and talk to them to make sure this thing doesn't get out of hand."

"Good luck, Frank. It's already out of hand."

As Frank and Mary walked back towards their offices, she said, "I'll try and get additional information from the NSA computer."

"Good idea. Will you have dinner with me tonight, Miss Webber?"

"Sure, Mr. McDermott."

"I'll talk to you about it when I get back from the coroner's office."

"See you then."

In Mark Denver's conference room, Mark closed the door so he and Mike Walker could talk again in private.

"Have you come up with a plan to insert yourself into the Black River Sheriff's Office, Mike?"

"Yes, and no. I have a plan, but it puts Ray Blackwell into their office, not me. Mary Webber may already have my name and maybe my picture. She would be unlikely to know about Ray."

"That makes sense. How would you get Ray into their office?"

"We send Ray in as a U.S. Marshal on the pretense that he has been asked to work with the Black River Sheriff's Office to make sure this Indian vs. archeologists thing doesn't get out of hand."

"Not bad, but what if they find out Ray's not with the U.S. Marshal's Office?"

"Well, he needs to be. Can you go through proper classified channels and get Ray appointed a U.S. Marshal?"

"I would have to go through the Attorney General and maybe all the way to the President and that would require an explanation to him of what's going on."

"The Attorney General and the President are cleared to REPEAT, aren't they, Mark?"

"Oh, yes. We couldn't do what we're doing without them knowing. I guess I'll just have to expedite the paper work and get Ray's appointment for this special assignment."

"I don't envy that task, but I think it's necessary, Mark."

"I'll get right on it. Meanwhile, let's assume I'll get Ray's appointment. Brief Ray on what we want him to do and start getting Ray the credentials he needs. I don't want to lose any time on this."

CHAPTER 12

When Frank arrived at the three-story red brick coroner's office, there was one local news crew, two others from nearby towns, and CNN. Frank had to park a block away. As he got near the front lawn, he saw his friend George Littlefield. George was dressed in street clothes, while several other members of his tribe were dressed in full ceremonial Indian outfits.

"Hey, George!" Frank cried as he walked up to him.

"Good to see you, Frank. I've been wanting to talk to you."

As Frank and George shook hands, a reporter from CNN came up to them, followed by another man holding a camera. Before Frank could say another word, the reporter stuck a microphone in their faces, and asked who they were? Frank and George both gave their names.

"And just what is your interest in this case, Mr. McDermott?"

"Well, I was the detective first assigned to this case when the bones were found."

"And why are you here now?"

"Well, I hope to make sure things don't get out of control any more than they already appear to be."

"And, Mr. Littlefield, where do you stand in all of this?"

"With my people. My father is the chief of our tribe. We're here to see to it that the remains of our ancestor are reburied on our land. My people believe it's a desecration to dig up the bones of our ancestors. Just how would you feel if someone dug up your grandfather's bones and wanted to put them on display for the whole world to view?"

"But, Mr. Littlefield, Mr. Farley has gone on record as saying he believes the bones are not the bones of an ancient Indian, but of a Caucasian. What do you have to say about that?"

"We believe our ancestors have lived on this land since the dawn of man. It doesn't matter to us that they may have looked different than we do today."

Just then Richard Farley arrived and came forward to shake hands with Frank.

The reporter immediately turned toward Richard and said, "Oh, Mr. Farley. We were just talking with George Littlefield about the possibility that the bones are not Indian bones. Could you elaborate on this for the news?"

Richard said, "Just let me say, this find of bones, dating seven thousand years before the birth of Christ, is a great find to the archeologists of the world. The number of other skeletons this old are very few. On behalf of all the archeologists of the world, we wish to come to some agreement with the Indians, who understandably identify with these bones, so that we might do further study to enhance our knowledge of ancient man. With that said, I wish to invite Mr. Littlefield to talk with me further on this subject, if he is willing to talk."

George looked at Richard and said, "Sure, we can talk. After all, we buried the hatchet ages ago."

With that, Frank motioned to both men to follow him into the coroner's office.

"That was pretty smooth, Richard. Have you met my good friend George Littlefield?"

"No. It's a great pleasure," was Richard's reply as he held his hand out to George.

George took hold of his hand and said, "Now I know how Sitting Bull felt when he was asked to make friends with the white man." They all smiled.

Just then, Joe Bianco greeted them and said, "I'm glad to see you guys friendly with each other. I haven't slept well, thinking this was getting way out of hand."

"What did you think we're going to do, Joe? Burn the place down."

"The thought had crossed my mind that you might do just that."

"Not today, Joe."

The four men proceeded to Joe's lab in the basement of the building where the bones were still carefully laid out on a table, forming an almost complete human skeleton.

Richard handed the skull to George, pointing out how the back of the skull was round and not flat. He went on to say, "Most ancient Indian skeletons have exhibited a flatter skull. We think this was because their mothers carried them on a board on their back from the time they were born. Also, this skeleton is of a man who would have stood about five foot ten."

"I'm five foot ten," said George.

"Yes, but most of your ancestors did not grow to that height. Also, note the narrowness of the portion of the skull that contained the brain, and the narrowness of the facial structure and projected jaw. These are features we normally attribute to a person of European or Southwestern Asian ancestry."

"If this guy wasn't one of my ancestors, then who do you think he was?"

"Oh, that's exactly what we wish to determine, my new friend. This man could have been a single Caucasian who crossed the land bridge that connected the Bering Straight into North America, or more likely one of many who migrated to this area over some centuries.

And if so, why did they do this, and why did they wander so far to the south east of the land bridge? These are burning questions we wish to answer. By studying ancient man we hope to understand more about ourselves. I hope you'll talk to your father and your people on our behalf. Will you do that for us?"

George looked at Frank and then back at Richard, and said, "I'll talk to them, but I can't promise you it'll change their minds. You must understand this is a religious issue with my people. We believe the spirits of our ancestors are still around us on our land guiding our way in life. But I'll talk to my people about the things I have learned here today."

"Thank you, George."

Frank suggested the four of them have lunch at the Back Alley Restaurant, a local spot where the press would not likely find them. They followed Joe out the back door and got into his Ford Explorer.

A round of beers at the restaurant tended to get everyone in a friendly mood.

After a while, Frank asked Richard, "Do you really think a man on foot could have crossed the land bridge at the Bering Straight and walked thousands of miles to this area?"

"Probably not. It's more likely that he was part of a family of people who gradually migrated to this area in search of a better place to live, much the way the white man migrated to the west. A DNA test of the bones might tell us more about this man's ancestry."

George said, "I'll discuss these things with my father, but I don't know if it'll have a positive or negative influence on him. He may view the things you say as a prelude to others coming to our land in search of more skeletal remains. My people would absolutely not tolerate this. We would consider it grave robbing on a major scale."

"You make a good point," said Frank. "Let's hope we can work together to find a middle ground that will not offend your people."

The four men finished their lunch, and headed back to the coroner's office. When they arrived, they found the scene had quieted from earlier that morning. The news crews had gone for the day. Frank invited George to take a walk with him while Joe and Richard went into the office.

As Frank and George walked along the sidewalk of the oak-lined street, the sun filtered through the branches of the green trees in the quietness of the summer day. Frank and George talked about some of their favorite times growing up together.

After a while, George confided in Frank. "One of the things that bothers some of my people is a fear that if these bones prove to be something other than of our ancestors, it might impact our rights to the lands we've claimed to be ours."

"That's understandable. A fear like that can drive men to do things which they would never consider otherwise."

"Do you think we have anything to be worried about?"

"I don't really think so. After all, how could anyone dispute the claim of a people who have inhabited land for thousands of years?"

"Don't forget, the white man didn't let that claim stop him from pushing the Indian from our lands in the past."

"Good point, but that occurred during a massive expansion of the white man to the west. At this point in time, I don't think anyone would try and push your people from your land."

"They better not try, Frank."

"Or you'll do what?" was Frank's reply as he turned in front of George with his fist ready to fight, but with a big smile on his face.

George smiled back and said, "I think I can still take you, Frank."

"In your dreams." They both laughed.

"You know," Frank said, as they started to head back towards the coroner's office, "there've been some strange things about this case that I haven't told anyone about, except Mary."

"Who's Mary?"

"Mary Webber is new to our sheriff's office. She grew up here in Black River, and recently returned to live with her mother, after her father died. We've become good friends. You might say, we are more than just friends."

"Sounds serious."

"Well, maybe."

"I'm glad for you, but what was it you wanted to tell me about this case being strange?"

Frank told George the whole story, starting with Harry's drawing.

When Frank finished, George said, "Do you remember how my people learn about their history?"

"Yeah. You told me the stories of the past are handed down from one generation to the next very carefully so that the entire history of your people is captured in your memories."

"Well, I'm one of the chosen ones who has been entrusted to carry down this history."

"That's great. Does it have any bearing on this case?"

"Maybe. I must talk with my father about this before I can say anymore."

"You're getting mysterious, George."

"I'm sorry. I'll let you know if I can say anymore."

Frank and George parted company at Frank's car. As it was getting to be mid afternoon, Frank started back to his office, while George joined his father in the tepee on the lawn in front of the coroner's office.

CHAPTER 13

Frank knocked on Mary's open office door and said, "Hi, Mary."

Just then Dave Tucker passed by, smiled at them and asked, "What happened to the Miss Webber, Frank?"

Frank blushed and said, "We're on a first name basis now."

"Okay, that's fine with me," Dave said as he continued towards his office with a smile.

Frank entered Mary's office and said, "I'll make a reservation at the Black River Restaurant for us if that's okay with you?"

"Sure."

"Can I pick you up at seven?"

"Sounds great."

"See you at seven."

Meanwhile, at the underground facility deep in the Virginia hills, Mark Denver was across his desk from Mike Walker and Ray Blackwell.

"I don't think I need to tell you how important this is. I had to get the President's signature on this to get you the U.S. Marshal's appointment. He wasn't too pleased with this whole thing, and told me not to screw it up. Did you give Ray all his credentials, Mike?"

"Yes."

Mark took a deep breath, looked at Ray and said, "How are you going to handle this?"

Ray sat up with his hands together on the top of the desk, and looked straight into Mark's eyes. "The Sheriff of Black River received a fax today from the U.S. Marshal's Office letting him know I will be working with them, starting tomorrow, to make sure this Indian thing doesn't get out of hand. I'll play the part while I try to get friendly enough with McDermott to get his confidence. I plan to take my team with me to work undercover. They haven't been briefed to REPEAT, so I'll continue to tell them only that we are trying to prevent a potential leak of a top-secret project, vital to the security of our nation. If any member of my team learns enough to be a risk, I'll brief them to the program, but only as a last resort."

"Did you get the wiretaps signed off?"

"Yeah. Ray has the authority to bug any suspect who's a risk to the program."

"What cover will your team use this time?"

"They'll have a truck identical to the ones used by the local phone-company. It's equipped with all the latest listening devices our guys cooked up."

"Okay, good luck, keep us up to date, and don't let them catch you watching them this time."

As Ray and Mike left Mark's office, Mark asked his secretary to send in Sam Magnum.

"Hi, Sam. How is the control coming along?"

"We stepped up production, and will have the prototype modification completed in no more than ten days. Jane Kirkpatrick and Jason Bedford have been a great help in coming up with a new resonance coordinator."

"Thanks for the update. I'll talk to you some more tomorrow."

Outside Mrs. Webber's home, Mary and Frank were just leaving for the restaurant as Mary's mother watched them from the front porch.

"You young people run along now," she said, with a smile indicating to Mary that she was pleased to see her daughter going out with this nice man.

As they drove down the road, Mary moved close to Frank and said, "I've been looking forward all day to seeing you."

"I've been looking forward to this, too."

They arrived at the restaurant and were taken to Frank's favorite table.

Mary said, "I saw you on TV when I got home tonight. That Richard Farley seemed to say all the right things to keep that reporter from starting a fight in front of the coroner's office today."

"Yeah, that could have been a shouting contest if the wrong things were said."

Frank went on to tell Mary about the other things that took place including his conversation with George.

"What history do you think George had on his mind?"

"I haven't the slightest idea. I guess I'll just have to wait for him to tell me, that is, if he is allowed to tell me. Did you find out anything more from your computer search?"

"Not much, except that the project Denver heads up doesn't take place at the NSA headquarters."

"How do you know that?"

"If it did, their computers would likely be networked to the other projects within NSA. The projects would have separate security lockouts, but I would've been able to get into Denver's project. As it is, I could only obtain the general information about the department size and personnel, which I already had. They probably required that much information in NSA headquarters for security, payroll, and government accounting."

"Then just where do they operate out of?"

"I couldn't find that out."

"That's very interesting, and so are your big blue eyes." Mary smiled.

Frank reached across the table and took hold of Mary's hand gently putting it into his own.

"Mary, do you believe in love at first sight?"

"I'm beginning to."

"I think I fell in love with you right from the day we met. From that moment, I haven't been able to get you out of my mind. I don't know if it's love or infatuation, but I love you. I don't know if I can describe my feelings for you."

"I think I know how you're feeling, for I have the same feelings for you. Every time we are together, I want you to hold me in your arms."

They smiled at each other, and as far as they were concerned they were the only people in the restaurant.

As they left the restaurant, Mary said, "When are you going to show me your etchings?"

Frank looked at her with a surprised smile and said, "Anytime you like; however, I've been living as a bachelor for some time now, and I'm afraid you might find a few things slightly out of sorts."

"Can I see your home now?"

"Your wish is my command."

As they entered Frank's beautiful old Victorian style home, Mary said, "This is beautiful. How long have you had it?"

"I was raised here. My parents left this home to me after they died. My wife and I raised our son here. After my wife died, I thought of selling it, but there are too many good memories here for me to do that."

Frank took Mary around the first floor showing off the kitchen, which he had modernized. He turned on music in the living room and they sat down together on the couch. Mary moved close to Frank and he put his arm around her shoulder. At once they could feel the desire in each other's body. They hugged and kissed tenderly. They kicked off their shoes and laid down on the couch so that they could feel the burning passion in each other.

About twelve thirty, Mary woke up in Frank's arms, and kissed him on the cheek. When he opened his eyes, she whispered, "Not that I want to leave, but I better be getting home."

"Oh, where did the time go? I can't believe it's this late."

"I don't want this night to end, but tomorrow is a workday."

They quickly made themselves presentable and he took her home. They walked up the porch steps to the front to the door and kissed one last, long kiss for the night.

The next morning at work, Harry noticed Frank and Mary talking with each other by the coffeepot in the hall and said good morning to them.

As he looked at their faces, Harry said, "Wonderful, you guys are in love."

"What are you talking about?" Frank replied.

"You can't fool me. After all, I've been reading faces all my life, but I don't think it would be hard for an amateur to read what you guys are putting out."

"Is it that obvious?" Mary said.

Harry smiled and said, "Yes," as he walked away.

"I guess there is no hiding it, Mary. We better try and keep up some sort of professionalism while we're in the office."

"If we can."

Just then Dave Tucker walked by and said, "Good morning. Would you two join me in my office please, and bring Harry with you?"

Frank looked at Mary and gave her a look that asked if she thought Dave was on to them. They followed Dave to his office, picking up Harry on the way.

On entering Dave's office, they were surprised to see a very official looking man, about thirty-five years old, standing in the corner looking out the window. He was wearing a brown suit with a white shirt, dark brown tie, and had a tan Stetson in his left hand.

He turned from the window to greet them as Dave said, "I'd like you to meet Ray Blackwell."

CHAPTER 14

Ray Blackwell shook hands with each of them.

Dave said, "Ray is a U.S. Marshal sent here from Washington to make sure things don't get out of hand over this Indian thing. Please everyone take a seat."

"Welcome to Black River," Frank said.

"Thanks, Mr. McDermott, is it?"

"Yes, but call me Frank."

Dave said, "Frank is my chief detective. We've been working together for some time now. Harry Packard is our resident expert sketch artist and senior deputy sheriff."

Harry took out his sketchpad and started drawing, as Dave continued. "Mary is new to our office. She comes to us from the FBI where she made quite a reputation as a computer expert."

"Nice to meet all of you," Ray said. "I'll try not to get in your way. I hope to get this business resolved and get back to Washington without disturbing you good people any more than I may have to."

"What do you know about this case?" Frank asked.

"Just what I was briefed by my office and what I've seen on television. I understand there were skeletal remains found along the Black River, which were later determined to be nine thousand years old from the carbon dating. And that the local Indians have pitched tepees on the front lawn of your coroner's office in an effort to get the bones released to them for reburial on their lands. I also was told the archeologists, lead by a Richard Farley, are intent on not giving up the bones before they study them in great detail."

"This is all correct," Frank said. "In addition, the Indians are worried the archeologists will want to start major archeological digs on Indian land. The Indians feel this would be akin to grave robbing on a major scale."

"One other thing worries the Indians," Frank continued, "the archeologists claim the bones are not Indian bones. Richard Farley believes the bones are of a Caucasian people who might have crossed the land bridge which is now the Bering Straight and migrated southeast to where the bones were found."

"Why would that worry the Indians?"

"Well, even though the Indians owned their lands before Christopher Columbus came to America, the Indians are concerned their land claim might be in jeopardy if it were proven white men lived here before the Indians."

"That's very interesting," Ray said. "Now I have a better idea why the two sides are at conflict over these bones."

"As a U.S. Marshal, just what authority do you have in this matter?" Frank asked.

"My superiors are looking for me to make a recommendation to the district court if this matter cannot be resolved peacefully."

"What sort of recommendation?"

"If things seem to be getting way out of control, I mean violent, I would recommend the skeletal remains be turned over to the district court for safe keeping until this dispute could be decided by the court."

"What would the district court do with the bones?" Mary asked.

"Probably lock them up in a safe in some bank or museum."

Frank said, "I know both parties in this dispute and I don't think you'll have to worry about it getting violent."

"That's good to know. Maybe you could introduce me to these people so I might impress upon them the consequences of violence in this matter."

Dave spoke up and said, "The sheriff's office will be glad to help you in anyway we can. Isn't that right, Frank?"

"Sure, Dave. I'll set up a meeting with both parties at the coroner's office as soon as possible."

Ray said, "That's good. Is there, anything else that I should know?"

Frank glanced at Mary, and then looked back at Ray and said, "No, that about covers it."

Dave Tucker looked at Frank with a puzzled look on his face and said, "Okay I guess that does about cover it. Good luck with your meeting. You're welcome to use the office across from Frank's during your stay, if you wish to, Ray."

"Thanks. That would be great."

As the group stood up to leave Dave's office, Dave asked Frank to stay for a minute.

After the others left, Dave said, "Frank, I suspect you didn't say anything about your missing person investigation because you don't feel you have enough of a story to relate it to a U.S. Marshal."

"Yes, that's about it. There's no sense making fools of ourselves. And thanks for picking up on my lead the way you did."

"Okay, see you later."

Ray Blackwell put his Stetson on the desk in the office he was given across from Frank's. He picked up the phone and dialed a number.

On the other end, Art Cox picked up his cell-phone and said, "Black River Phone Company, Truck 10, what can I do for you?"

"Where are you now?"

The other man recognized his voice and said, "We're at the Webber home where we're giving Mrs. Webber the newest model phones."

"Good. Talk to you later."

Meanwhile, Frank got on the telephone and made arrangements to have a meeting in Joe Bianco's office at eleven o'clock to discuss the controversy over the bones. Frank found out from George Littlefield's wife that George was staying with Chief Joseph Littlefield in a tepee outside the coroner's office to show support for the Indian side.

At ten thirty, Frank drove Ray Blackwell to the coroner's office. On the way in, Frank stopped at the Chief's tepee and introduced George and his father to Ray Blackwell. George was a little taken back upon meeting an U.S. Marshal and asked if they were going to be arrested. Frank calmed George down and asked if he and his father would care to have a little meeting with them inside, along with Joe Bianco and Richard Farley. George and his father agreed.

The four men entered the coroner's office building and went directly to Joe's office. Frank made all the introductions. They sat down around Joe's desk.

Ray explained why he was there and what powers he had been given to resolve the situation. He went on to say, "I hope both sides can come to a solution without government interference."

Everyone listened, but neither side was quick to respond.

Finally, Chief Joseph spoke up and said, "What right does the government have to take the bones of our ancestors?"

Ray replied, "The government has the right and obligation to keep the peace."

"The government can keep the peace by letting us rebury the bones of our ancestors."

"Unless you can come to agreement with Mr. Farley on this, I'm afraid the government will step in to help you resolve the matter."

Richard said, "As representative of the Archeological Society, we wish to come to an agreement everyone can live with; but I must remind you, if we go to court over this matter, I believe I can prove the bones are not the bones of your ancestor."

Frank could see that both Chief Joseph and George Littlefield were slightly more red-in-the face than usual, and suggested, "Let's end this meeting for now so both sides can consider the things that were said here today."

The meeting ended with everyone agreeing to get together again after they considered what was said.

Frank and Ray stopped for lunch at a local deli before returning to the sheriff's office.

After ordering soup and sandwiches, Frank asked Ray, "How often do you have to travel on assignments like this?"

"Actually, this is my first traveling assignment with the U.S. Marshal's Office. I've mostly been involved with routine business in Washington."

"Do you have a family?"

"No, never found the right woman. How about you?"

"I was married for twenty years, but my wife died from cancer about a year and a half ago. I have one son who is grown up with a family of his own now."

Frank started to ask more questions about the U.S. Marshal's Office, but Ray just said that he hated to talk shop while at lunch. Ray changed the subject back to Frank by asking him what he liked to do for fun.

"Well, I like to read. I keep up to date on the latest tools of our trade and I like mystery novels. How about you?"

"I play golf when I can find the time."

The remainder of the luncheon conversation continued along the same friendly lines with Frank finding out little about Ray or his work.

When they returned to the office, Frank asked Mary if she had any plans for the night.

"I have offers from three other men, but I might be persuaded to cancel them if a better offer comes along."

Frank smiled and said, "Do you like Italian food?"

"Sure."

"I know a wonderful Mom and Pop place where we can get great food and have a quiet place to talk."

Mary picked up her phone and said, "Cancel all my other dates for tonight."

Frank smiled and said, "Pick you up at seven?"

"Okay."

By mid afternoon, Art Cox and Jimmy Norton were just starting the job of bugging Frank's home. They parked the truck on the street in front of the house. Jimmy expertly worked the lock on the back door and let himself in without being seen. Art kept watch from the truck while Jimmy worked inside. They kept in contact with each other with headsets. Jimmy finished his work and left the way he came in. He casually walked to the truck and they drove away.

Art asked, "Everything go okay?"

"Like a charm, but while I was working in McDermott's home, I remembered I forgot to connect the R85 in the phone in the living room at the Webber's this morning."

Art immediately raised his voice and replied, "I'm getting tired of your screw-ups, Jimmy. We're getting well paid for this job, and we were told if we screw it up, we'll never work again."

"I'm sorry, Art. You know how hard I try to get things perfect. It won't happen again."

"If it does, we are out of the best job we've ever had."

Jimmy said, "Why can't we just go back and tell the old lady we forgot to do something. It'll only take me a minute to make the connection."

"And what if Mary Webber or McDermott are there?"

"We can swing by and check it out. If they're home, we do it tomorrow."

"No. Ray told us to have it done today, and you know when Ray says today, he doesn't mean maybe tomorrow. And you know what Ray said about keeping a low profile. If we get made, we never work again."

"We have the rest of the day and night to fix this," Jimmy said, "so don't get yourself so worked up. Let's wait till the old lady goes to bed. I'll ease in and out without the old lady knowing I was even there. We can either wait until both ladies go to bed, or maybe Mary Webber won't even be home by then."

"Okay," Art relented, still steaming. "We'll do it your way."

Late in the day, Ray pretended to be busy at work on his laptop computer. After everyone left the sheriff's office, he planted bugs in Frank's and Mary's phones and offices. When Ray left the office, he went out for dinner, and then back to the local Comfort Inn where he was staying.

Frank picked up Mary at seven and they left for dinner. Art and Jimmy were parked four doors down the street and watched Frank and Mary drive away. They waited until after dark to make their move.

At quarter to ten, Art and Jimmy saw the front porch light come on at the Webber home. A minute later, the upstairs light went on. After fifteen minutes, they watched the upstairs light go out. They waited fifteen minutes more and Jimmy made his move.

He casually walked down the street like someone taking an evening stroll. As he reached the driveway, Jimmy simply walked to the back of the house like it was his own. He skillfully worked the lock and entered through the back door, all the time staying in touch with Art on their headsets.

Jimmy entered the living room as Mary and Frank returned home and drove into the driveway. Art immediately warned Jimmy to get out.

Mary unlocked the front door and went in, with Frank a few steps behind her. She saw a dark figure sliding to the back door as she flipped on a light. She screamed and Frank ran to see what was the matter. She pointed to the back door just as Jimmy went out.

Art started the truck and moved down the road in the direction of the Webber home.

Frank yelled, "Stop, or I'll shoot!" even though he wasn't carrying a gun.

Frank followed Jimmy out the back door in pursuit.

Jimmy saw the truck pass the front of the house as Art had just told him on their headsets. Jimmy ran diagonally across the front yard to the right, following after the truck. As he ran, he pulled out a gun and fired one shot in the direction of his pursuer.

Frank reached the street side of the house just in time to hear the bullet go over his head. As the truck pulled away, Frank didn't have a chance to read the plate because it was too dark, but he did get a glimpse of the truck. He ran back into the house through the front door to make sure Mary's Mother was unhurt.

Mary's mother was just coming down the stairs and said, "What on earth is going on?"

Mary gave her mother a hug and said, "I'm glad you're all right."

"Why wouldn't I be?"

"Frank just chased a burglar out the back door."

Mary's mother sat down and said, "I never heard a thing."

Frank called the dispatcher and reported the incident. He told him to have the night patrol keep an eye out for a white or light gray utility truck with two people in it.

"Maybe it would be a good idea if I stayed the night," Frank suggested.

Mary and her mother both agreed. Mary made hot chocolate and the three sat around for an hour talking about what happened. Nothing had been stolen, but they were all shaken up a bit over the incident.

Mary's mother went back to bed after she calmed down. Mary and Frank sat together on the couch in the living room and talked about the incident.

"I'll get fingerprints in the morning. Since nothing was stolen, I suspect we surprised the guy soon after he got in. What I can't figure out is why burglars would be using a utility truck for their getaway."

"Maybe they work for one of the local utilities and don't have cars of their own."

"That's one answer."

"I feel a lot safer with you here tonight," Mary murmured, putting her hand in his.

Frank took her in his arms and they kissed. Mary turned out the lights in the living room and later they fell asleep together on the couch.

Frank woke up a little after five the next morning. He kissed Mary as she started to come awake. He stood up and stretched after sleeping on the couch all night with Mary.

She woke up and said, "I'll get cleaned up and make us some breakfast. How does bacon and eggs sound?"

"Sounds great."

"Orange juice and coffee?"

"Sure."

After breakfast, Frank got his detective kit from the trunk of his car and dusted the area from the back door to the living room for fingerprints. He got many good prints to check out later at work. Frank noted to himself that whoever came in the back door either found the door open, or so skillfully unlocked it that there were no indications of a break in. Frank asked Mary's mother if she had left the back door unlocked.

She said, "Ever since my Ed died, I've been careful to make sure the doors are locked at night."

She thought about it for a minute and said, "Yes, I remember making sure the back door and front door were locked and I put on the porch light for Mary before going to bed."

Frank thanked Mary for breakfast and said, "I'm going home to get cleaned up. I'll talk with you at work."

When Frank got to work, Sheriff Dave Tucker asked, "What happened last night?"

Frank told him the story and said, "I'm going to check out the fingerprints I found this morning."

Dave reminded Frank that he was going on his annual fishing trip, starting the next day, and that Frank would be in charge until he returned. Frank told him to have a good time and not worry about things while he was away.

Frank got to work checking for a match. By the time Mary arrived, Frank had determined one set of the prints belonged to himself.

Mary said, "I'll check the others using the FBI database."

With Frank looking on, Mary identified one more set of prints as her own and that there was only one more set of individual prints. They knew the third set must be her mothers.

"She probably never had her finger prints taken," Mary commented.

She then said, "After you left this morning, I was talking more to my mother about you seeing the man get into a utility type of truck last night. My mother told me a phone truck was at our home yesterday installing new phones."

"Did your mother give you a description of the men?"

She pulled out a piece of paper from her purse with the descriptions her mother gave her.

"Good work. I think we have some leads to consider."

Meanwhile, Ray Blackwell was getting hot under the collar. He had been pretending to be doing paperwork at the desk in his new temporary office. Instead he was listening to Frank and Mary's conversation using the bug he had planted in Mary's office the day before.

Ray took a walk outside to have a cigarette and called Art on his cell-phone.

When Art answered, Ray said, "You better have a good excuse."

Art stammered and then told Ray the whole story. Ray was steamed, but he knew he couldn't do anything at this point, except damage control. Ray told Art to get the truck out of town.

Art said, "We did that last night. We're a hundred miles away."

"Good." Ray thought for a minute and said, "Okay here's what I want you to do. First, put me on the speaker so Jimmy can hear it, too."

"Okay you're on the speaker."

"Rent two cars and come back to town. Make sure the cars aren't anything flashy. Check into the local Comfort Inn on the edge of town where I'm staying. I want one of you to follow Frank and the other to follow Mary if they go anywhere other than home or work. I'll let you know when one of them leaves the sheriff's office so you don't need to hang around outside where you might get caught. We already have a bug in Frank's car, but we need to get one in Mary's. I'll try and do that myself. Dress in ordinary street clothes. Stay way out of sight. Listen and record any conversations they have together. Got all that?"

"Ah, yes sir," said Art.

"Have you got that, Jimmy?"

"Sure, Boss."

"This is your last chance. Don't call me; I'll call you for reports on a regular basis." He rang off, went back inside, and continued to monitor Frank and Mary's conversation.

Frank and Mary were in the middle of their conversation.

Frank said, "Okay let's go over what we know. We know the man who broke in last night was no amateur because he left no traces of a break in and no prints. We also know the men who installed the new phones yesterday wore hospital type gloves from what your mother said. We don't buy the explanation the men gave your mother that the gloves keep them from getting acid from their fingers on the components. Nothing was stolen last night. These men may have bugged your home yesterday. The only explanation we can come to is someone is watching us. And the only other time we felt we were being watched was on our return trip from Washington. Mary, I think we have stumbled onto something big."

"This scares me. I know too much about how the FBI does things to know you're probably right."

"And it all seems to be connected somehow to our visit with Denver and our inquiry about Jack Spencer."

"I wonder if Denver could have had Jack Spencer killed, Frank."

"That's one possible explanation, but why would Denver think we knew anything?"

"Maybe this Denver is real paranoid."

"To hire people to watch us, he must be. Maybe Denver will back off when he finds out we don't know anything about him. In the mean time, let's you and I watch each other's back until we either figure out what's going on, or they figure out we really don't know anything."

Ray Blackwell removed the tiny listening device from his ear to pick up a call on his cell phone.

Mark Denver asked, "How's it going, Ray?"

With a quiet voice, Ray proceeded to bring Mark up to date.

Mark had all he could do to keep his blood pressure under control.

He took a deep breath and said, "Okay let me know of any new developments."

CHAPTER 15

Frank contacted George Littlefield and asked him if he would meet he and Mary for lunch at the Back Alley Restaurant at noon. George agreed.

Frank introduced Mary to George at the Restaurant and the three sat down together in a comfortable corner booth.

"I've been looking forward to meeting you, Mary, after all the good things Frank has said about you."

"I'm happy to meet the other half of the legendary Black River high school champion team duo."

After several more pleasantries were exchanged, Frank commented, "I can see you two are going to be friends; but in addition to wanting you to meet Mary, the real reason I set up this meeting was because we need your help."

George sat up with a bit of surprise and said, "What can I help you with?"

Frank proceeded to bring George up to date on what had been going on.

George took it all in and said, "Where do I come into this?"

"I was hoping you would ask. Would you be interested in helping us catch the people who are watching us?"

"Sounds like fun."

"It could be dangerous, George. If these people are working for a killer, they may be killers themselves. The guy took a shot at me last night."

"You and I are blood brothers. If you want my help, you have it."

"I appreciate that. We haven't filled in the Sheriff on all this because we don't have hard evidence yet that we're right. And I'd rather have you watching our back in an unmarked car."

"Jeep, in my case, Frank."

"Right. Can you start tonight by following Mary home from work at five o'clock?"

"Sure."

"Here, take my cell phone."

"I don't need it. I'll just send you a smoke signal." George smiled and pulled out his Nokia cell phone.

They exchanged cell phone numbers and Mary commented, "We can expect bugs in our cars and homes based on my FBI experience. We better use our cell phones outside our homes and cars for all communications between the three of us."

"If you call us, George, we'll go outside and call you back within five minutes unless you have emergency information for us."

"Okay, Frank."

Ray Blackwell watched them leave the restaurant a little after one o'clock, looking as if they had had a family reunion. He had been unable to listen to their conversation in the restaurant. Ray figured he better follow them himself until the others got back to town. George parted their company, and Ray followed Frank and Mary back to the sheriff's office.

Assuming they might be overheard in Frank's car, Mary and Frank watched what they said to each other. Mary thanked Frank for introducing her to his best friend and asked him if he would like to come to dinner that night.

"Sure, I'd love to."

They kept the remaining conversation to the Indian bones-situation to throw anyone listening off the track.

Ray was listening. He didn't think anything was unusual about their lunch with George.

While following them back to the sheriff's office, Ray called Art Cox. "Art, how soon can you get back to town?"

"We're almost at the edge of town now. Jimmy is right behind me."

"Good. I suspect Webber and McDermott will each go home after work. Art, you watch McDermott and have Jimmy watch Webber. McDermott is going to Webber's home for dinner tonight. If they go anywhere together after dinner, follow them. Report back to me at ten o'clock."

George followed Mary home at five o'clock, staying some distance back from a tan Ford Escort that was following her car. When she pulled into her driveway, the Escort pulled over to the curb a block away from Mary's home. George parked his Jeep at the curb a block behind the Escort, so he could observe both the car and Mary's home. He saw only one man sitting in the front seat.

George called Frank, and a couple minutes later, Frank returned the call, as prearranged, from his back yard. "What have you got, George?"

"A guy in a tan Ford Escort just sitting in the car, about a block from Mary's."

"Just one?"

"Yeah. That's all I can see from here."

"Were you able to get the plate?"

"Got it, Frank."

"Good job."

"Do you want me to confront him?"

"No, just watch him and find out where he goes."

"Okay."

"I'll be at Mary's home tonight by six-thirty for dinner."

To a casual observer, Jimmy Norton appeared to be listening to music on a Walkman radio while reading the newspaper in a tan Ford Escort. If anyone had asked Jimmy what he was doing there, his answer would be: "Oh, I'm just waiting for my brother-in-law to finish selling life insurance to the people who live in that house."

Frank got cleaned up and drove to Mary's home for dinner. He drove past George and then past the Ford Escort. Frank casually glanced at the man behind the wheel as he went by.

George and Jimmy both watched Frank pull into the driveway and go into Mary's home. Then George saw a dark blue Ford Taurus pass his Jeep and pull behind the Escort. A big man, about thirty, got out and went over to the man in the Escort. The two men talked for a few minutes and then the big man got back into the Taurus.

George got the numbers on the plate from the Taurus and watched, from a slumped position in his Jeep, as the man in the Taurus turned his car around and retraced his way past him.

A half-hour later, the man in the Taurus returned. The big man got out with a bundle and got into the Escort. George watched as the two men in the Escort ate their dinner. George pulled out a sandwich from a bag and ate his dinner as well.

At ten, that evening, George saw the big man make a call on his cell phone. Then he saw the smaller man get into the Taurus and drive away.

At eleven o'clock, George watched the big man in the Escort follow Frank's car as Frank left Mary's for the night.

George followed the Escort to Frank's street. The Escort parked a block away from Frank's home. George kept well back so he would not be seen.

After the lights went out at Frank's home, George followed the Ford Escort to a local Comfort Inn on the edge of town. He watched the big man go into a motel room. George drove through the parking lot and was not surprised to see the Blue Ford Taurus with the license plate number he wrote down earlier.

George drove back to Frank's home and woke him up. They went out on the back porch where he told Frank about his surveillance.

"George, if you ever need a job in the sheriff's office, you've got one. Good work!"

George gave all the information to Frank and asked him, "What do you want me to do next?"

"Well, you've verified we're being watched. I'll have Mary check out the plates from her computer tomorrow. Let me mull this over tonight, and I'll let you know tomorrow what I think we should do next."

"I think you still need me watching your back, Frank."

"Have you got a hand gun?"

George pulled out a nine millimeter automatic from a shoulder holster under his brown leather jacket. George then pulled up the pant leg of his blue denim pants to reveal a small holster with a snub-nosed thirty-eight in it.

"Good," said Frank. "I think I'll start carrying my thirty-eight. You better get some sleep. I'll stop over to see you tomorrow about mid morning outside the coroner's office. And thanks, George. I owe you one."

The next day, Frank got up early and went immediately to Mary's. She answered the front door bell and seemed pleasantly surprised to see Frank. She greeted him with a kiss after he entered the house. "This is a nice surprise, but you didn't give this lady enough time to look presentable."

"You always look great to me. Breakfast was so good yesterday, I hoped I might do it again."

"Sure, Frank," as he motioned to her to watch what she said.

Together they walked through her home and outside to the back yard. Frank filled Mary in on what had transpired the night before.

Mary moved into Frank's arms, "I'm scared, Frank."

Mary felt something hard against the inside of her right arm. She reached under Frank's sport coat and felt his thirty-eight in a shoulder holster.

She looked up into his eyes, and Frank said, "Yes. I think you better carry one, also. Do you know how to shoot a hand gun?"

"They trained me in firearms at the Bureau, but I never needed to carry one."

"Do you have a hand gun?"

"No."

"I'll get you one at the office today. Here's the description of the two men and the cars they were driving last night including the license plates. They're staying at the Comfort Inn at the edge of town. Will you check these out at the office this morning?"

"Sure."

They went back inside and ate breakfast. Frank thanked her and told her he would see her at the office. As Frank drove out of her driveway, he noticed the blue Taurus parked down the street. As he passed the car, there didn't seem to be anyone in it.

Art Cox waited a few seconds and sat up in the driver's seat of the blue Taurus. He pulled out his cell phone, and called Jimmy. "McDermott just left Webber's house. He's probably on his way to the office. I'll stay here and wait for Mary. You find a good place to camp out nearby, but some distance from the sheriff office."

"Okay, Art. Do you want me to let Ray know what's going on?"

"No, there isn't much to report, so let's wait until he contacts us."

When Frank went into the office, he noticed Ray Blackwell and Harry Packard standing around the coffeepot having a conversation.

He greeted them with, "Good morning," and asked Ray, "Do you want to go back to the coroner's office with me about ten o'clock if I can arrange for both Littlefield and Farley to be there?"

"Sure, if you can arrange it. We can see if they've come to any mutual understanding about the bones."

Frank went to his desk, called the coroner's office, and asked for Richard Farley.

A minute later, Richard picked up the phone and said, "How's it going, Frank."

"Not bad. Have you and Joseph Littlefield come to an understanding about the bones?"

"We're on speaking terms and have talked with one another several times. The Chief is a reasonable man and just wants his people to retain their rich heritage."

"Can you and the Chief meet with Ray Blackwell and me this morning about ten thirty?"

"Sure. I'll ask the Chief to join us in Joe Bianco's office. I'm sure Joe won't mind."

"Thanks, Richard. I'll see you then."

Frank went to Ray's office door and told Ray, "We're all set to meet the others at the coroner's office. I'll come by for you at ten."

"Okay, Frank."

Frank went to Harry's desk and asked him to pick out a small handgun for Mary to carry in her purse.

Harry said, "Sure, but why should she need one?"

"I'll fill you in later."

Harry gave him a puzzled look and said, "I'll see what we've got."

"Thanks."

At ten o'clock, Frank stopped at Ray's open office door and asked, "Ready to go, Ray?"

Ray picked up his Stetson from the corner of his desk and followed him to Frank's car.

As they were driving to the coroner's office, Frank asked, "How are you getting along in our quiet little town?"

"Just fine. It's a pleasant change from the beltway traffic."

"Where are you staying?"

"I found a nice little Comfort Inn on the edge of town. There's a convenient restaurant within walking distance that has pretty good food."

Frank's radar was turned on by the revelation Ray had just made. Since there were several other motels and one hotel in the town of Black River, Frank wondered if this might be just a coincidence. Frank thought to himself, 'I think I'll keep certain things from Ray until we have a chance to check him out.'

Then Ray asked, "How long have you known Mary?"

"Not vary long. Only since she started working with us at the sheriff's office."

"Oh, I thought you two were an item?"

"What made you think that?"

"Oh, I can see how you look at one another."

"I didn't know we were that obvious."

"She seems to be a really nice girl."

"She was raised right here in Black River, like me, so we have a lot in common."

"That's real nice."

When they arrived at the coroner's office, Frank suggested Ray go inside and find Richard Farley while he located the Littlefield's. Ray agreed and went inside.

Frank went inside the Littlefield's tepee and was greeted with handshakes from both men. "Good to see you both," said Frank. "George, please don't say anything about last night in front of the others inside, including Ray Blackwell."

"Do you think he is on the wrong side?"

"I don't know, but on the way over here, Ray told me he's staying at the Comfort Inn."

"Hmm," said George.

"Yeah" said Frank. "I don't like the coincidence. I'm going to check him out."

With that, the three men left the tepee and went inside.

Frank kidded with the other two as they walked into Joe Bianco's office. "Aren't you two getting tired of sleeping on the ground in your tepee?"

Chief Joseph said, "I'll be glad to get back to my Sealy Posturepedic." Everyone laughed as they sat down in the room where the others were already gathered.

Ray said, "I'm glad to see there's no tension in this group now. Have both parties come to a mutual decision on what to do with the bones?"

Richard spoke up saying, "We've agreed to keep the bones here at the coroner's office for now to allow more of my colleagues to inspect them. I've promised Chief Joseph to keep him advised on everything we find out about the bones."

Chief Joseph chimed in, "You've also promised to not allow any more archeologists to come on our land without getting permission from me."

"That's correct," said Richard.

"We've also agreed on a three month time period for your people to view the bones," Chief Joseph commented. "After three months, we expect to either rebury the bones on our land, or continue the discussion over this matter."

"That seems very reasonable from both sides," Ray commented. "Will the examination of the bones include destructive testing?"

"Nobody told me there would be destructive testing," said Chief Joseph with a raised voice.

Richard said, "Only small slivers of bone have been removed for carbon dating so far. We would want to do DNA testing to determine the most likely heritage of the bones. This would require only very small samples for this testing."

George spoke up and said, "I think you better show us in detail just what you want to do with the bones before we agree to anything more."

"I'll be more than glad to show you exactly what we would like to do and just what we expect to get from the testing."

George said, "Is this all right with you, Father?"

"We shall listen and then make our agreement. Until then, we do not have an agreement on anything. After we listen, I will take your words to our council where my people will help me decide."

"Fair enough," said Richard. "When would you like me to review our procedures with you?"

"How about after lunch?"

"Sure."

Frank said, "Can we agree on going to the Back Alley Restaurant for lunch?" Everyone agreed.

After lunch, Frank and Ray returned to the sheriff's office. Ray told Frank he wanted to catch up on some paper work and went into his office. Frank went into Mary's office.

"Hi, Mary," as he closed the door to her office behind him and motioned for Mary to watch what she said.

"Oh, hi, Frank. How did your meeting go at the coroner's office?"

"Very well, I think they're making progress," as Frank wrote on a paper, "Please check out Ray Blackwell. I'll explain later."

Mary raised her eyebrows and nodded.

Frank said, "Would you like to go out for dinner with me tonight?"

"Sure. What should I wear?"

"Your blue dress looks nice on you. I'll surprise you on the restaurant. Is seven okay?"

"That'll be fine."

At seven that night, Frank and Mary drove to the Black River Restaurant. Art Cox and Jimmy Norton followed them in the Ford Taurus.

Once in their favorite corner table overlooking the river, Frank said, "I think we're alone now."

Mary followed with, "And the beating of our hearts is the only sound."

Frank smiled and took Mary's hand. "You're a wonder, Mary. I'm sorry for all this secrecy."

"That's okay. Wait till you hear what I've found out." Frank sat up showing all attention. "First, I traced the licenses to a Hertz car rental place about two hundred miles from here. The cars were rented to an Arthur Cox and a James Norton. I checked them out and found they do private investigation work for special government agencies."

"Like the NSA?"

"Like the NSA, Frank."

"Were you able to find out anything about Ray Blackwell?"

"Sure did. It took some special hacking. Ray was appointed U.S. Marshal just before coming here. And guess what he did before that?"

"Something connected to the NSA?"

"You guessed it. Ray was in security assigned to Michael Walker who works for Denver."

"No kidding!"

"Not only that, do you realize what Denver would have to do to get Ray appointed a U.S. Marshal?"

"No. What?"

"Mark would have to get approval through the Attorney General all the way to the President."

"Then that means whatever we've stumbled onto has some national security significance."

"I came to the same conclusion."

"And we don't have a clue about what it is they think we know."

"What's our next move, Frank?"

"Good question. To add to the mystery, George Littlefield took me aside after lunch today, and asked me to meet him at ten-thirty tonight at the reservation. George says he might have some information for me about all of this."

"This is really getting weird."

"You said it, Mary. Did Harry give you something extra to carry in your hand bag?"

"Yeah, a snub-nosed thirty-eight."

"Good. Better safe than sorry, as they say."

They finished their meal and headed back to Mary's home. They went inside the front door, held each other, and kissed for a few minutes. Mary whispered, "You be careful tonight."

"Don't worry. I'll see you in the morning."

He drove directly home, and soon after turned out the lights, making it look like he had turned in for the night.

At ten o'clock, Art picked up his cell phone in the Ford Taurus and said, "Ray, just checking in. We followed them to the Black River Restaurant and back to the Webber house. We followed McDermott to his house and he seems to have called it an early night. He turned out the lights fifteen minutes ago. Do you want us to stay here or go back to the motel?"

"Wait around another hour, and if nothing happens, call it a night"

At ten-twenty, Frank backed out of his driveway and went past them down the street. They quickly turned the car around and followed. When they saw Frank get stopped at the gate to the Indian reservation, they passed the gate and parked the Taurus under some trees several hundred yards down the road. They collected their listening equipment from the trunk of the car and climbed a chain link fence to the reservation. They picked up the entrance road and followed it to the main camp. There, they saw a compound of small homes and Frank's car parked next to one of them. A large tepee was located in the center of the compound with smoke swirling out of the top. Under the cover of trees, out of sight, Art and Jimmy aimed the parabolic-cone of the listening device towards the tepee.

In the tepee, George was introducing Frank to one of the elders of the tribe who had not met him before. Most knew Frank from boyhood. The group of eleven men, including Frank, sat in a circle around the fire with Chief Joseph in a prominent position opposite the entrance.

"Let this special meeting of the council come to order." The Chief motioned for his son to begin.

George addressed Frank and the others. "Ever since my father and I have been camping out in front of the coroner's office, we've been discussing the bones found on our land. When we were told the bones were not of a person from our ancestry, Father and I have pondered about our special history. As you know, Frank, this history is handed down to us by word of mouth from generation to generation. It is not written anywhere, except in our minds and hearts. My father and I have talked at length with this tribal council of elders about revealing a little of our history to you tonight. If it were not for this history, Frank, my people would not be in negotiation with Richard Farley over the rights to the bones. Instead we would be insistent that the bones be reburied. What I am going to tell you now is from my people's very early history."

With that, George began the story. "In our ancient history, there is a story of a pale- faced stranger who visited our ancestors. This man wore unusual clothes and spoke with a strange tongue. Our people did not befriend him at first. One day during a hunt, he jumped out of nowhere, and killed a large bear with a fire-stick in his hand that sounded like thunder. The stranger lived with our people for one moon. One night, this man and my people observed a strange fire coming from the mountain. The next morning, the man thanked my people and left. He was never seen again."

George stopped talking and looked at Frank.

Frank said, "Is there anything more you can tell me about this man?"

"Only that his chest armor was made from a strange material, and that the man learned my people's language in the short time he was with them."

"Are you saying this man might be the bones found on your land?"

"It's one possibility that answers the question of how a nine thousand old non-Indian might have died on our land."

"But just who was he?"

"We don't know, Frank, but we have been asking ourselves if this man could be from another time."

"A time traveler, George?"

"Remember when you first told me about the lead you were following on your case, Frank? You had identified a person from our time who matched up to the bones found on our land."

"Yes, George, go on."

"Well, when you told me this, a light bulb turned on in my head. I matched my ancient story with the missing man story you told me. From the time I was a young man and first heard this story, I've wondered about the fire-stick that sounded like thunder. It never made any sense until you call the fire-stick, a gun."

Frank and the others were silent for a moment, and then Frank said, "Assuming you might be correct, I think we all better keep this idea to ourselves until we can prove it."

"That's exactly why we called you here tonight, Frank. We wanted to share this with you because we trust you. We feel you should know everything we know, so you can help us, and we can help you."

With that said, Chief Joseph stood up and said, "This concludes our special meeting for tonight. Thank you all for coming."

As the men started coming out of the tepee, Art and Jimmy made their way back to the Ford Taurus, so they could follow Frank when he left the reservation.

Frank thanked George and said, "Mary checked out the leads you gave us. She found out the men following us likely work for Ray Blackwell, and Ray probably works for that NSA person, Mark Denver."

"So Ray Blackwell, the U.S. Marshal, is spying on you?"

"It looks that way. When I found out Ray is also staying in the Comfort Inn, I had Mary check him out. Ray indirectly worked for Denver until Ray was appointed to the U.S. Marshal position just before he came here. Mary told me it takes an appointment by the Attorney General with the Presidents approval to become a U.S. Marshal. We figure this must be a national security issue."

George said, "Doesn't this reinforce my story?"

"Maybe, but we need more proof. Do you mind if I let Mary know what was said tonight?"

George looked pensive, but he said, "Okay, Frank, but no one else."

"Agreed," said Frank. "Let's sleep on this, and talk some more tomorrow. We better get some rest."

Art and Jimmy followed Frank home and then went back to their motel. The next morning, they called Ray at 6:00 A.M. and asked him to meet them for breakfast. At breakfast, Art and Jimmy relayed everything they overheard the night before.

Art asked Ray, "Does this case have anything to do with time travel?"

Ray just answered, "Don't be absurd." He paused, smiled at them, and said, "You guys did good last night." Then he removed the smile and added, "But keep your mouths shut!"

Frank went into work early and met with Harry Parker.

"Harry, do you still have the hat pin listening device we used on the Underwood case?"

"Oh, you mean the micro-miniature bug?"

"That's the one."

"Yeah. I think I know where we stored it."

"Can you get it for me?"

"Sure, Frank. When are you going to let me in on what you're working on?"

"Well, let me just say, I plan to bug Ray Blackwell because I think he's here to spy on us."

"Are you forgetting Ray Blackwell is a U.S. Marshal?"

"No. This case is rather complicated. I do appreciate your help and loyalty, Harry."

"Frank, you know I've got your back."

"Thanks. I'll tell you more if my suspicions turn out to be correct. Until then, please keep this to yourself."

About five minutes later, Harry brought him the small device, and showed him how to use the miniature bug.

Harry asked Frank where he planned to put it and he said, "In Ray's cell-phone if I can manage it"

"I don't know how you're going to do that, Frank, but good luck."

Half an hour later, Ray came into the office. Mary arrived shortly after Ray. Frank said good morning to both of them at the coffee pot station as if it were just another day. He figured Mary was probably dying to know what happened the night before. So on the way back to their offices, Frank quietly asked Mary if she would have lunch with him. Mary responded eagerly with a nod of her head and a smile.

Later, when Ray used the rest room, Frank quickly went into Ray's office. He found Ray's cell phone in the pocket of Ray's suit coat hanging over the back of the chair. Frank looked for a way to put the bug into the cell phone, but decided he didn't know how to manage it in the few minutes he had. Frank put the cell phone back and noticed Ray's Stetson sitting on the corner of the desk. He quickly picked it up and hid the micro-bug in the hatband. He replaced the hat and left Ray's office. Frank crossed into his office just before Ray returned.

For the next hour of the morning, Frank kept the listening device in his ear, as he did some paperwork in his office.

About eleven o'clock, Frank saw Ray go outside for a smoke. Frank listened as Ray called Mark Denver on his cell phone. He could hear everything Ray said, and as luck would have it, he could hear most of what Denver was saying, as the bug was located in the hatband near Ray's right ear.

Ray told Denver about the things overheard at the Indian reservation the night before.

Denver paused and said, "They're close to being a real threat to national security."

"Do you want us to eliminate the risk?"

Just then, Ray moved the phone to his other ear.

Frank could not hear Mark's reply and only overheard Ray say, "Okay, Mark, I'll get back to you."

CHAPTER 16

Frank went into Mary's office and said, "Mary, can you break for lunch now?"

She answered, "Sure, " with a smile.

On the way out, they passed Ray and told him they decided to break for lunch.

Ray watched them leave and called his team, "They're on their way to lunch. Follow them."

Frank took Mary to a local deli where he knew the noise would likely make listening to their conversation difficult from an outside monitor. As they were seated in a booth, Mary was bursting to ask what happened the night before. Frank related the story he heard from his Indian friends.

Frank then told her, "You were supposed to be the only other one to know of this story. I asked George for permission to tell you."

"Supposed to be?"

"I planted a micro-bug in Ray's hatband and listened in as Ray talked with Denver this morning. His people overheard everything that was said at the Indian Council meeting last night. They must have one of those cone-shaped listening devices. They're more professional than I gave them credit for. I couldn't hear Denver's response to Ray's question, 'Do you want us to eliminate the risk'?"

"What do you think he answered?"

"I don't know, but we better monitor Ray and have George continue surveillance until we find out. I figure the best defense is a good offence."

He took Mary's hand and said, "I don't want anything to happen to you. I think we should stick together like glue until this gets resolved."

She looked at him lovingly and said, "Just until this gets resolved?"

Frank looked into her eyes with a smile that answered her question.

After lunch, they drove to the coroner's office. They found George Littlefield sitting on the front steps.

Mary handed George a note she had written on the way to the coroner's office. The note said, "Your meeting last night was overheard by the men following us. They might be listening now, so watch what you say. Frank planted a bug in Ray Blackwell's hatband and overheard Ray's conversation with Denver. It seems they think we are a risk to national security."

George took out a pencil and wrote, "Let's go inside and find a way to talk without being overheard."

Frank looked at his note and nodded agreement. They went into the building and found Joe Bianco in his office.

Frank introduced Mary to Joe and said, "Is it all right to take another look at the bones?"

"Sure, you'll find the bones on a table in the basement. Richard Farley is down there looking at them."

They found their way to the room where Richard was looking at the bones under a high powered magnifier.

As Richard greeted them, Frank introduced Mary. "Nice to meet you, Miss Webber. Frank speaks highly of you."

Frank noticed a radio not far away and asked Richard if he minded them putting on some music.

Richard looked at the new arrivals with a questioning look on his face. He paused and said, "I don't see why not."

Frank put on music and turned up the volume. The look on Richard's face turned from one of questioning to a look of irritation.

Frank said, "Don't worry, Richard, we haven't lost our minds yet. We just need a place to talk where nobody can overhear our conversation. Would you mind if we took our conversation to that corner and leave you to your work?"

He looked at them with more wonder, and said, "Sure, I don't mind. Can you tell me what's going on?"

"Not just yet, we're talking over some options."

Frank moved the radio to the corner of the basement where the three pulled up four wooden chairs. Frank put the radio on one chair and they sat down on the others.

As they huddled around the radio, George said, "What's this about being over heard last night and about being a risk to national security?"

Frank repeated what he had told Mary.

"George said. "What did Denver say in answer to Ray's question?"

"I don't know. Ray must have moved the phone to his other ear. I couldn't hear Denver's answer. That's why Mary and I wanted to talk this over with you."

"What's our next move?"

"Well, I don't think we can run away and hide. To protect ourselves, I think we need to keep tabs on Ray to find out why he has men following us, and just what his next move might be. We also need to find out what it is Ray thinks we know."

Mary asked, "How can we possibly keep track of Ray and his men when there are at least three of them and only three of us?"

"That's a good question. I don't think they'll follow George around, but they might. It's more likely they'll try to find out what we are thinking through you and me, Mary. Let's start carpooling to work to make it easier for George to follow us around."

George chimed in, "So I follow your car around, Frank?"

"Yeah, if you don't mind continuing to watch our backs."

"Okay, Frank."

"But be careful, I don't want to lose my best friend."

George said, "I've been thinking a lot about how to prove my time traveler theory. You know at the time the bones were found, the searchers also found some plastic pieces with the bones."

"Yeah, I think you're right."

"Well, what if the plastic was nine thousand years old and found to be of a modern type of plastic. That would be, sort of, proof of my theory, wouldn't it?"

"I guess it would," said Frank. "Let's ask Richard if he still has the pieces of plastic."

The three got up and went over to Richard.

Richard looked up from inspecting the bones and said, "What can I do for you?"

"Do you still have the pieces of plastic found with the bones?"

"Sure, we cataloged everything."

"Would you humor us and have one or more pieces of it carbon-dated?"

Richard smiled and said, "What do you hope to gain by doing that?"

Frank said, "Just humor us. I'll have the sheriff's office pay for the test if that's an issue."

"Okay, Frank. I'll ask Joe to send it out right away."

"Thanks. If you get any surprising results, try to keep it under your hat."

Richard looked at them with a skeptical look. Frank turned off the radio and thanked him for being so accommodating.

Later that day, at the office, Frank got a call from Richard Farley. "Hey, Frank, you'd better come over here."

"I'll be right there."

Frank grabbed his sport coat and drove to the coroner's office. When Frank got there, he found Joe and Richard waiting for him.

"Look at this, Frank."

Joe passed over a fax from the carbon dating lab confirming George Littlefield's theory. Frank said, "follow me," and led them to the far corner of the basement. He turned on the radio and asked them to gather around.

"What's this all about, Frank?"

"George Littlefield has a theory that I felt worth looking into. First, let me ask you guys a question. Is it possible for plastic like this to have occurred in nature nine thousand years ago?"

Richard spoke, "I don't think so. The plastic pieces look like some kind of a molded composite to me."

"Anyway you can find out what kind of plastic it is?"

Joe said, "Sure, I have a friend in a materials lab who might help us."

"Would you ask him to check the plastic out for us? It could be important to our case."

"If my friend is in, I'll run the plastic piece over to the lab myself, right now."

"Great, Joe. Mind if I come with you?"

"Okay, Frank."

"You're not going to leave me out of this," said Richard. "I'm coming along, too."

Joe confirmed his friend was available.

The three got into Joe's Ford Explorer and headed for the materials lab. When they got there, they were greeted by Joe's friend, Scott Baker, and led to one of the labs.

"What have you got there, Joe?"

"It's a piece of plastic we'd like to find out more about. Can you tell us what kind of plastic it is?"

"Shouldn't be too hard. You guys grab a cup of coffee in our little cafeteria. I'll get back to you in half an hour."

About forty minutes later, the lab technician came to see the three men in the cafeteria. The technician gave the piece of plastic to Joe, and said just one word, "Samsonite."

Joe looked at the others and said, "Are you sure, Scott?"

"I can give you the chemical composition, but the fact is, the common name for this plastic is Samsonite, made by the people who give you rugged suit cases and brief cases."

Joe thanked his friend. The three got into Joe's Explorer and headed back.

When they got on the road, Richard said, "Do you want to fill us in on what's going on, Frank?"

Frank figured Joe's Explorer was probably as safe a place as any to talk.

He decided to use the opportunity to fill in much of the story for Joe and Richard. "Okay, guys, but before I do, I must tell you what I'm going to say might put you in as much danger as I think I'm in. Do you still want to hear the story?"

"You've got more than our attention now."

"Well, George Littlefield came up with a theory, as impossible as it might seem, that the bones are the bones of a time traveler."

"Time traveler! How did George come up with that theory?" asked Richard.

"Well, that's another story, but George figured one way to prove the theory might be to prove the plastic pieces were as old as the bones. There is a lot more to this story."

"Like what?"

"Well, do you remember when Harry made a picture of a man from the bones and we thought we would play a joke on Mary Webber?"

"Yes. You were going to ask Mary to run it through missing persons."

"That's right. Well, Mary did, and she found a match."

"A match?"

"Yeah, a Jack Spencer of Warrenton, Virginia. He's been missing for six months. Mary and I drove to Warrenton and visited with his wife."

"Go on, Frank."

"Well, to shorten the story somewhat, we found out this Jack Spencer worked for a special agency of the NSA. Mary and I started looking into this further and have drawn more attention to ourselves than we ever wanted."

"What do you mean?"

"Well, at this point, Mary and I are being watched by three men including Ray Blackwell."

"Ray Blackwell, the U.S. Marshal?"

"That's right. We've stumbled onto something big."

"And now you think our government is engaged in time travel?"

"I don't know, maybe."

"That's a hell of a story, Frank."

"I figured you guys would figure out the time travel angle yourselves now that we know the plastic is Samsonite. Can you think of any other explanation for the plastic being nine thousand years old?"

Joe and Richard said nothing and sat there pondering the information they had just been given.

After a few minutes, Richard said, "If you're right about the bones being a missing man and a time traveler who worked for a special agency of the government, then they could be carrying out who knows what kind of business, and for who knows what reasons."

"That's what I've been thinking, too. They certainly wouldn't want the world to know they have this power. They might kill to protect it."

"So if they think we know what they are doing and that we can prove it to the world, our lives aren't worth squat," said Joe. "Why, the hell, did you tell us, Frank?"

"I'm sorry to involve you guys. I don't think they know you know at this point. I figured you would start doing your own speculation about the plastic being Samsonite. I also figured I better fill you in before you told anyone else, and so you would know what you're up against."

"What do we do now?"

"Good question. I've been considering this question and have come up with a few options."

"Like what?"

"Well, we could go to the government and disclose what we know. We could take the knowledge we have public and try to get an inquiry into whatever the government is doing. Or we could keep completely quiet about what we know and let them make the next move."

"Their next move might be to eliminate us, considering what they are doing and its possible impact on the world," said Joe.

"We can only hope what they are doing is planned to protect the world from catastrophe," said Richard.

"Do you guys have any other options?"

"I don't like your second or third options. If they think we'll go public, they'll probably stop us right away. And if we play dumb too long, they'll have no choice but to eliminate the possibility we'll go public."

"That's kind of how I was leaning, also, Richard."

"Frank, how many people know?" said Joe.

"Besides the three of us, George Littlefield, Mary Webber and possibly others who know some of the information; but not all of it, like the members of the Indian Council, and the guy who did the carbon dating for you, Joe."

"That's a lot of people already. You know they'll do their own speculation, and before long the grapevine will spread this to the world."

"How many people know about the last carbon dating?" asked Frank.

"Besides us, only Brian Philips who did the carbon dating for us only hours ago."

"We better see if we can stop Brian from saying anything about the plastic being nine thousand years old."

"I'll give him a call right now."

Joe pulled out his cell phone and called Brian at his laboratory. "Can I speak to Brian Phillips, please? This is Joe Bianco from the coroner's office."

"He went home early today, Mr. Bianco. His wife is expecting a baby and had some false labor pains."

"Can you give me his number at home please?"

A minute later Joe had the number and called Brian at home. "Brian, this is Joe Bianco."

"What can I do for you, Joe?"

"You know the last specimens you carbon-dated for me earlier today?"

"Yeah, the plastic that was nine thousand years old. I didn't understand how plastic could be nine thousand years old."

"That's why I called you at home. I wanted to correct my error. I misheard Mr. Farley. Farley laughed like crazy when I told him. I should have said prehistoric, not plastic. I wanted to let you know about my error before anyone else found out, and made something out of nothing. Did you tell anyone about it?"

"I didn't have time. Right after I faxed you the information, I got an emergency call from my wife, and went right home."

"Is your wife okay?"

"She's just fine, Joe. She's expecting our first child and had false labor."

"I'm glad she's all right. Give her my best."

"Thanks. I'll put the official report and specimen in the mail for you tomorrow."

Joe said, "Thanks," and rang off.

Frank said, "I think that eliminates Brian. We could eliminate Mary and George as well as the Indian Council if I lie to them and tell them the plastic was modern day."

"That statement is true if you leave out the part about it being carbon-dated as nine thousand years old," said Joe. "After all, it's for their own protection."

"Good idea, except that leaves me with no explanation to give Mary and George why Ray Blackwell and his men are following us around."

"Couldn't you just say you don't know?"

"That wouldn't be fair to them, Joe. They would have no knowledge of how much danger they are in if I don't tell them the truth. No, I'm afraid I must tell them. I'll let them know how important it is to keep this information to themselves."

Richard said, "Can I make a suggestion? From now on, when we talk about this situation to each other, let's refer to it as the *bones situation* so anyone listening will think we are referring to the confrontation between the archeologists and the Indians over possession of the bones."

They both agreed.

As they returned to the coroner's office, they didn't notice the Ford Escort following them with Art Cox at the wheel. A quarter of a mile behind Art, George Littlefield was following in his Jeep.

By the time the three men arrived at the coroner's office it was dark, so Frank thanked the others and went home. Art Cox followed Frank in the Escort and parked down the street. George also followed and parked one street over from Frank's street. George walked through yards until he reached Frank's back door, and knocked on the door. Frank welcomed George onto his back porch, and, after making coffee, filled George in on the events of the day. George told Frank he had been following the Ford Escort all day.

Meanwhile, Art Cox called Ray Blackwell and filled Ray in on the day's events.

"You say, you followed McDermott, and two other men from the coroner's office to a materials laboratory thirty miles away?"

"That's right."

"Do you know why they went there?"

"No. They were riding in the other man's Ford Explorer, so I couldn't hear anything they said."

"Could you take me to this laboratory?"

"Sure, anytime you want."

"I may just want to check it out myself tomorrow. I'll let you know. Where's Jimmy?"

"Jimmy called me a little while ago and said he would follow Webber home."

"Okay, stay on them until eleven and then call it a night, unless something unusual happens."

"Okay, Boss."

Frank thanked George for his help and congratulated him on figuring out their puzzle.

George said, "What's next?"

"I guess we try to survive one day at a time. We need to keep a close watch on each other's backs until we figure out our best move."

"One thing football taught us is to make a plan for every contingency."

"That's a good idea. I'll try and get our team together tomorrow so we can start cooking up some plans. Do me a favor and call Mary on your cell phone. She should be home by now, and should call you back within five minutes as we planned."

George did as Frank suggested. Mary put down her regular phone and called back from her back yard on her cell phone.

"George?"

"No, It's me, Mary. George is with me on my back porch."

Frank filled in Mary with the day's events. He told her he would pick her up at seven-thirty to start their carpooling to the sheriff's office in the morning, and said good night.

"George, since it is already eleven thirty, why don't you stay here tonight."

"Okay. I'll just get my Jeep and drive it around the block to your driveway. I'll park it in your back yard."

George walked down Frank's street, and didn't see anyone.

When he came back into Frank's house, he said, "I think they called it a night."

"Good."

Frank made them dinner and they turned in.

CHAPTER 17

The next morning, Ray Blackwell met Art and Jimmy for breakfast.

"Okay, guys. Let's go over what happened yesterday."

Art pulled out his pocket notebook and said, "We both followed McDermott and Webber to a deli at a little after eleven. We couldn't make out anything they said because it was too noisy. After lunch, McDermott and Webber went to the coroner's office and met George Littlefield outside on the front steps. The three talked for about five minutes, and then disappeared into the coroner's office for twenty minutes."

"What do you mean disappeared?"

"I mean we couldn't hear anything they said after they asked some guy if they could take another look at the bones. They were told they could find the bones in the basement. A few minutes later, all we could hear was loud music."

"Go on, then what happened?"

"We followed McDermott and Webber back to the sheriff's office. About four hours later, I followed McDermott back to the coroner's office. Jimmy stayed outside the sheriff's office to follow Webber."

"What happened at the coroner's office?"

"I overheard two guys talking with McDermott. They were talking about some plastic that was carbon-dated to be nine thousand years old. They also said something about George Littlefield's theory."

"Did you record what they said?"

"Sure, Boss."

"You can play it back for me after breakfast. What happened next?"

"I followed McDermott, and two other men to that materials laboratory about thirty miles away that I was telling you about last night."

"Anything else happen yesterday you haven't already told me about?"

Art started to say something and stopped.

"What were you going to say, Art?" asked Ray.

"Only that it seems like they know we're following them."

"Why do you say that?"

"I've been doing this work for a lot of years and after a while you can feel when the other guy is on to you."

"How?"

"They clam up. You don't hear anything but routine stuff. And when they seem to go out of their way to have noise around them when they're talking, it's a dead giveaway."

"Do you have anything else for me?"

Art looked at Jimmy who just shrugged, and said, "No, that's about it."

Ray thought for a minute and said, "You guys are doing a good job. I've also noticed they clam up around me. Jimmy, I want you to follow McDermott today. Art, I want you to go with me to this laboratory."

After breakfast, Ray listened to the tape confirming that plastic was carbon-dated to be nine thousand years old. Ray called McDermott at the sheriff's office, and told Frank he had to do an errand, so not to expect him today.

Ray and Art left for the materials laboratory. When they got there, Art waited in the car while Ray went inside. Ray looked very official dressed in his brown suit and Stetson hat. He stopped at the reception desk and inquired who might have talked with sheriff's detective Frank McDermott the day before.

When Ray drew a blank look, he said, "I think McDermott came in with two men from the Black River Coroner's Office."

"Oh, you mean Joe Bianco. Yes, they came in late yesterday afternoon and talked with Scott Baker. Want me to get him for you?"

"Please."

A few minutes later, Scott came to the lobby and asked if he could help. Ray introduced himself as the U.S. Marshal working on a case with Frank and Joe. He then said, "Yesterday when the others were here, they failed to get an official report."

Scott said, with a little surprise, "I was just doing a favor for Joe and didn't think he needed a report. I told Joe it was Samsonite. What more does he need?"

Ray thought quickly and said, "Oh, just the chemical analysis. I told Joe I was going this way and could pick it up for him."

"Sure, I'll get you a copy."

Scott came back a few minutes later with a copy of the chemical analysis. Ray thanked him and left.

When he got back to the car, Art asked, "Did you find out what you wanted?"

"Sure did. Let's head back to town."

When Ray and Art got a few miles down the road, Ray pulled into a restaurant parking lot and asked Art, "Will you get us some sandwiches and coffee while I make a call to the head office?"

"What kind do you want?"

"Oh, chicken salad if they have it. Whatever looks good if they don't."

Ray got out of the car and called Mark Denver. Mark's secretary broke into his meeting and told Mark that Ray was on the phone.

"Okay. I'll take it in my office." Mark stepped into his office and picked up the phone. "Ray, what's going on?"

"Bad news. I'm pretty sure they've figured it out."

"How do you know?"

"I better not go over the details over the phone, but I'm sure, Mark. I'll FedEx some details to you right away."

"How many of them know?"

"At least three, maybe two or three more."

"Try and find out exactly who knows, and get back to me as soon as you can give me a list. I'll look for your FedEx."

"Okay." And they rang off.

After lunch, Ray called the coroner's office.

"Coroner's office, Joe Bianco speaking."

"Joe, this is Ray Blackwell. How's it going today?"

"Just routine."

"My superiors have asked me to get a few records to document this case. Can you tell me who to call to get a record of the carbon dating of the bones?"

From Joe's point of view, he figured this wasn't just a routine request, but he complied. "Yes, just a minute. I've got it now."

Joe told Ray how to contact Brian Phillips at the carbon dating lab.

Ray called Brian Phillips and made a similar request. After Brian said he would be glad to fax him a copy of the report on the bones, Ray made another request. "Can you also send me a copy of the report on the plastic?"

"What plastic? Oh, you mean the other prehistoric bone specimen Joe sent over yesterday."

"Wasn't there a sample of plastic?"

"No, sir. Joe made a mistake. He thought Richard Farley said plastic when Richard really said, prehistoric. We had a good laugh over that one. In fact, I just sent out the official report on the last sample to Joe this morning."

Ray paused and said, "Oh, I guess I got it wrong, too." He pretended to laugh to try and add credibility to his last comment. "I guess that makes more sense. I'll get copies of Joe's reports and save you any more trouble."

"I'd be glad to send you copies, Mr. Blackwell."

"No, no, that's all right. I'll just get copies from Joe. Thanks for your time."

After lunch, Ray and Art stopped at the nearest Federal Express Office and Ray sent a "Same Day" Federal Express to Mark Denver. It read:

> *"Joe Bianco, Richard Farley, and Frank McDermott have carbon-dated some plastic found with the bones at nine thousand years old. They have identified the plastic as Samsonite. See the enclosed lab report. Others who likely know are Mary Webber and George Littlefield. Brian Phillips did the carbon dating of the plastic, but was told the samples were bones. I talked with Phillips and think he believed the samples were bones, but I wouldn't completely rule him out. I will get back to you when I have more information."*

Earlier that same morning, Frank picked up Mary at her home and they drove to the parking lot of the sheriff's office. As they walked from the parking lot to the office, Frank whispered, "I'm going to set up a meeting with the others at the coroner's office as soon as possible. I'll give Ray some excuse for us leaving the office."

After entering the building, they walked to Mary's office with the usual morning chitchat. As they entered her office and closed the door behind them, Frank took Mary into his arms and they kissed. They held each other for several minutes.

Frank opened the door to Mary's office to see if Ray was in the area. Just then the phone rang at Frank's desk. He quickly moved to his office and picked up the phone. A minute later, He returned to Mary's office and said with a smile, "Ray just called saying he had to do an errand and not to expect him today."

She smiled back, and he said, "I'll go set up the meeting."

Half an hour later, Mary and Frank drove to the coroner's office. George, Joe, and Richard greeted them as they came in. Frank suggested they go to the basement to look at the bones as they had done the day before. Everyone agreed, including Richard who now understood the need for the music. This time all five sat in the corner with the radio playing loudly near by.

Joe Bianco started by saying, "I didn't get much sleep last night."

"I don't expect any of us did," Frank replied.

Frank then reviewed the three options they discussed the day before and said, "Yesterday, we came to the conclusion that waiting for the government to make the next move is a mistake. They might decide to eliminate us before anyone else finds out what they're doing."

"I agree," said Richard. "I've been giving this a lot of thought. We really only have two courses of action: try and stop the government by going public, or let the government know what we know, and take a chance they won't kill us."

"Either way, they might try to eliminate us, said Frank."

Joe commented, "I've got a wife and two kids to think of."

Richard said, "Me, too, Joe. That's why we need to figure out what we're going to do and act before they kill us."

Frank said, "Then are we all agreed, we must act right away, whatever we do?"

They all nodded agreement.

George said, "I don't think it's wise for the government to be fooling around with history. What if they change one thing and something else worse happens that is completely unexpected? It could be worse than what the government planned to fix in the first place."

"Yeah," said Joe. "And what if their motives are not so pure? In the hands of a greedy person, or government, the ability to change history could be a catastrophe."

"We can only hope what they're doing is planned to protect the world from catastrophe," said Richard.

Mary chimed in and said, "During the time I've worked for the FBI, I've always felt their motives were as pure as possible, but of course with the good of the United States in mind."

"I suspect we all gave these ideas a good going over in our minds last night," said Frank. "That's why I want to propose we come up with a solution that allows us a 'back door,' as Mary would call it."

"What do you have in mind?" said Richard.

"Well, one thing Mary taught me about software programs is the writer always puts in a contingency plan for getting back into the program to fix it if something goes wrong. She calls it a 'back door'."

"Go on."

"Well, I think we should go to the government and tell them what we know, but first put together a file explaining what we know with all of our evidence. We somehow make this file visible to the world if ever we detect the government is using time travel for the wrong purpose."

"And just who decides when to release this file, Frank?"

"I guess we do, George. Of course we don't tell the government the file exist. If the government ever found out the file existed, they would find a way to eliminate it."

"What's to keep the government from killing us once we tell them what we know?"

"The government is going to find out we know, soon enough, Joe, if they haven't already."

Richard said, "It sure would be nice to use the file to protect our lives as well as the world, Frank."

"I don't know of a way to do that, do you, Mary?"

"Just maybe. What if I put everything we know on a disc. Then I entrust this disc to a friend to keep with instructions to send the file out over the Internet if one of us dies unexpectedly, or if we contact this person with instructions to send it out. My instructions would include a clause that allows us to contact this person within twenty-four hours, and stop the file from going out, if we know the person's death was not caused by the government."

"Might work," said Joe. "What do you think, Frank?"

"Might work at that. We could put the pieces of bone and plastic into a safe deposit box, along with the carbon dating reports, as evidence. We would have to give the key and box number to the person you give the disc to."

"Who could you trust to do this for you, Mary?" asked Richard.

"It might not even need to be a person," said Mary. "I believe I can write a program and put it on several computers that, when triggered by a message from one of us, will send out the file and the location of the evidence over the Internet. In fact, I can set it up to automatically send the file out if the computers do not receive a weekly message from me to not send it out."

"That's brilliant, Mary," said Frank.

Richard said, "But what if something happens to you, Mary? God forbid, the rest of us wouldn't know how to stop the computers from sending out your message if you died accidentally."

"I could teach each of you so that any one of us could send out the message or prevent it from being sent out. And of course we tell the government the story that someone else sets off the alarm if one of us dies unexpectedly. Maybe that will keep the government from invading our computers, trying to figure out how my computer plan works."

They all looked at each other with some degree of maybe it could work; except George, who said, "Just how do we know, if and when the government is fooling around with history, is a good idea or not?"

"That's a tough question," said Frank. "Since we are the only ones who will have a chance to stop the government with our 'back door' plan, I guess we'll have to accept the responsibility of being a committee of independent judges over what the government is doing."

"You mean we blackmail the government into letting us vote on every use of this power?" asked Richard.

"I guess that's what I'm saying. We would have to get the government to agree on us taking over this responsibility for the rest of our lives."

"Mary raised her voice a bit and said, "That would mean we would each have to give up our jobs and become government employees, Frank."

"Maybe, maybe not. We could force the government to allow you to put a control gate into their computer that makes the time travel possible. The control gate would trigger a review by our committee before the time travel is allowed."

George asked, "Just how would we be so smart as to know when it should or shouldn't be done?"

Mary said, "We could insist on having the government give us all their information why they think time travel should be done. We then try to judge, as an independent committee, that the government has the best of intentions."

George asked, "Who was it that said, 'The road to hell is paved with good intentions'?"

"Yeah, I guess we've all heard that, but do we have any other plan to consider? At least this plan might keep us alive and maybe keep the government's motives as pure as possible at the same time," Frank replied.

"What do the rest of you think?"

"I like it," said Mary.

"Me, too," said Richard.

"Count me in, too," said Joe.

"How about you, George?"

"Yeah, Frank, count me in, too. I don't have a better plan."

"Good. Then let's put the plan into motion."

They spent the remainder of the morning going over the details of who does what to make their plan work. The group decided they would have both Richard and Joe get safe deposit boxes in different cities and place evidence in each box. The location of each box and key would be accounted for in Mary's computer program.

George planned to take evidence and bury it somewhere on the Indian reservation. Mary was to start creating the computer program to be stored on several computers. The program would be triggered by an encrypted Internet message.

Mary figured she better get out of town for a few days and find a safe place to work on the program.

Around noon, the group went to a noisy deli in town to continue making their plans. Mary called a girl friend in the Washington area and made arrangements to stay at her friend's place for a couple of days. She planned to leave her home at 2:00 A.M. the next morning and drive to the Washington area.

Frank told her he didn't like the idea of her going alone, but he didn't have a better idea. George planned to follow Mary for several miles to make sure she wasn't being followed. This made Frank feel a little better about Mary going alone.

"After all," she told Frank, "I lived there on my own for several years."

She promised Frank she would take the gun Harry had given her for protection.

The group decided to confess to Ray Blackwell what they knew, as soon as their 'back door' plan was in place.

CHAPTER 18

The next day, Ray Blackwell met with Art and Jimmy for breakfast to update the previous day's events.

"How did it go yesterday, Jimmy?"

"I followed McDermott to the Webber home at seven-thirty. McDermott picked up Webber, and I followed them to the sheriff's office. They went inside for a half-hour. I then followed McDermott and Webber to the coroner's office where they disappeared until noon."

"Disappeared?"

"They must have turned on the radio again because that's all I could hear. About noon, McDermott, Webber, Richard Farley, Joe Bianco, and George Littlefield came out of the coroner's office. I followed them to a deli in town, where again I was unable to hear their conversation. They stayed there for over two hours. When the group came out of the deli, I followed McDermott and Weber to her home. McDermott went inside with her for about fifteen minutes and then he returned to the sheriff's office."

"Just McDermott?"

"Yes."

"Did you follow McDermott home?"

"Yes, he left the sheriff's office about six. I stayed there watching his home until eleven. Nothing interesting to report."

Ray took a sip of coffee and said, "Sounds like they're playing the 'I know you are watching us' game."

Jimmy said, "Yeah. How'd you guys make out yesterday?"

"Just fine." Ray changed the subject, not wanting to divulge any secrets to them. "Jimmy, you watch McDermott again today. Art, I want you to log who comes and goes at the coroner's office, in particular the people Jimmy watched yesterday. Record anything they say if you can hear them."

At the underground facility set deep in the Virginia hills, Mark Denver assembled his senior staff. "Sam, how about an update on the control."

Sam Magnum took off his titanium-framed glasses and laid them on the table. "We've been working twenty-four-seven as you know, Mark. We think we have the control ready for trials."

"That's the best news I've heard in a while. Jane, have you and Jason figured out the minimum number of control trials you'll need to perform?"

Jane Kirkpatrick looked across the table at Jason Bedford. She then looked at Denver and said, "We've narrowed it down to the fewest possible number of trials to ensure the risk is less than one in one thousand."

"How many?"

"We figure thirty trials, minimum."

"Thirty?"

Jason spoke up and said, "That's the smallest number needed to give us any statistically meaningful data."

"How long will that take?"

"About two weeks working around the clock and assuming everything goes well."

"All right."

Denver stood up and paused before saying, "As you probably remember, I mentioned to you that Mike Walker and I have had people working on a security problem. This problem has escalated to the point where I think you should know what's going on, but I want you to keep this information confined to this senior staff. Have any of you followed the news stories about the finding of the nine-thousand-year-old-bones a couple hundred miles south of here?"

Sally Stevens spoke up and said, "Yes, the bones were found on an Indian reservation in a small town about a hundred miles west of where I went to school. The town of Black River, wasn't it?"

"That's right. The bones were of a white man about five foot ten." Denver's last comment brought the others to full attention.

He continued. "A sheriff's detective named Frank McDermott and a computer expert named Mary Webber came to me some weeks ago and showed me a picture they'd made from the bones found along the river. I don't know how they came up with the picture, but it was a perfect likeness of Jack Spencer. At that point, Mike and I had Ray Blackwell appointed U.S. Marshal and sent to the Black River area. Ray has been watching the investigation by these people. He's using the excuse that he was sent to Black River to keep the peace between the Indians and the archeologists who are fighting over control of the bones. At this point, these people have carbon-dated some plastic found with the bones at nine thousand years old. They've also determined the plastic is Samsonite." Denver paused to take in the amazed expressions on the faces of his team.

Paul Andrews spoke up and said, "You just made my retrieval job easier. Now I know where to find Jack."

"Yes," said Jason, "and we now know how far back in time to go."

"You're both right, but the downside of this is these people are now in the position of enough evidence to prove we know how to go back in time," said Denver. "At the very least, they could start a public inquiry into what we are doing and maybe get us shut down."

"If they do that," said Paul, "we wouldn't be able to retrieve Jack."

"Now you know why I've had you working around the clock to get ready for a retrieval. I want you all to know, I appreciate everyone's efforts. I need you to continue."

Dylan O'Grady asked, "How many people know about the nine-thousand-year-old Samsonite?"

"At least five, maybe more. I figure they could take their knowledge public at any time now and we aren't ready for the retrieval. That puts us in a very vulnerable position."

Mike chimed in, "Can't we pull these people off the street?"

"We've got two solutions as I see it," said Denver. "We can either try for a retrieval now without the trial testing, or bring in these people and give them a top secret briefing."

Jane spoke up, "Without the trials, I wouldn't give you any hope of a successful retrieval."

"That's what I thought you would say. So I think we should have Ray Blackwell bring in the five people. My hope is that if we confide in them how important this project is, we can get them to help us squelch any further information release to the public."

Paul commented, "Theoretically, if we can retrieve Jack, we can change the timeline that allowed these people to get this close to us in the first place."

"What do the rest of you think?" Denver looked around the room as the nine members of his senior staff considered his question.

Jason looked Denver straight in thee eyes and said, "We definitely need more time, Mark."

Sam agreed, "We all know Jack was supposed to go back nine years, not nine-thousand. I definitely vote for doing the trials and tweaking the control until we know it's correct this time."

Mike said, "I don't see what other choice we have, Mark, short of killing these people." The others looked at Mike with scowls on their faces. Mike looked around and said in his own defense, "There are those in our government who wouldn't hesitate." The other team leaders started a commotion in the room.

Denver broke in and said, "Calm down, we aren't going to kill anyone. Not only would this be against our beliefs, it also would be stupid in my estimation. We would only draw more attention to what these people were working on." He then said, "Are there any other questions or comments?" When he didn't get a reply, Denver said,

"Good. Then I'll have Ray bring them in as soon as he can. Let's get the trials started. That's it for today. Keep up the good work."

Back at the sheriff's office, Ray Blackwell knocked on the open door to Frank's office and asked, "Where is Mary?"

"Oh, Mary wasn't feeling well so I suggested she stay home."

"Is there anything new to report on the Indian vs. archeologists situation over the bones?"

"No, nothing new. How did your day go yesterday?"

"Very well. I was able to clear up some business I needed to take care of."

Ray put his listening device in his ear to pick up any phone conversations Frank might have. Meanwhile, Frank did the same in his office to pick up Ray's phone conversations. About half an hour later, Ray got a call on his cell phone from Mark Denver. Ray told Mark he would call him right back. Ray put on his Stetson and went outside. Once outside, Ray called Mark.

"Mark, I'm outside the sheriff's office on my cell phone now. What can I do for you?"

"Ray, I've been discussing your situation with my senior staff. I've decided I want you to bring in these people as soon as you can."

"All five?"

"That's right, and the sooner the better."

"Do you want me to arrest them?"

"No, not unless they won't come of their own free will."

"How much should I tell them?"

"Tell them that you've been working in Black River under false pretenses for a special agency of the U. S Government. And at this point in time, you have been asked to bring them in for a special briefing of information critical to the security of the United States."

"Should I say anything more about the project?"

"No. You better leave all details for the briefing, in case one or more of them decide not to cooperate. I also suggest you round them up and tell them all at the same time, so that one doesn't spook the others. And, Ray, you better do this as informally as you can, so that their sudden departure doesn't alert others. Try and get their cooperation. Have them each make excuses as to why they won't be in Black River for a couple of days."

"Okay, Mark. What do you want me to do with Art and Jimmy?"

"Tell them there's no longer a need for surveillance and thank them for doing a good job."

"Mark, I'm worried that Art and Jimmy heard things that might allow them to put things together."

"Okay, you better have them report to the office in Washington for an upgrade of their security clearance. Just tell them they must report for a debriefing of this assignment within two days. I'll have Mike Walker take it from there."

"Will do, Mark."

"Do you have any other questions about this?"

"No, I've got it."

"Good. I'll see you at the facility as soon as you're able. Let Mike know when you're on your way."

Frank caught the entire conversation. His first feeling was one of relief that the government wanted to talk with them. Frank then thought about their 'back door' plan. He didn't know how long it would take to put the plan in place. The hardest part of the plan belonged to Mary. Frank figured he better get in touch with Mary and find out how long it would take her to do the programming. Without saying anything to anyone else, Frank quietly got up and went outside. He got into his car and went to the Back Alley Restaurant.

Ray noticed Frank leave and called Jimmy on his cell phone. "McDermott just left the sheriff's office."

"I'm on him."

"Good. Let me know where he goes."

"You've got it, Ray."

Jimmy followed Frank to the restaurant and waited outside, a block away in his car. Jimmy called Ray and told him where Frank went.

"Any sign of the others?"

"No. I don't see any sign of the others."

"Okay, thanks. Stay on him."

From a corner booth, Frank ordered a cup of coffee, and pulled out his cell phone.

"Mary, it's me. How was your night drive to the Washington area?"

"I made out just fine, but I laid down on the couch after I got here and just woke up."

"Oh, sorry to wake you."

"I'm glad to hear from you."

"I'm calling from the Back Alley Restaurant because I have some good news. I overheard a conversation this morning between Ray and Denver. Denver asked Ray to bring the five of us into their facility for a special briefing of information critical to the security of the United States."

"No kidding?"

"No kidding. The conversation seemed to confirm all our speculations."

"Including time travel?"

"That wasn't specifically mentioned, but what else could it be?"

"When is Ray supposed to bring us in?"

"As soon he can. That's why I'm calling. How long will it take you to do your program?"

"I was thinking about how I would design the program during my trip last night. I figure the smaller I can keep it, the less likely it will be detected. I think I can write a simple program, to do all the things we planned, in a day or two."

"That long?"

"Frank, do you know how long it would usually take a programmer to do this?"

"No."

"Probably a month unless the person was as good as me."

"I'm sorry. You know I'm a novice around the computer. I don't like to be away from you any longer than I have to be."

"I miss you, too, Frank."

"What did you tell your mother?"

"I told her I wanted to visit my friend in Washington for a few days. I also told her I was planning to leave at two in the morning to avoid the D.C. traffic."

"Maybe you had better call your mother and let her know you arrived safely. Tell her, if anyone from the office should call, to tell them you're sick and probably won't be back to work for a couple of days. I'll try to keep Ray in check until you finish. Give me a call when you're ready."

"Okay, Frank. I love you."

"I love you, too, Mary."

Frank then called Joe at the coroner's office. He asked him to set up a meeting with the others as soon as he could.

Joe said, "What's up, Frank?"

"I better wait to tell you the good news when we get together."

"Okay. Why don't you come to the coroner's office and I'll round up the others?"

"I'll be there in fifteen minutes."

Jimmy followed Frank to the coroner's office and parked his car next to Art's. He got into Art's car and they both watched Frank enter the coroner's office. Art said, "I just saw George Littlefield go in, also."

"Isn't that Richard Farley pulling into the parking lot?"

"Yeah, that's him."

They watched Richard enter the coroner's office. They set their listening equipment to the most sensitive levels. They heard someone say, "Let's go downstairs where we can look at the bones." The next thing they heard was a radio playing The Beatles' "I Want to Hold Your Hand."

"Okay, Frank, what's the big news?"

Frank told the others about Ray Blackwell's conversation with Denver. They were relieved to hear this news.

Frank said, "I also talked with Mary. She made it okay to her friend's apartment in Washington. She said it'd take her at least two days to write the program. I figure the three of you better try and do your part of our 'back door' plan today."

Joe looked at Richard and George and said, "I was planning on doing just that, anyway."

"Me, too," said both George and Richard.

"Good."

Joe then gave George and Richard two small packages that he had made up that morning. "In each package, I put a bone and a plastic fragment along with copies of the lab reports. I have a third package like yours that I'll put in a safe deposit box this afternoon."

Frank said, "That's good, Joe. When you and Richard get the locations and numbers of the boxes, I'll send them on to Mary to put into the program."

"And I'll hide the third package on the reservation somewhere," said George. "Shouldn't I also give Mary the location to put in the program?"

Frank answered, "I was thinking about this. Let's keep the sample you hide on the reservation out of Mary's program as an ace in the hole. What do you guys think?"

"Sounds like a good idea to me," said George. The others nodded agreement.

Richard was puzzled. "One thing about this was bothering me last night. Why would anyone send someone back in time nine thousand years?"

"Yeah. It doesn't make sense," said Joe.

George commented, "Maybe it was just a trial and they felt this would have the least chance of affecting the future."

"I don't know," said Frank. "Maybe they'll tell us. Anyone have anything else to add?"

Joe said, "How do we get the information to Mary?"

"Good question," said Frank. "I think one of us should deliver it in person. It's too important to leave to the chance of it getting lost."

George asked, "Do you plan to deliver it yourself, Frank?"

"I'd like to, but I'm pretty sure they're still following me."

"I could take it to her."

"They could follow you, also, George."

"They will never know what direction I went. I'll give them the old Indian slip."

The other two smiled and Frank said, "Okay, George, I'll give you the phone number and address of Mary's friend in Washington."

George said, "I'll wait here for Richard and Joe to get their parts back to me later this afternoon. Then I'll go back to the reservation, have dinner with my family and leave after dark."

"Sounds like a plan."

By the next morning, Ray was concerned about not being able to round up all five people at the same time. He had his usual breakfast meeting with Art and Jimmy. They filled Ray in on the previous day's events offering no new information about what the five were doing.

Ray then said, "I think we've come to a dead end on this job. My boss wants me to pull the surveillance and return to home base. I've been asked to have you report to Washington within two days for a debriefing of this assignment."

Art and Jimmy looked at each other with a little surprise and Art said, "I don't understand, Ray. These people knew we were watching them and were going out of their way to keep us from knowing what they were doing."

Ray shook his head. "We've got our orders guys. I've been asked to return, also. These people are not doing anything illegal."

Art said, "What about the national security issue?"

"You'll be debriefed in Washington. I advise you both to say nothing to anyone about this case until you're debriefed."

"Okay, Ray, we'll pack up and leave today."

"Good. Thank you both for your help."

Jimmy said, "It's because they found out we were watching them, isn't it Ray?"

"Don't worry about it," said Ray. "It wasn't your fault."

After breakfast, Ray went to the sheriff's office. He went straight to Frank's office and knocked on his open door. "How's Mary doing?"

"Oh, getting better. She might be back to work tomorrow."

"I'd like to talk with you about something if you have a minute."

"Sure, have a seat."

Ray sat down across from Frank and said, "I need to have a meeting with you plus Mary, Joe Bianco, George Littlefield, and Richard Farley as soon as possible."

"Oh?" said Frank, as he noticed some sweat on Ray's forehead. From Frank's point of view, Ray looked like a little kid getting caught with his hand in the cookie jar.

Ray hesitated for a second and said, "I haven't been completely truthful about my reasons for being in Black River."

Frank smiled at Ray and said, "Can I see that nice Stetson hat of yours for a minute?"

Ray said, "Sure," with a little surprise, and handed Frank his hat.

Frank pulled out the micro-listening bug from Ray's hatband and handed the hat back to him.

Ray smiled back at Frank and said, "You guys were too smart for us. How did you catch on?"

"Several ways: Mary and I knew we were being followed as early as the day after our first meeting with Denver. We had George Littlefield follow Mary and me around to see who was following us. George followed your friends to the Comfort Inn Motel. We traced the plates on their rental cars and identified them as NSA operatives. When we found they were staying at the same motel as you, Mary investigated your background. She found out who you really work for."

"I guess I shouldn't have underestimated you. Then you must know what I want to do now."

"Yes. Can the six of us get together tomorrow and go over just where you want to take us?"

"Then the others already know?"

"Yes, and we'll be glad to help the government in any way we can."

"That's great news, Frank. Why can't we meet today?"

"We could meet with everyone except Mary today. I'll fill in Mary afterwards if you like."

"Good! Will you set it up?"

"Sure. I'll give the others a call and see if they'll meet us at the coroner's office at three this afternoon. That'll give you time to make a list of the locations of all the bugs you planted so we can find them and give them back to you."

Ray smiled and said, "I'll make the list."

"I'll start setting up the meeting." Frank picked up the phone as Ray left.

Frank called Joe and told him about the meeting he just had with Ray. He asked him to contact Richard for the three o'clock meeting at the coroner's office. Frank told Joe he would contact Mary and George himself.

Taking no chances that Ray might still be listening, Frank went outside and used his cell phone to call Mary.

"Hello!"

"Hi, Mary. Did George make it all right?"

"Yeah, he's on his way back after staying the night on my friend's couch."

"That's good. How are you coming on the 'back door' plan?"

"I'm sure I can finish it today."

He then told Mary about his meeting with Ray, and the scheduled three o'clock meeting that afternoon. Frank then said, "I told Ray I would update you after the meeting."

She said, "I can't wait to hear what Ray has to say. I miss you, Frank."

"I miss you, too, Mary. I'll call you later." And they rang off.

Frank then called George on his cell phone.

"Hello!"

"George, it's me. How close to Black River are you?"

"About two hours away."

He told George about his meeting with Ray and the planned meeting at three o'clock. "Do you think you can make the meeting this afternoon?"

"Sure. I might even have time to get cleaned up."

At three o'clock, everyone but Mary was assembled in Joe Bianco's office. Ray thanked everyone for coming, and said, "I've been working in Black River under false pretenses for a special agency of the U. S. Government. At this point, I have been asked to invite you four people, and Mary Webber, to our facility for a special briefing of information critical to the security of the United States. I would like you to each make informal arrangements to come with me so that we draw as little attention as possible to your sudden departure. Frank has assured me I can count on your cooperation."

Joe looked at Ray Blackwell and said, "Is that it? Is that all you're going to tell us? We are right about this nine-thousand-year-old man being a time traveler, aren't we?"

Ray said, "That's all I can tell you at this time. If you come with me to our facility, you will be briefed in more detail."

Frank looked at the others and said, "How soon do you want us to leave?"

"How soon can you make your excuses?"

CHAPTER 19

Two days later, Ray Blackwell drove a white government van to an underground facility just forty minutes outside Washington, in the Virginia hills. Ray turned off the main road and proceeded down five miles of back road. The van passed through two gates at barbed wire fences. Each gate was operated remotely with cameras. A quarter mile farther down the winding road, the van came to a place where the road seemed to disappear into the hillside through large, thick metallic doors, also operated remotely with cameras. The doors opened and Ray drove into an underground garage. He parked in his designated space, and his group from Black River exited the van.

Two armed guards had them pass through a metal detector, one at a time. After confirming their identities, they were given badges and led to a large conference room. Outside the conference room door, there was a box at waist level where Ray placed his hand to unlock the door.

As Ray's group went in, Mark Denver and Mike Walker followed them into the conference room. Mark greeted them. "I've met Mary and Frank already. My name is Mark Denver."

Mark shook hands with Joe Bianco, George Littlefield, and Richard Farley. "I'd like you to meet my chief of security, Mike Walker. The work we do is classified. Normally it takes six months or more to obtain clearance to a program like this, but in special situations, as in your case, we expedite the process. Before I can tell you anything about our program, it is necessary for you to fill out security clearance paperwork. Mike will help you fill out the documents and answer any questions you might have. This is a normal routine for anyone not cleared for the program. I'll turn this over to Mike and see you a little later this morning." With that said, Mark left the conference room.

Mike Walker shook hands with each of them and said, "Please take a seat and make yourselves comfortable. We have a full day planned, starting with the security issue. Unfortunately, because of the nature of the work we do here, my first task at hand is to have each of you read the papers in front of you and sign them. These papers basically say that, as United States citizens, you will be briefed to a special program for the security of United States. You will never divulge any of the information you are about to learn. If you do, you can be fined, imprisoned, or put to death by the United States Government. We will be obtaining security clearances for each of you."

After the better part of the next hour of going over the papers, and upon getting answers to their questions, the papers were signed. The biggest compulsion for signing the papers was that it was for the security of the United States.

After the group signed the security papers and took a coffee break, Mike brought in Denver and his senior staff. The door to the conference room was bolted from the inside so that no one else could enter while they were in conference. Mark sat at the end of the table and had the five newcomers sit to his immediate right and left. Adjacent to them going around the table, Mark introduced his senior staff.

"You already know U.S. Marshal Ray Blackwell. Ray works for my chief of security sitting next to him, Mike Walker who you met this morning. Next to Mike is Sam Magnum who heads up our Controls Section. Next to Sam are Jason Bedford and Jane Kirkpatrick. Each heads up a special section that has to do with quantum physics and magnetism.

"Next, Sally Stevens heads up our History Section. Next to Sally is Dylan O'Grady who heads up our Mechanical Engineering Section. Sitting next to Dylan at the other end of the table is Captain Paul Andrews."

George Littlefield looked directly at Paul Andrews with a look of surprise. Mark took notice of this. "Do you already know Paul, Mr. Littlefield?"

George regained his composure and said, "No. I've never had the pleasure." George stood up and walked over to Andrews and shook his hand as if Paul was some sort of a celebrity. He then returned to his seat so that Mark could continue. Frank gave his best friend a puzzled look.

"Paul heads up our Logistics Section. Next to Paul is Dave Owen who heads up our Environmental Section. Lastly, Steve Harrington heads up our Computer Graphics, Drafting and, Computer Simulation Section. Each of these people have staffs of their own working on our project."

Mary Webber spoke up and said, "I think you left off one senior staff member not present, Jack Spencer."

Mark raised an eyebrow and said, "You're correct. Jack headed up the section we call Travelers." Frank smiled at Mary as Richard, Joe, and George looked at her with surprise.

Mark continued. "Our project is called REPEAT- Respect Environment, Preserve Earth and Time. The purpose of our group is to protect the world from calamity. To do this, we project future events by mathematically extrapolating past and current events. We plug large amounts of information into our main computer and use algorithms to have the computer extrapolate the data and make projections of what logically will happen in the near future. We then use this information to prepare for events that might upset the national security of our country and the world.

"About ten years ago, some leaders of our country decided they wanted us to go one step beyond. Knowing our limitations to solve global problems once they are out of control, we expanded our group to create a way to travel through time. To do this, we first had to assemble some of the smartest people in the world, many of whom are in this room. This group then started working on the project known as REPEAT.

"After nine years, we developed a time travel machine and a good reason to use it. Our first usage of the time machine was to send one man, Jack Spencer, back in time nine years. Jack was to have gone back to the time before the Gulf War of January 1991 when Saddam Hussein's Iraqi Army invaded Kuwait. Jack was to have contacted certain people in the past to enact a plan to prevent the Gulf War oil fires from ever happening. This was and still is important in our present time. The hundreds of oil fires started by retreating Iraqi troops near the end of the Gulf War, when combined with years of pollution and the destruction of the tropical rain forest have started an irreversible green house effect on the earth. This greenhouse effect has caused global warming and depletion of the ozone layer of the earth that scientist predict will have fatal consequences."

"What went wrong?" Frank asked.

"That's a good question. Our time control malfunctioned. It was not adequately tested at the time we sent Jack on his mission. We evidently sent him back nine thousand years instead of nine. We have your group to thank for helping us determine this. Our problem now is we need time to make sure our control won't malfunction again. We want to do trials until we are satisfied the chances of retrieving Jack are almost one hundred percent."

Joe Bianco asked, "What's stopping you from using all the time you need to get it right?"

Frank said, "I think I can answer that question. You're worried the public will find out about your time traveler, like we did, and use public opinion to shut you down."

"Correct. That's why I had the President approve the appointment of Ray Blackwell to U.S. Marshal and allow us to send him to Black River to watch your situation. In fact, we're hoping you will now help us by going back to Black River and making sure no one else finds out what the five of you have learned."

Frank looked at his friends and said, "I hope I'm talking for the others when I now say, you can count on our help."

Mark looked at the other four and waited for their comments.

Mary said, "You can count on my help."

"Me, too," said both Richard and Joe.

George said, "Sure, but one thing really bothers me about going back in time to change things. How do you know you won't negatively affect life by doing so?"

Mark said, "That's an excellent question. We have debated this for years and have come up with a list of rules to govern when time travel may be used. I had planned to go over these rules with you later today, but we can do it now." Mark dimmed the lights and turned on an overhead projector that was tied into his laptop computer. Mark searched a menu and quickly pulled up a list entitled: The Rules of Time Travel.

The Rules of Time Travel to the Past:
Failure to act will cause irrevocable damage to the world
It must benefit mankind in general; not just the United States of America
To minimize the impacts, only the specific world-threatening event(s) may be changed
No advanced objects from the present may be left in the past
No one in the past is to be killed without the 100% agreement of the Council
Interactions with persons in the past are to be minimized
A Council of twelve persons will be appointed by the President of the United States to review and approve all uses of time travel (These persons will have Top Secret Clearances)
The persons on this Council will be chosen from a diversity of backgrounds
The persons on the Council may not be chosen from the REPEAT organization
The REPEAT organization must recommend and provide justification to the Council for each use of time travel

Mark Denver reviewed each rule on the list. He pointed out that, in going back to the Gulf War, only the oil fires started by retreating Iraqi troops near the end of the war were to be stopped.

George asked, "Just how was Jack Spencer to keep people in the past from doing more than stopping the oil fires."

Mark said, "I'll let Captain Andrews, our logistics expert, answer that one."

Paul Andrews looked older than his forty-two years with almost white hair and dark eyebrows. Paul was a powerful looking black man with his six foot two frame and two hundred and twenty pounds. His expertise in logistics came, not only from institutions of higher learning, but also from many real life experiences including the Gulf War.

Paul stood and said in his deep voice, "During the Gulf War, I worked for Norman Schwarzkopf. Jack Spencer was carrying a special advanced computer that was programmed to play a small disc, like a newsreel. I personally made the newsreel telling about the timing and location of the retreat of the Iraqi troops and the setting of the oil fires. I explain, to the listener, the significance of the oil fires to the future of the world. I included footage of the fires as shown around the world on the news."

George broke in and said, "Sort of a 'Mission Impossible' tape?"

"That's right, but with all the high tech presentation we could provide today. Jack's job was to contact me before I left Washington for the Gulf. He was to show the newsreel to Schwarzkopf and me, only. The introduction to the newsreel shows the President standing next to Jack. The President asks Schwartzkopf and me to believe the incredible story we are about to hear. Of course, since I'm the presenter on the newsreel, it's expected I will trust myself and convince the General to do the right thing. Jack was then to return to our time with everything he took with him."

George said, "In other words, Jack only leaves the General and you in the past with enough information to stop the oil fires."

"That's it exactly."

George then asked, "And what keeps Jack Spencer or anyone you send into the past from, say, contacting himself and telling himself to mortgage his home and put the money into Intel stock in 1991?"

Mark answered, "Integrity and the knowledge that he might be negatively affecting his own future. The people hired for this program were screened and continue to be screened in every way this side of Sunday. Our government knows how important this project is."

George commented, "It sure would be a temptation."

Mark replied, "We understand, so we are working on ways to detect and prosecute any traveler who commits this crime."

Richard Farley said, "I have a question regarding Spencer's mission. What was made out of the Samsonite we found?"

Paul replied, "We had Jack's special computer built into a Samsonite briefcase to protect it"

Frank said, "Well, I guess that leaves no doubt about whose bones we found. What about time travel into the future?"

Mark responded, "We hope to travel into the future as well some day to better understand how the things we do today affect the world. We also have a list of rules for time travel into the future." Mark displayed the list.

The Rules of Time Travel to the Future:
Failure to act may cause irrevocable damage to the world
It must benefit mankind in general; not just the United States of America
The Future may only be studied. Nothing may be changed in the Future
No advanced objects from the future may be brought to the present or the past
No one in the future is to be killed or changed in any way
Interactions with persons in the future are to be minimized
A Council of twelve persons will be appointed by the President of the United States to review and approve all uses of time travel (These persons will have Top Secret Clearances)

The persons on this Council will be chosen from a diversity of backgrounds

The persons on the Council may not be chosen from the REPEAT organization

The REPEAT organization must recommend and provide justification to the Council for each use of time travel

Frank said, "I noticed you changed number five so that no one in the future may be killed."

"That's right. Even a person who seems intolerable in the future may have a child who invents a cure for the world's most damaging disease. We do not have enough information in the present to determine life and death in the future."

Frank commented, "I, for one, am glad you have thought things out pretty well, but how will you determine if you have negatively changed something by time travel?"

"Dave Owen, who heads up our Environmental Section can field that question."

Dave Owen was five-feet-ten, a little overweight, with thick gray hair. He looked every bit of forty-five. Dave had a slight southern drawl and talked very slowly but precisely.

Dave started talking like a professor to his students. "The purpose of my group is to continually monitor changes in the world. We use banks of computers to compile news events from all over the world twenty-four hours a day. We input world weather conditions, temperatures and chemistry of the oceans, quality of the air, outbreaks of disease, and millions of bits of other data. My people program the computer to constantly sift through the data and alert us to small changes to the world we know today. We have the computer extrapolate the changes and make predictions of near future events. It doesn't matter whether the event is a political assassination of a government leader or the statistics of how many teenagers in Philadelphia got cavities in a particular week. We try to account for everything changing. Having said all that, I can assure you this job is an ever-expanding task. We are continually updating and adding to our computer banks. Alarms go off when the changes exceed the threshold of normal daily changes. We are currently working on ways to better calibrate the magnitude of changes beyond normal daily changes."

Dave paused and asked, "Do you have any other questions?"

George Littlefield asked, "What happens when the computers go down?"

Some of the people in the room laughed.

Dave smiled, "Good question, George, but from the time this facility was first conceived, our people recognized this problem. We have our own source of power and it has many redundant systems, as does the hardware and software in our computers. We also have fire and or overheat protection systems throughout our computers and the facility."

Mary asked, "Do you have protection against computer hackers and viruses?"

"Another good question. We think we have the most secure system in the world."

"Then how did I get into your computers?"

"Yes, Miss Webber, you thought you got in. That's exactly what we wanted you to think. We allow hackers into one separate computer allowing them to get some basic background information. We then use this computer to track the hacker down and have the FBI pay this person a visit."

"But I was able to obtain the backgrounds of the people in this room and that they reported directly to Mark."

Dave said, "Ah, we may have a problem. Would you be willing to let us know just how you did this?"

Mary said, "Sure. I think for the security of the country, I'd better."

Mark spoke up, "Thank you, Mary. I'll arrange it for later today if you agree."

"Sure."

Mark then said, "Why don't we break for lunch. We have a special room next to our cafeteria that is set up for all of us today. We can continue this discussion after lunch." With that, everyone got up, stretched, and followed Mark to the cafeteria.

As Frank and Mary walked with the people to the cafeteria, they talked to each other about their 'back door' plan, in a code only they could understand.

Mary said, "You know your back door may not need fixing after all. It may be all right the way it is now."

Frank caught on to Mary's thought that Denver's people already had a well thought-out means of deciding when a time travel event should occur and said, "Well, you might be able to make it look better. It just might need a woman's touch."

"I'll take another look and see if I can recommend improvements. If I can't think of any, we'll use the old back door."

"Okay."

The group had a good lunch and got to know one another a little better. Frank spoke with Captain Paul Andrews about Jack Spencer's planned retrieval in more detail. Paul told Frank how he and Jack were best friends and that he was determined to bring him back to the present.

After lunch, Mark suggested his senior staff take thirty minutes to make sure their sections were running smoothly. He also suggested that Mary Webber could go with Dave and show Dave how she hacked into their computer. Mary agreed. Mark took the other four visitors on a brief tour of the facility.

Dave led Mary to the main computer room. The room was accessed through another special access door. Dave placed his hand on the box and said his name. The door opened.

Mary asked, "Is that both hand and voice recognition?"

"That's right."

Once inside the well air-conditioned room, Dave led Mary to a booth with a computer terminal. "Here's your chance to show me how you accessed our computer."

Mary sat down and typed in a command.

"I've never seen that command before."

Mary was able to get to their main menu with just a few more commands.

"How'd you do that?"

Mary smiled, "Before I went to work for the Black River Sheriff's Office, you might say my job was chief hacker for the FBI." With that Mary typed in a few more commands.

"That looks suspicious. What did you just do?"

"I put in a special command. I'll tell you about it when we get back to the meeting."

"I don't like the sound of that at all. You had better undo what you just did."

Mary took the opportunity to complete the commands she had started, and said, "There, all set." She stood up and said, "Can we get back to the meeting now?"

Dave called over his top programmer, Walt Martin, and ordered, "Walt, check out the entries made in the last fifteen minutes and make sure everything is normal. If you find anything wrong, come to the main conference room and let me know what you've found."

"Sure, Dave."

When Mary and Dave got back to the conference room, they found the others already there standing around talking.

Mark saw them arrive and said, "Okay, now that we are all back, lets get started again." Dave went over to Mark and whispered into his ear.

Mark looked at Mary, "Dave has just informed me Mary was able to get into our computer and that she made some entries Dave didn't understand." This comment raised some general chatter around the room. Mark asked, "Mary, would you comment about this?"

"Sure. My job before going to the Black River Sheriff's Office was chief hacker for the FBI. Your computer system was easy for me to get into. As important as your project is, you need to improve your computer security."

Mark questioned, "What about the entries you made?"

"First let me apologize to Dave. I took advantage of you treating me as a guest in your own house. Sorry, Dave, but I made a small revision to your control for starting a time travel event."

"What did you do?"

"I simply injected a command that stops the event until it is reviewed by the five of us outsiders."

Just then there was a knock on the door. Dave opened the door and asked Walt Martin to come in.

Dave then said to the group, "I asked Walt to delete any entries that Mary put into our computer. How did you make out, Walt?"

Walt looked a little sheepish and said, "I wasn't able to delete a thing she entered. Whatever she did, I think only she can fix it."

Denver turned red in the face. He raised his voice and said, "Young lady, do you know you can be imprisoned for what you did?"

Frank jumped up and said, "Hold your temper until you hear the rest of the story."

"I'm listening."

There was tension throughout the room. Frank continued, "Mary and the rest of us felt that we wanted some way to help protect the world from the wrongful use of your powerful new tool. The five of us put together a file explaining what we know with all our evidence. We have devised a way to make this file visible to the world if ever we detect the government is using time travel for the wrong purpose."

Mark's face got one shade redder. "And just what do you expect us to do?"

"Put the five of us on the council that reviews each time travel event."

"And if we don't choose to do this?"

"Well, Mary's control in your computer will keep you from initiating the time travel event."

"And what's to keep me from throwing you all in a special jail until Mary fixes our computer?"

Mary spoke up, "If any one of us fails to do something every day, a program will go out on the Internet with the story of the nine-thousand-year-old man. It will include the record of where our evidence is located."

Mark took a deep breath. He looked around the room and said, "Does anyone on my staff have any ideas how to get out of this?"

When there was no answer, Frank asked, "May I comment?"

Mark said in a loud voice, "By all means."

"Well, since you already have a council set up to do the same job we five had planned to do, maybe you could introduce us to your council. Hopefully, we will be so impressed that we can bow out of the picture gracefully."

Mark looked directly at Mary. "If we do, will you fix the computer and agree to help us make our computer impenetrable?"

Frank looked at Mary.

Mary said, "Sure. All we really wanted to do was try and make this new tool of yours less likely to fall into the wrong hands. If you want, I can reprogram your computer to give one designated council person the final say of go or no go."

Mark said, "Sort of like a presidential veto."

"Yes. That way, if the wrong people overpowered this facility, there would be a fail-safe measure in place."

Mark commented, "I like that idea."

Frank, Mary, and the other three breathed a sigh of relief.

Mark then said, "And will you stop your back-up plan to automatically send out data on the Internet?"

Mary said, "Yes."

Mark smiled, "You know you people are a royal pain in the ass!" Everyone laughed, even Mark Denver.

When the laughter died down, Mark said, "You know we really need your help to also make sure nobody else uncovers the truth about the bones found in the Black River."

Frank looked at the other four and said, "We'll take an action item from this meeting to come up with a reasonable plan to stop someone else from finding out the truth about the bones."

"Good."

Mark then said, "The next thing I had planned to do this afternoon was to fill you people in on where we are in this program.

Art Cox was waiting for Jimmy in a Hertz parking lot, standing next to the Ford Taurus he'd rented. Jimmy Norton pulled his Ford Escort rental next to the Taurus and got out. Together they started for the office to turn in their keys.

Jimmy commented, "You know, Art, I've been thinking about what we heard in Black River. I've been thinking time travel."

When Art and Jimmy entered the Hertz office, there was only one other man in a brown suit ahead of them renting a car. They went up to the counter next to the Hertz agent and the man in the brown suit.

Jimmy continued. "They were talking about some plastic that was carbon-dated to be nine thousand years old, right?"

Art said, "That's none of our business. You know what Ray said. That's probably why we're supposed to get debriefed today."

"But what if the plastic was found with the nine-thousand-year-old bones? Wouldn't that prove my case?"

Art realized the man in the brown suit was listening and pulled Jimmy over to some chairs in the corner.

"Wait until we get debriefed. You know better than to make comments like that. I think that guy overheard you."

Back at the counter, the man in the brown suit asked the Hertz agent if he knew the way to Black River. The agent had recognized Art and Jimmy as men who had asked him the same question when they rented their cars and said, "Why don't you ask those guys. I think they just came from there."

"Thanks, I will." He walked over to the two men and said, "Say, the Hertz guy tells me you just came from the little town of Black River."

"That's right."

"Well, I'm on my way there and could use a little help with directions."

"Let's see your map." One of the two men obtained a red marker from the Hertz agent and marked the route to Black River. He then described the way for the man.

The man thanked him and said, "I couldn't help but overhear you and your friend talking about finding plastic with the nine-thousand-year-old bones in Black River."

"We didn't say Black River. You misunderstood my friend. Who are you, anyway?"

"I'm a freelance reporter for several archeological magazines. I'm on my way to Black River to get the story about the nine thousand year-old bones found there. So naturally your comments are of interest to me. Can you tell me anything else about the bones?"

"No, we're just a couple of hard working guys who had to deliver something to Black River. Anything you might have overheard was just my friend's imagination."

The reporter looked at the man's face, and realized he wasn't going to get anything else. "Thanks a lot for your help." He returned to the counter to pick up the paperwork for his rental car.

After getting his car, the reporter pretended to be checking out his rental. He watched the two men come out of the Hertz office. The reporter couldn't hear them, but it was obvious one man was mad at the other. He watched them get into another car parked in the far corner of the lot and drive away. He thought to himself, 'Maybe there is more to this story than I thought.'

Chapter 20

Mark Denver displayed his organization chart showing his chiefs of staff and their responsibilities. He then explained the interaction of the control section with the two test sections. "Sam is an expert in creating controls, both mechanical and electrical. Jane and Jason each run special test sections. Their sections are responsible for making the time travel device work with a high degree of success. At this point in our project, Sam has given us a new control, but first Jason and Jane's groups must work together to test it out. This is going to take another two weeks to complete the trials."

With that said, Mark looked at Jason and Jane for confirmation and said, "Right, two weeks?"

They replied, "Right."

Mark continued. "Our entire team has been responsible for the creation of the time machine from its initial conception, design, detailing, construction, and check out."

Frank asked, "Are you going to tell us how it works?"

"Yes. I guess I could give you an overview. If I get too deep into the sciences, just ask questions and I'll try and put things into laymen's terms. And for my staff, please chime in if you want to correct me or add anything."

Mark paged quickly through a presentation and said, "Let me show you the meat of the slides I used to brief the top officials in Washington.

"The time travel device puts a man in a diamagnetic bubble chamber that is suspended in a magnetic field. We then can transmit the bubble chamber by laser to any place on earth and to any time by adjusting the magnetic resonance frequency of the bubble to the special frequency of that space-time. The time machine uses the laser as the transmitting road to the new place, and sensitive frequency changes to go to the desired time. Our satellites send and track the bubble chamber to the destination using the laser beam as the road."

Richard broke in and said, "You lost me at 'diamagnetic bubble'."

Mark said, "Jane, would you care to help me on this question?"

Jane Kirkpatrick was in her late thirties with brown hair and a pleasant smile. She wore a white laboratory smock over her blue suit and had tan glasses.

Jane stood up showing her slight five seven frame and said with authority, "Sure, Mark. All matter in the universe consists of small particles called atoms. Each atom contains electrons that circle around a nucleus. If you put an atom, or a large piece of matter like a man containing billions of atoms, in a magnetic field, electrons going in circles inside the man do not like the presence of the magnetic field. The electrons alter their motion in such a way as to oppose this external influence. The disturbed electrons create their own magnetic field and as a result, the atoms behave like little magnetic needles pointing in the direction opposite to the applied field. If you've ever played with magnets, you know that like poles push each other away. Our magnets create enough magnetic energy for all the atoms inside the man to act together and repel the large magnetic field. The upward force on the man is enough to compensate for the force of gravity pulling him down. The man is then suspended in space."

Frank asked, "What does this magnetic field do to the man?"

"Good question. We don't subject the man to the magnetic field directly. Instead, we put the man in a superconducting chamber where a series of computer controlled magnetic fields all around the chamber keep the chamber suspended in space without affecting the man at all. In the purest sense, a diamagnetic material, like a superconductor, expels a magnetic field. In our device, the superconductor chamber expels the magnetic field, suspends the chamber, and protects the man."

Richard said, "I thought superconducting materials had not been invented yet for use at room temperature."

"This is true. Our chamber must be super-cooled with a thin layer of liquid nitrogen. But we also oscillate the current at the inner boundary of the chamber to generate a levitating force, making it less necessary to have a perfect superconductor. This allows us to minimize the weight of the chamber. We now have a big enough chamber to carry two people."

"So the chamber protects the person inside from the magnetic field," said Richard.

"That's right. We call the chamber a magnetic bubble."

Frank said, "So now you have a chamber suspended in space with a man in it. How do you move the chamber to another time?"

Mark answered, "Time, we've discovered, is really a magnetic wave having frequencies that constantly vary. If you can exactly match the chamber frequency with the magnetic field frequency of the time and space of your destination, you can put the chamber, and the person in the chamber, in that time.

"First we had to learned how to record the magnetic frequencies of space-time. This took us three years and was a significant breakthrough. If you think of each point in particular space-time location as a crumpled up piece of paper, you can mathematically express the model of this paper as an algorithm of frequencies. The shape of the piece of paper is constantly moving to a new shape as time passes. Using sophisticated computers, we learned how to make a tape recording of this changing mathematical algorithm.

"Our team used computers to study these algorithms until they developed a mathematical model of space-time for the past and the future. Using our model of the near future, we verified this model worked by recording the near future and seeing that it matched the model. We then projected the model into the past and used the model to go back one day. It worked. The team then computerized the model to past, present, and future. We ran numerous trials going only a few days either way at first, until we gained confidence in the entire theory. Our theory has proven itself time and time again, forgive the pun."

"Well, what went wrong when you sent Jack Spencer back in time?" asked Frank.

"That's what we have been working on for the past six months. Our electronic projector sent Jack back nine thousand years instead of nine. We think we have solved the projector control problem. Sam Magnum's team came up with a magnetic resonance computer control time calibrator that precisely locates the bubble chamber to the desired time. Sam, would you explain how you finally fixed the problem with the control."

Sam took off his titanium-framed glasses and laid them on the table. "After months of playing with the control, we finally determined we simply needed to reduce the power to our electronic projector by a factor of one thousand. We think it's as simple as that. There is one drawback, however, the error in going back nine thousand years might be give-or-take a month."

"A month!" said Paul Andrews. "That means someone will have to arrive a month before Jack to be sure we don't miss him."

Sam looked directly at Paul. "I'm afraid that's right, and the person might have to wait the better part of another month if we're unlucky."

Richard raised his hand and said, "Okay, I think I have a vague idea of how you project a person to another time, but how do you move the person to another place at the same time?"

Mark said, "Good question. The answer is, it's a two step process. We use a laser system to project the chamber to a desired location. This is always done in present time using satellites around the world for sending and tracking. Once the chamber is at the desired location, we match the chamber frequency to the frequency of the desired time we are traveling to. We currently can not leave the chamber at another time for more than five minutes. After five minutes, the chamber frequency automatically returns to the present, using its onboard memory circuits, and residual magnetic power supply."

Frank asked, "Then how do you return the time traveler if you don't know where he precisely is or in what time he is in?"

Mark replied, "We are still working on this. We have the time traveler carry a homing device that, for the lack of a better way of describing it, omits a signal that lets us know where and when the person is. The homing device sends a unique frequency signal for the point in time the traveler is located in. We monitor this frequency on a computer tuned like a radio receiver to listen constantly for this unique signal. Once the signal is activated by the time traveler, and is detected by the computer, the time travel device locks in on this signal and projects our bubble chamber to the correct place and then to the correct time. The time traveler then has five minutes to enter the bubble chamber and be transported to the current time. Once in the current time, the chamber is projected back to here."

"Why then does someone need to go looking for Jack?"

"Because the homing device Jack had was never calibrated for the nine thousand years he went back. The only way to retrieve him is to send another time traveler after him with an updated homing device. Jason and Jane's people are working on this homing device even as we speak; right?"

Jane answered, "That's right, Mark."

Mary Webber said, "One thing is bothering me. Why go back nine thousand years to retrieve Jack Spencer when you could just as well go back to the day Jack left here? You then could simply stop him from going back nine thousand years, give him a new homing device, and send Jack on his original mission."

Mark answered, "Don't think we didn't think of this, Mary. We considered sending Paul, with a computer filled with the events from this timeline, back to this location before Jack left. Here we have a paradox. If Jack never went back nine thousand years, how did we find out the control malfunctioned? And if we didn't find out the control has a problem, how did we know to fix the control?"

Mary answered, "You knew you needed to fix the control from the first timeline."

"That's one simple answer, Mary, but we are just learning about time travel and are not sure we can simply stack timelines in series to repeat events many times. In addition, we want to go back nine thousand years to prove our device is fully capable of this. We are still in the experimental stages of this operation and need to gain all the experience we can. If we are successful in going back nine thousand years, think of the possibilities. We might try to go back to a time before the great flood and prove there was an Atlantis."

Frank commented, "I read Jules Verne and H. G. Wells when I was a kid, but I never expected I would ever see anything like what you people just described. Will you actually show us the device?"

Mark said, "Perhaps Paul could take you to see it after we finish here." Paul nodded.

Mark then said, "Now I'd like to talk to you some more about the real reason we have shared so much of our project with you. Earlier this afternoon you agreed to take an action item from this meeting to come up with a reasonable plan to stop someone else from finding out the truth about the bones. This is not only important to our project, but just maybe, critical to the existence of the world. If someone else finds out what you five have learned, that we are engaged in time travel, they might enlist public opinion to shut us down.

"We live in a complicated time by comparison to life one hundred or even fifty years ago. The Internet, with all its advantages, is a double-edged sword. It opens up the world to knowledge that can be used for both good or bad. Someday children around the world will be able to receive the same high standard of education that we now have in the more developed countries. Internet classrooms will teach everything from languages to higher mathematics using the most effective teachers in the world. The only thing lacking is to provide the means to the Internet to the children of the world. This new knowledge will allow these children to eventually solve the problems of the world. Poverty, sickness, and the lack of enough food to feed everyone can become a thing of the past. Someday, people can spend their days seeking the higher goals of life instead of trying to just survive. However, the Internet is also a storehouse of information that can be used by terrorists around the world. The blue prints for the atom bomb or how to make deadly viruses are available on the Internet, as is the means to deploy them. If and when catastrophe strikes the world, we will need a way to counter it.

"We all know how countries, with our own country at the top of the list, have been polluting the earth during the industrialization of the twentieth century. Until now, we have not had any tool to reverse the situation. We discussed earlier about the concerns of time travel, but we must also consider the potential good things that it could accomplish, given a chance.

"I'd like to leave you five people in this room for the next hour to come up with a reasonable plan to stop someone else from finding out the truth about the bones. In our work here, we use brainstorming sessions to come up with new ideas. Paul is a good facilitator for this type of session and will stay here with you to help facilitate your meeting."

Frank looked at the others and got a general nod of agreement.

Mark said, "Ray Blackwell has lived with you for some time now. Would you like Ray to sit in and help you, also?"

Frank said, "Sure, how about taking a break first? "

After taking a fifteen-minute break, Paul re-assembled the five outsiders and Ray in the conference room. Paul took the lead as facilitator. He stood up at the front board and wrote *Ideas to keep others from knowing the truth about the bones.*

Paul turned from the black board and said, "The way we do this brainstorming is we go around the room and ask each person for an idea. You can pass if you can't think of one at the time. We find someone says something that may sound preposterous, but this idea may stimulate someone to come up with a better idea. Therefore, one main rule we have is that no one may criticize another's response. I'll record the responses and we can get started. Frank, how about you leading it off."

Frank said, "Give the bones to the Indians and let them bury the bones in a secret place on the reservation."

Paul wrote down on the board, *have Indians bury the bones.*

"Mary, you're next."

"Somehow corrupt the evidence we've uncovered so that it will dispel the idea of possible time travel."

Paul wrote down, *corrupt the evidence.*

"Joe?"

Joe paused for a moment and said, "I'll pass this time around."

Paul said, "Okay, how about you, Richard?"

Richard said, " 'Piltdown Man Hoax'."

Joe said, "What does that mean?"

Paul said, "Now remember, we don't discuss these items until we have a complete list. How do you spell *Piltdown*, Richard?" Richard spelled it for him. "It's your turn Ray."

Ray said, "Corrupt the facts, a slight addition or revision to Mary's idea."

"Okay." Paul wrote it down on the board. "George, you're next."

George said, "I like Frank's idea."

Paul then said, "Okay, we've been around once. Let's go around again. Frank?"

Frank said, "I'll pass."

"Mary?"

"I'll pass, also."

"Joe?"

Joe said, "I could claim we made a mistake on our findings."

"Okay." Paul wrote down, *mistake on official findings.*

"Richard?"

Richard smiled and repeated, " 'Piltdown Man Hoax'."

The others looked at Richard smiling and Paul said, "Ray, do you have anything to add?"

Ray said, "I'll pass."

George said, "Me, too."

Paul then said, "Anyone else have anything to add?" Everyone looked at each other without saying anything.

Paul said, "Okay, Richard. It's time for you to explain what you mean by the *'Piltdown Man Hoax'*."

Richard smiled and said, "In 1912, in Piltdown, England, someone fooled anthropologists into believing they found the 'missing link'."

Frank asked, "What do you mean by, 'missing link'?"

"That will take a little explaining in itself. Most anthropologists believe that man slowly evolved from the ape or a modern relative of the ape that we call Neanderthal man. Some scientists believe, more like the book of Genesis, that man evolved from a single generative in Southern Africa or the Middle East rather than a gradual evolution from the Neanderthal. These scientists refer to this as the 'Eve Hypothesis'. So there is a dispute between these scientists and most anthropologists.

"The modern understanding of human evolution rest on known fossils, but the picture is far from complete. Only future fossil discoveries will enable scientists to fill in many of the blanks in the present picture of modern evolution.

"Now you have to understand the skull of the Neanderthal evolved from the skull of the modern ape. The Neanderthal skull is characterized by a small brain cavity. He had a large protruding jaw with large canine teeth. The modern human skull is characterized by a much larger brain cavity. The face is flattened, the chin is recessed, and the teeth are decreased in size.

"Getting back to the discovery in 1912: A scientist named Charles Dawson discovered fragments of a modern skull along with the jawbone of an ape. They called this discovery 'Piltdown Man' because it was found near Piltdown, England. The scientists gave this man the name Eoanthropus or dawn man. They thought the 'missing link' between the Neanderthal and modern man had been found. It wasn't until 1953, that scientific analysis proved the fossil was a forgery. They proved the skull fragment was a modern human cranium and the jawbone was of an ape.

"People today still don't know for sure who perpetrated this hoax. Some think Charles Dawson did it to gain fame, but others including myself think that Sir Arthur Conan Doyle did it."

Frank said, "Sir Arthur Conan Doyle, the creator of the Sherlock Holmes novels?"

"That's right. Sir Arthur lived only seven miles from the site where the fossils were found. He was known to play elaborate practical jokes and had the knowledge to salt the site."

"But what motive would Doyle have for doing this?"

"Good detective question, Frank. Sir Arthur had just completed his new book, 'The Lost World' and sent the book to his publisher the very week of the 'Piltdown Man' discovery. Some believe Sir Arthur used the 'Piltdown Man' discovery to get publicity for his new book about the ancient world. There was even a map from the book that located a site similar to where the 'Piltdown Man' was found. Sir Arthur probably died with a smile on his face that nobody at the time discovered the hoax."

Paul chimed in, "So I take it you plan to make the public think the nine-thousand-year-old bones are a hoax."

"That's my plan. We'll go back to Black River and maybe Joe will discover that I salted the test samples."

"What would your motive be?" Frank asked.

"Why, as an archeologist, I wanted access to Indian land to further study the bones of the Indians."

Frank said, "You'll be taking a lot of heat. It will destroy your reputation."

"I know. That's why it will be doubly important to me that Paul retrieves Jack Spencer. If Paul retrieves Jack, history will be rewritten, and I'm off the hook; but if Paul fails, I'm screwed."

Paul said, "Thanks for your faith in us, Richard. Does anyone else have a better solution?"

Frank said, "Sounds like Richard's plan encompasses all our other ideas and provides a workable plan."

"Well then, Richard, I guess you're our scapegoat."

CHAPTER 21

After the brainstorming session ended, Mary returned to the computer room with Dave Owen to repair the software changes she had made earlier. This time she returned the computer back to its normal operation. Dave thanked her and escorted her to another room where Paul Andrews was waiting with the other visitors from Black River to begin a tour of the area where the time-travel device was located.

Paul led the small group through a maze of security doors. Before entering the main area, the group had to put on special, white, protective clothing similar to a hospital operating room. Paul led them into the main room. They found themselves in an enclosed room the size of two side-by-side basketball courts. The ceiling was one hundred feet high. In the center of the room, they saw a giant erector-set like object that could be described as a huge science experiment with scaffolding all around it. Twenty-five people were busy at work doing all sorts of task around the device. To one side of the room was another enclosed room with windows looking out onto the main room. Paul walked the group to within ten feet of the outside of the scaffolding and started describing the device.

Pointing to the windowed room off to the side, Paul said, "That's the control room. From that room the laser projector is activated to transport the bubble chamber to the correct destination. Then the electromagnetic frequency projector transports the chamber to the correct time." Paul pointed upward to the center of the scaffolding, and said, "The round chamber in the center is the bubble chamber. It's big enough to hold two people."

Frank asked, "What's that steam coming off the top?"

"That's water vapor coming from the air around the liquid nitrogen cooling system that surrounds the super-conducting surface of the chamber. Just outside the cooling system is the magnetic layer that is used to create the diamagnetic bubble. The inside of the chamber itself is insulated from the magnetic field by the super-conducting layer."

Richard asked, "What is the large hole just above the chamber?"

"That's a magnetic plenum leading directly upward into the laser stream tube. If you look up and to the right of the laser stream tube, you'll notice this tube extends into the laser projector."

They looked at the laser projector and saw what could be described as freight-car-sized device mounted on a bed. The entire bed appeared to be mounted on vibration dampers. It had two glass tubes located above the main stream tube running in parallel to each other and connected at the ends by mirrors. The bed had slotted surfaces from which some sort of metal tubular device extended upward into the slots. There were cryogenic tanks located below and connected to the tubular device.

"On the other side, where the magnetic tube connects into the main laser tube, you will notice the main laser tube extends through the ceiling. From the ceiling the main laser tube goes above ground to a turret that can target and project the chamber to a mirrored satellite and to the final destination."

Joe asked, "How do you project light around corners?"

"With mirrors. We have mirrors inside the tubes that reflect the light around the corners. The chamber, itself, is suspended in a kind of plasma light as it travels along the laser light."

"How do you move the chamber through the laser light?"

"Good question, Frank. The chamber has its own very strong positive magnetic charge. The laser projector has the capability to make the outer plasma of the laser light either magnetically positive or negative by a simple throwing of a switch."

"I get it," said Frank. "To project, you use the positive charge. To retrieve, you use a negative charge."

"Go to the head of the class."

Richard said, "That's incredible. Where does all the power come from to run this machine?"

"We have a direct tie into a nuclear power station. I wouldn't want to pay our electric bill. The power comes in through that wall over there and goes through the control room and directly into the laser projector along this line, and to the magnetic generators along that line over there. The control room contains our computer banks for the device and all the controls."

Mary said, "So let me see if I've got this right. You walk up these stairs and get in the bubble chamber. People in the control room, over there, charge up the chamber and the laser. They magnetically move the chamber that is floating in a magnetic field into the main stream of the laser. The chamber is then suspended in a magnetic plasma of laser light. They then project the chamber in the laser stream to a predetermined destination using the nation's satellite system. Right, so far?"

"Right, so far."

"They then change the magnetic field of the chamber to the exact resonance frequency of the desired time you plan to go to, and poof, you're there."

"That's about it."

Mary continued, "And when you get out of the chamber, the chamber returns here."

"That's correct. After five minutes, the chamber will start its return trip, whether you are in it or not."

"And when you want to return, you activate the homing device to let the people in the control room know you are ready to return."

"That's correct."

Richard asked, "How long does it take?"

"Anywhere from thirty seconds to many minutes depending on where you are going and how far back in time you go."

Joe said, "I've heard Steven Wright, the comedian, say, 'I put instant coffee into my micro-wave oven, and it went back in time.' He had nothing on you guys." Everyone laughed.

Frank looked at George and said, "What do you think of all this?"

George looked up at the huge invention and said, "The technology is incredible, but I still feel uncomfortable with the idea of man fooling around with time."

Paul responded, "In many ways so do I, but I figure someone is going to travel through time sooner or later. I feel obligated to make sure it's done correctly for the good of man."

George said, "The area you are planning to go to, Paul, is the land around my reservation, right?"

"That's right."

"I've been thinking. I could take you on a camping trip around this area so that you would have a better idea of where you are when you travel back in time. After all, this land has never been developed. The mountains in particular may not have changed that much. There are caves in the mountains that you could use to keep you sheltered until Jack arrives."

"That's a great idea. Could we go next week?"

"Sure, just let me know when."

Paul asked if there were any other questions. When he didn't get a reply, the group left the secret area. Paul escorted them back to the main entrance underground parking area where a government car was waiting for them.

They were driven back to Warrenton, Virginia and dropped off at the Hampton Inn where they had spent the previous night. They were glad they had booked rooms for a second night, having spent a long day at the government facility. They agreed to meet for dinner at seven-thirty that night. Joe and Richard shared one room. Frank and George shared another, while Mary had a room to herself.

At seven-thirty, all five piled into Frank's car and drove to a local restaurant. They picked a table in a corner where their conversation could not be overheard.

Frank started the conversation. "It's been some day."

"I've never experienced anything like it," Joe replied.

Mary said, "Even working for the FBI never got this intense."

Richard said, "You know I volunteered to be the scapegoat in this matter. I'm having second thoughts. What if Paul's mission fails? I'll be left holding the bag. Can you people think of any way of working my 'Piltdown Man' plan without me hanging so far out on a limb?"

Frank said, "Well, we could work it so you and Joe figure out the site had been salted, but without knowing who did the salting."

Richard said, "That wouldn't work. The only way I could've made the results turn out as they did was to send real nine thousand year-old samples to be carbon-dated. I would be the most likely suspect. I think I've answered my own question. I'll have to take the blame.

Joe, I think you'll turn out to be the good guy. Here's how we should work it. I'll give you a two-hundred-year-old sample of bone. You send the sample to be carbon-dated. When the results come back, you'll say you confronted me about the differing results. I'll break down under the scrutiny and confess. What do you think?"

Joe said, "Unless someone can come up with a better idea, your plan makes sense. How do we deal with the press?"

Mary said, "Maybe you can leak the story to the press somehow, so that the press thinks they have a scoop."

Richard said, "That's not a bad idea, Mary. How do you think we can make that happen?"

"I don't know, but I'll work on it."

Frank said, "George, how do you think your people will react?"

"Badly. I suspect they'll accuse Richard of fraud to get access to the reservation just as Richard said earlier today. In fact, if you want, I can start a small riot and you can arrest Richard for his own protection."

Frank said, "Just like in the old west, George?"

Everyone but Richard laughed. "You guys are forgetting, I've got a family and reputation at stake."

The smiles faded and Frank said, "We know, Richard. We wish there was a better way."

After dinner, Frank drove the group back to the Hampton Inn. They said good night and Frank told George he would walk Mary to her room. George smiled back and said, "Good night, I'll leave a light on in case you decide to come back to your room."

Frank smiled and said, "Good night, George."

Mary and Frank entered her room and She threw her arms around him. They fell on the nearest bed.

When they came up for air, Mary said, "I've been wanting to do that all day."

"Me, too."

"You know, one thing has been bothering me."

"I think I know what you are going to say, Mary, but go ahead."

"When Paul goes back in time, the timeline may change so that we never fall in love."

"That has been bothering me, too. What do you think we can do about it?"

Mary started to cry and said, "I don't know what we can do about it."

"Well, you know we will still meet when you come to work at the sheriff's office. That shouldn't change."

"But how do we know we'll fall in love again?"

"I can't imagine any way I wouldn't fall in love with you again, Mary."

"Oh, I hope you're right."

"I know I am, so stop crying and give me a kiss."

An hour before the group agreed to meet for breakfast, Frank entered his own room and found George up and getting ready for the day. George said, "Good morning, Frank," with a smile on his face.

Frank smiled back and said, "Good morning."

The group met in the help-yourself breakfast area of the Hampton Inn at seven-thirty.

Frank asked, "Richard, do you feel any better this morning after a good nights sleep?"

"Not much, Frank. I had a hard time getting to sleep thinking about our plans."

"It'll work out just fine. Keep the faith."

Just then Mary came into the room and Frank stood to greet her with a kiss. "You're looking lovely this morning, Mary."

"Thank you. You look very handsome yourself."

George said, "How about the rest of us?"

"You all look very handsome," was her reply.

Frank raised his orange juice glass and said, "I just want to say, having gone through yesterday and this adventure with this group, I hope we'll always be friends regardless of how difficult things may get; 'friends forever'."

The others raised their glasses in agreement and repeated, "friends forever."

After breakfast, the group from Black River got into their two cars and started for home. Traveling together, they stopped both cars at a roadside diner to have lunch. The five travelers found another corner booth and ordered their meals.

Joe Bianco started the conversation, "We forgot to discuss our reason for this short trip. We better have a common alibi."

Frank said, "You're right. What if we say you and Richard needed to go out of town to obtain some archeological data that Richard thought relevant for the study of the bones?"

"Okay. What excuse will you use?"

"We can say Mary and I wanted to get away together and we brought George along for a chaperone."

Mary said, "Really, Frank! In this day in age, do you think anyone would believe we brought George along as a chaperone?"

"Well, I guess you're right. How do we explain George coming along then?"

George said, "Maybe you just happened to be going in the same direction and you agreed to give an old friend a ride to visit a sick relative."

"Not bad, George."

When the group arrived back in Black River, Mary and Frank dropped off George at his home and went directly to the sheriff's office. Sheriff Dave Tucker was back from his fishing vacation and asked where the two of them had been. Dave believed Frank's story that he and Mary wanted to get away together for a couple of days to explore their relationship.

Dave smiled at them and said, "Harry Packard held the fort while you were gone."

Frank asked, "How was the fishing?"

"I caught my limit every day I fished and you should have seen the one that got away. It was this big."

"Did you get a picture of that fish?"

"Not exactly, but it was big."

Just then Harry Packard walked up, "I'm sure glad all of you are back in town. I was getting tired of making the decisions around here."

Frank said, "Were things that busy?"

"We had several domestic squabbles, one fire in a home on River Street, two cases of breaking and entering, and one car accident caused by a heart attack. Oh, and some freelance reporter for archeological magazines stopped in yesterday asking questions about the bones found along the Black River."

Frank said, "What kind of questions?"

"The reporter said he had tried to talk with Richard Farley and Joe Bianco over at the coroner's office, but they were not available. So he came here to get the story. I told him the bones appear to be the bones of a nine-thousand-year old man based on the testing done so far. He seemed real interested. I told him you could probably tell him more when you came back from your trip. The reporter said he would be staying at the Black River Hotel and gave me his card. He wants you to call him, Frank."

Harry passed the card to him and Frank read out loud, "*Charles Barton, Freelance Reporter, New York, N.Y.*"

CHAPTER 22

Mary and Frank sat at their favorite table in the Black River Restaurant and ordered drinks before dinner. Mary started the conversation. "I've got an idea of how we might use this freelance reporter to facilitate our plan."

Frank smiled, "What do you have in mind?"

"We could steer the reporter to Joe Bianco, who could claim he felt something was fishy with the latest test results. Joe could show the reporter the conflicting two-hundred-year-old results along with the nine-thousand-year-old results."

"I get it. We let the reporter discover that Richard salted the site so that the reporter thinks he has a big scoop."

"Exactly. The reporter tells the world the bones are actually only two hundred years old and that Richard used the situation to gain access to Indian land."

"That sure is a good way to get the story turned around in a hurry, Mary. Let's start working the plan tomorrow. I'll call the others tonight and fill them in."

After dinner, Frank took Mary home and returned home himself to make the calls. The next morning, Frank called Charles Barton.

"Mr. Barton, my name is Frank McDermott. I'm a detective for the Black River Sheriff's Office. I understand you wished to speak with me about the bones found along the Black River."

"Thanks for calling, Mr. McDermott. Can I come by and talk with you this morning at your office?"

"Sure, how about ten o'clock?"

"I'll be there."

At ten o'clock, Barton knocked on Frank's open office door.

Charles Barton was about six feet tall with light brown hair and was a little overweight. He wore a light brown suit with a white shirt and dark brown tie.

Charlie had worked on a newspaper after college, but found he could not work on the kind of stories he really liked. So after a year with the newspaper, he had become a freelance reporter. Charlie had been doing this for over ten years and found he was able to make a comfortable living. He was not married and liked to travel. It seemed to Charlie that there could be no better way of life.

Frank reached out his hand, "Mr. Barton?"

"Charles Barton, freelance reporter. Please call me, Charlie."

They shook hands and Frank said, "Call me Frank. Have a seat." When Charlie sat down, Frank asked, "Why are you interested in the bones?"

"I'm doing an article for archeological magazines about the nine thousand-year old bones. It's quite a sensational story to those who follow archeology. I understand there was some plastic found with the bones that was also carbon-dated to be nine thousand years old?"

This comment caught Frank by surprise. Frank tried to keep a poker face and said, "Where'd you hear that from? I don't think that's true."

Charlie looked directly at Frank and said, "I heard it from a confidential source."

Frank recovered his composure and said, "As a sheriff's detective, I was called in when the bones were found to investigate the possibility of a murder. But when we learned the bones were nine thousand years old, I've only stayed involved out of curiosity and to keep the peace between the local Indians and the archeologists. The Indians claim the bones were found on their land and therefore must be an ancient relative. They want the bones returned to their land for reburial."

Charlie said, "I understand the archeologist, Richard Farley, believes the bones are not Indian bones, but of a Caucasian with European features."

"That's correct and that's why there's a big dispute between the Indians and archeologists that may have legal ramifications."

"Where do I go from here, Frank, to get more information for my article?"

"The bones are being kept at the local coroner's office. You can talk to Joe Bianco, the Coroner, about seeing them. He can fill you in with more details."

Charlie stood and said, "Thanks, Frank. I'll do just that."

Frank watched Charlie get into his car, and then called Joe. Frank warned him that the reporter, somehow, knew about the nine thousand-year-old-plastic being found with the bones. Frank told him that he denied knowing anything about the plastic and suggested that Joe also deny the fact. Joe agreed and told Frank that he would let Richard know about this, also.

By the time Charlie introduced himself to Joe and Richard at the coroner's office, they were prepared to deny knowing anything about the plastic. After initial introductions, they took Charlie to see the bones laid-out on a table in the basement.

Charlie's first comment after looking at the skull was, "I'm not an archeologist like you, Richard, but I understand why you think these are the bones of a Caucasian. I've seen enough skull bones in my time, doing stories for archeological magazines, to know that this skull looks more like a white man's skull than an Indian's skull."

Richard agreed with Charlie and went on to give the technical reasons why it was so. Charlie listened intently and took notes while Richard was speaking.

Charlie then asked, "I understand you had the bones carbon-dated and found to be about nine thousand years old?"

"That's correct," said Richard.

"I also understand you found some pieces of plastic along with the bones and had the plastic carbon-dated to be about nine thousand years old, also?"

Prepared for this question, both Joe and Richard pretended to look puzzled. Richard said, "That's not true. Where would you possibly have gotten that idea?"

Charlie said, "I have my sources. Would you tell me what lab you used to do the carbon dating?"

At the sheriff's office, Frank called Ray Blackwell. "Ray, I think you better consider coming back to Black River."

"Why, what's up?"

"A freelance reporter by the name of Charles Barton is in town asking questions about the nine-thousand-year-old plastic found at the site."

"What did you tell him?"

"We're denying it, of course, but you know how nosy reporters can be."

"I'll pack a bag and meet you in your office in the morning."

Thirty minutes later, Frank got a call from Joe. "How'd you make out with Charles Barton, Joe?"

"That's why I'm calling. Charles brought up the question of the carbon dating of the plastic. We denied it, but he asked what lab did the carbon dating for us."

"Did you tell him?"

"Yeah. What else could I do?"

"Better call your friend at the lab and let him know who's coming. Remind him the specimen was mislabeled and should've said prehistoric, so your lab friend gets the story straight if Barton comes nosing around for information."

"Good idea. I'll give Brian a call. We can use the mislabeled specimen story to our advantage. We can say that must be where the reporter got the wrong idea about the plastic."

"Good thinking, Joe. Oh, I almost forgot! I called Ray Blackwell and told him about the reporter. Ray will be here in the morning to help us ward off any problems."

"Okay Frank, see you later. Oh, Frank!"

Frank said, "I'm still on the phone."

"I also sent the two hundred year-old bone specimen over to the lab this morning as we planned."

"Thanks, Joe. I'll bring Mary and George up to date and talk more with you later."

That afternoon, Barton visited the radio carbon dating lab at the address given to him by Joe Bianco. Charlie introduced himself to the receptionist and asked to speak to Brian Phillips, who Joe had indicated as the person to contact at the lab. When Brian came out to greet Charlie in the reception area, Charlie introduced himself and said he was doing a story for archeological magazines about the nine thousand year-old bones.

Brian said, "I got a call from Joe Bianco. He told me you might visit. What can I do for you?"

"I understand you did the carbon dating of the bones for the coroner's office?"

"That's right, for Joe Bianco."

"And the specimens of the bones found along the Black River turned out to be nine thousand years old."

"That's right."

"What about the specimen of plastic?"

Brian laughed and said, "Joe said you might ask me about that. Actually, the specimen was mislabeled. It should have been labeled, prehistoric, not plastic."

"How did you know the specimen was mislabeled?"

"Joe called me late the same day that I did the carbon dating and told me the specimen was mislabeled."

"And you believed him?"

"Yes."

"How long have you been doing this job?"

"Seven years, but what does that have to do with anything?"

Charlie realized he was pushing a bit too hard and decided to back off. So he asked Brian how the carbon dating process worked, even though Charlie already knew. Brian answered his question in detail. Charlie complemented Brian on his knowledge and thanked him for his help. Charlie said good-by and turned to leave. Just as he got to the door, he turned and asked Brian, "Do you think you could tell the difference between a specimen of bone and a specimen of plastic by sight?"

Brian paused and said, "Maybe."

Charlie then asked, "Would you say the prehistoric specimen was bone or plastic?"

Brian said, "I thought it might be plastic until Joe told me otherwise."

"Then you didn't actually determine if the material was bone or plastic?"

"No. That would have to be done at a materials lab."

"Do you still have the specimen?"

"No. I sent the specimen back to Joe along with my official report."

"Are there any labs around here that might be able to identify a specimen as bone or plastic?"

"Sure, there are a few within about a hundred miles of here."

"Could you give me the names of these labs?"

"Sure, but what's this all about?"

Charlie said, "I don't really know myself. I've been a freelance reporter for ten years and it's just my way to be nosy about things."

Brian smiled, wrote down the names of three material labs, and asked, "Is there anything else I can help you with?"

Charlie shook Brian's hand and said, "No. You've already been a big help."

Charlie decided to follow his lead. He stopped at a restaurant to get a cup of coffee and look up the phone numbers of the material labs on Brian's list. After getting the numbers, he started calling the labs to ask if anyone there had done any work recently for the Black River Coroner's Office. Charlie thought he had reached a dead end after calling two of the three labs on the list and getting a negative answer. But he hit pay dirt when he called the third lab.

The person who answered the phone said, "Yes. What about the work? Who's calling please?"

Charlie said, "I'm calling about the material specimen you checked for Joe."

"Yes. Who is this?"

"Well, I work for Joe. He wondered when you were going to send him the official report."

"I already told Joe the specimen is Samsonite."

Charlie just hung up the phone. That was all he wanted to know.

Late in the afternoon, the phone rang at the coroner's office. "Joe Bianco."

"Hey, Joe, this is Scott Baker at the materials lab."

"Yes, Scott."

"I got a strange call this afternoon from some guy who said he worked for you."

"Did you get his name?"

"No. He asked me about the last test I did for you to find out what material your specimen was. He wondered when I was going to send the official report."

"I think I know who that was. What did you tell him?"

"I told him I had already told you the material was Samsonite and he hung up on me."

Joe paused for a second and said, "Don't worry about it. I know who that is. I don't need an official report, and thanks a lot for the call, Scott."

"Sure, Joe, catch you another time."

Joe called Frank, "Barton found out about the Samsonite."

"How'd he find out so quickly?"

"He must be a real blood hound, Frank."

"We better get together tomorrow at the coroner's office when Ray arrives."

CHAPTER 23

The next day, the reluctant conspirators met in the coroner's office. Frank and Joe brought the others up to date on what Barton had found out the day before.

"What do we do now?" Frank asked.

Ray pulled out his cell phone. "I'll run a background check on this guy."

"I already have, said Mary. Barton has been working freelance all over the world for about ten years. He's written stories about people, places and things for many magazines and newspapers. He likes to sensationalize his stories."

Frank asked, "Like what? Do you have any examples?"

"Yes. Barton did a story about a fire in a high-rise apartment building in Mexico City about eight years ago. I read the story and it made me feel as if I were one of the people trapped by the fire on the top floor. A young woman jumped to her death only minutes before rescuers arrived in a helicopter. Barton really made the reader feel the tragedy of the situation.

"I also read an article Barton did about the drug trade in Colombia. The article told stories of how local officials were either paid off or killed. Barton made it a point to describe in detail how one local official and a priest were tortured and murdered. He described how fearful the people were to do anything to oppose the drug dealers."

"It sounds like Barton has a social conscience," Frank commented.

Mary nodded, "Yes, and I think he has a nose for a good story."

"Well," said Frank, "we better make sure Barton latches onto the story we want him to have. Joe, how soon can you get the results back from the two-hundred-year-old bone sample you sent to the carbon dating lab?"

"I'll try and get the results right away."

"Good. The sooner you can leak the hoax story to Barton, the better."

Ray looked at Frank, "But even if you get this guy to buy the hoax, how will you explain the Samsonite to him?"

"Good question." Frank turned to the rest of the group. "Does anybody have any ideas?"

Joe responded, "I've been thinking about this. I could tell Barton the Samsonite has nothing to do with the bones found along the river; that I got the information for my son, who is doing a science experiment for school. I would stick to our story that the specimen sent to the carbon dating lab was mislabeled."

Ray asked rhetorically, "Would you buy that? I think I better keep an eye on this guy and make sure he buys your story. At the first sign Barton is onto us, I'm going to pull him off the street."

Mary asked, "What do you mean, 'pull him off the street?'"

"I mean I'll have to take him aside and let him know what's going on the way we did with you."

"Oh. I got the impression you might do him some harm."

"Not if I can help it, but you realize what's at stake. If Barton starts calling people and telling them he's onto something, I'll have to act fast."

Frank asked, "How can we help?"

"I guess the first thing is for Joe to let me know what this guy's reaction is to your story. I'll get my people back here to bug Barton's rental car and hotel room."

Joe asked, "How do we get Barton back here for me to tell him about the dilemma I'm having over the two-hundred-year-old bone specimen."

"Unless I've misread Mr. Barton, he'll be back here today."

Frank said, "Mary's probably right, Joe. You better get the carbon dating results right away."

As the meeting broke up, Ray asked Frank if he could continue to use the sheriff's office as home base.

"Sure, I don't think Sheriff Tucker even knew you were gone. So just act like the office is still yours."

"Thanks, Frank."

Joe said, "I just got a message from my secretary that Barton has been trying to talk to me. I'll give him a call as soon as I have the results from the carbon dating lab."

"Good, Joe. We'll talk with you later."

On the way out of the coroner's office, George walked with Mary and Frank. George said, "You know, next week I'm planning on taking Paul Andrews on a camping trip around the river area and mountains where the bones were found. Why don't you and Mary come along?

Later that afternoon, Barton arrived at the coroner's office to see Joe.

"What can I do for you?"

Barton told Joe how he had contacted the Carbon Dating Lab, and also that he talked with a person at the materials lab and found out about the Samsonite. He asked Joe to explain the carbon-dated plastic and the Samsonite.

Joe answered, "The Samsonite was sent to the materials lab the same day as another bone sample was sent to the carbon dating lab. The bone sample should've been labeled prehistoric bone. Instead it was mislabeled as plastic. The Samsonite had nothing to do with the bones. My son is doing a science experiment and asked me if I could find out what kind of plastic his teacher gave him to study."

Joe then told Barton, "You know there's something about this case that is bothering me though."

Barton raised an eyebrow, "Oh, what's that?"

"The first bone specimens sent to the carbon dating lab were dated to be nine-thousand-years old. But yesterday I sent another bone sample to the lab and the results came back only two-hundred-years-old."

Barton said, "And the two-hundred-year-old specimen was from the same bones found along the river."

"That's right. At least I think that's right."

"Why do you say that?"

"Because the specimen I sent yesterday definitely was from the bones found by the river. But the earlier specimens were given to me by someone else, supposedly from the bones found along the river."

"You mean, you didn't select them yourself?"

"That's correct. I trusted the other person to pick out the specimens."

"Just who was that?"

"The archeologist, Richard Farley."

"Are you saying Richard Farley sent specimens that were not from the bones found along the river?"

"I don't know what I'm saying. I haven't even had a chance to talk to Richard about this yet. I just got the results this afternoon."

"When do you plan to talk with Farley?"

"As soon as I can."

"This could change the whole story about the bones," Barton made some notes.

"I know."

Barton was still making notes as he asked, "Can I assume you'll talk to Farley by tomorrow?"

"I'm certainly going to try."

"Can I come back tomorrow for the rest of the story?"

"As long as you promise not to go off with this story before I have a chance to talk with Richard Farley."

"You have my word. I'll see you tomorrow."

At the sheriff's office, Ray Blackwell picked up his phone and made a call. Art Cox answered his cell phone.

"It's Ray Blackwell. I've got another surveillance job for you and Jimmy."

"Sure, Ray. What do you have in mind?"

"It's basically the same case in Black River. I'll fill you in when you get here. Now that you've had your security clearances upgraded and know this area, I believe you'll be able to do a better job for me."

"We will. When do you want us in Black River?"

"Right away. Call me when you get here."

"We'll be there by 8:00 A.M. tomorrow."

Ray then put in a call to Denver. After a few minutes, Mark's secretary was able to get him on the phone.

"It's Ray, Mark. I'm back in Black River to ensure the correct story goes out to the press."

"Is everything under control?"

"Should be. There's a freelance reporter snooping around the case. We're feeding him bits of our story hoping the reporter will be the person who finds out that Richard was playing a hoax in order to gain access to the Indian reservation. We want this reporter to be the one who breaks the story to the world."

"Good, so everything is proceeding as planned?"

"Yes, I think that is a fair statement, but to be sure, I'm bringing in my surveillance team to keep a watch on the reporter."

"Good idea, Ray. Don't spook him. We don't need any more trouble."

"Right. How's the team doing, Mark?"

"We're finishing up the trials. Paul Andrews is going on a camping trip with George Littlefield next week to get the lay of the land and then we're ready to go. Anything else you wanted to tell me, Ray?"

"No, I'll keep in touch."

"Thanks."

Barton returned to the coroner's office at 10:00 A.M. the following day. The secretary led him to Joe's office where Joe was already talking with Richard Farley. Joe reintroduced Barton to Richard.

Barton extended his hand to Farley. "It's an honor, Mr. Farley, or should I call you Professor Farley?"

"Richard will do. I understand you're doing an article about the bones found along the river for some archeological magazines."

"That's correct." He told Richard the names of the magazines in which the article would appear.

Richard looked forlorn. He said, "Joe just told me that he had another specimen of bone carbon-dated, and the results showed the bone was only two hundred years old. Joe has just asked me if I can explain this discrepancy."

Both Joe and Barton continued to look at Richard for the answer.

Richard hung his head. "I guess it's time to come clean as they say on the TV shows. When I first saw the bones, I knew right away that they were not ancient; I knew the bones were probably at least a hundred years old. The river made the bones look older than they were. I also recognized right away that the bones were likely of a white man and not an Indian. This gave me an idea. For years we archeologists have wanted to investigate this Indian reservation land, but have always been turned away. I thought about it for a while and came up with the story we all know went out to the public."

Barton pulled out his note pad, "So you salted the specimens to get the results to match your story."

"That's right. I had some bone samples that came from a site in England that I already knew were nine thousand years old. I simply gave them to Joe to send to the radio carbon dating lab to confirm my story."

"I didn't have any part in this," Joe said very defensively.

"No, that's right. I'm sorry, Joe, to involve you in this."

"What do we do now?" asked Joe.

Richard answered, "I guess it's time the world knows the truth. Maybe they'll give me some sympathy because I did it to advance man's knowledge of ancient people."

Barton looked Richard directly in the eyes, "I'd like to write this story. I think I can show the human side of it and maybe get you some sympathy, at least from your colleagues."

Joe looked at Richard. "It's up to you. One way or another, I've got to make sure the correct story is told to set things right."

Richard looked at Barton. "You seem like a nice young man. Go ahead with your story."

Barton smiled like a kid who just got a new baseball glove and thanked Richard as he went quickly out the door. Joe and Richard watched Barton go out of the building, get into his car, and drive off. They walked back to Joe's office suppressing smiles and shut the door. Only then did they laugh and congratulate themselves.

When Barton came out of the coroner's office at ten-thirty, Art Cox and Jimmy Norton were already on the job. Ray had briefed them on their assignment earlier the same morning. As prearranged, Joe had called Ray when Barton arrived at the coroner's office. Ray had asked Joe what kind of car Barton was driving and Joe told him a blue Ford Taurus. Art and Jimmy parked their white van next to the Taurus and quickly bugged the car. They then moved to a shady spot in the parking lot some distance away and waited for the driver to come out.

When Barton came out and got into his rental car, Art said to Jimmy, "Hey, I know that guy! Isn't he the one we gave directions to back at the Hertz office?"

Jimmy looked through binoculars and said, "You're right."

Art said, "Get down, we better not let him see us."

When Barton pulled out of the coroner's office parking lot, they tailed him at some distance. Barton went directly to his hotel room at the Black River Hotel. Art and Jimmy flashed their new NSA badges to the hotel clerk and found out what room Barton was staying in. They checked into the room next door and waited for Barton to leave his room. An hour later, Art followed Barton to a local restaurant and called Jimmy. He told him where he was and that it was safe to go into Barton's room.

Jimmy wasted no time. Once inside, he quickly planted a bug in the phone. He found Barton's lap top computer open on the desk and decided to check it out. He turned on the computer and checked the files to see what the last entry was.

Jimmy found the "Microsoft Word" file that Barton had last been working on. He quickly read the article titled, *"Noted Archeologist Creates Hoax to Gain Access to Indian Reservation Land."* The article clearly indicated that archeologist Richard Farley had intentionally salted the site where the supposed nine-thousand-year-old-bones were found in order to gain access to the Indian reservation. Jimmy took notes and carefully returned the computer to the condition in which he found it. He looked around to make sure he hadn't disturbed anything, and quietly left the room.

Later that day, Art called Ray to report what they found. Ray was pleased and said, "Stay on Barton, but give him plenty of leash. We don't want him to know he's being watched. Make sure you disguise yourselves to blend in."

By the next day, Barton had reviewed his article with both Richard Farley and Joe Bianco. They made only minor suggestions to his story and agreed he should go ahead and send it out to the press. A day later, the story made the front page of the local newspapers and the second page of many major newspapers.

When Frank went to work, he found Sheriff Dave Tucker waiting for him.

"Frank, have you seen the news about the bones found along the river?"

"Yes. The story is all over the local news this morning."

"You better get over to the coroner's office and make sure things don't get out of hand. And I'd take your U.S. Marshal friend with you, if I were you."

"Good idea!"

Frank waited for Ray to arrive, and together they went to the coroner's office. When they got there, they found a small uprising of reporters and Indians mulling around the entrance of the building. A reporter had taken George aside and was doing an interview with a camera rolling. Frank and Ray watched the interview with the rest of the crowd. George was calling for the arrest of Richard Farley and the return of the bones to the Indian reservation. When he saw Frank in the crowd, George immediately called for him to support his cry for justice. Playing the pre-arranged scene with George, Frank walked through the crowd with Ray and joined the interview.

The reporter recognized Frank and stuck a microphone in his face, "Mr. McDermott, do you care to make a statement for the sheriff's office?"

Frank looked into the camera. "This is U.S. Marshal, Ray Blackwell standing next to me. We're here to talk with Richard Farley. We plan to ask Mr. Farley to accompany us to the sheriff's office where we'll determine if this hoax story is true."

The reporter asked, "And if the story is true?"

"Well, then we'll detain Mr. Farley until we determine who's at fault and if there are grounds to make any arrest."

George grabbed the microphone, "What about the bones? We want them returned to the reservation."

Frank talked into the microphone held by both the reporter and George. "That may well be the final course of action in this case, but first we need to get some questions answered."

As Frank and Ray walked into the coroner's office, Ray commented, "You're playing your role very well."

They went directly to Joe's office where they found Joe and Richard enjoying a cup of coffee. Joe waved to them, "Come on in. How's it going outside?"

Frank sat down and crossed his leg, "Great! George is playing his role to the hilt. I just told the news people I would be taking Richard to the sheriff's office this morning for questioning."

Joe raised his coffee cup, "You might as well have some coffee and relax for a few minutes before we all go to the sheriff's office."

Richard looked worried. "I'll be glad when this thing is over."

For the next couple of days, the little town of Black River was bustling with news people and cameras. The courts could not decide if any prosecution was required. George Littlefield assured his people that the bones would be returned to the reservation as soon as the courts deliberated on the case. Richard Farley was escorted out of town to return to the safety of his own home near the University of Virginia.

Ray Blackwell and his surveillance team left Black River to follow Charles Barton. They continued to observe him until Ray was satisfied that Barton was on another assignment and no longer seemed to have any interest in the Black River story.

Meanwhile, George Littlefield was busy planning the camping trip he was to take with Paul Andrews, Mary, and Frank. George was really looking forward to this trip.

CHAPTER 24

It was a beautiful, early-fall morning on the Indian reservation. George Littlefield waited anxiously for his guests to arrive. He was visibly relieved when he spotted Frank's late model Mercury Marquis followed by Paul Andrews in his rented Ford Taurus.

George greeted them warmly. "Hi, Mary. Hi, Frank. Are you ready to get back to nature?"

Mary smiled. "I've been looking forward to this camping trip ever since you invited us."

Paul got out of the Taurus and joined them. They pulled their backpacks out of the trunks of both cars. Each had a sleeping bag, one change of clothes, trail food, a mess kit, a lighter, and bottled water. Paul came prepared for anything. He brought along his Glock automatic and Swiss Army knife.

George looked at all their gear, and said, "Remember now, we're only going for three days. You'll be carrying your own gear up to the top of that mountain over there."

The other three looked at the mountain in the distance, and decided they had better reconsider what to bring with them. They took an inventory of each other's things and decided to leave behind the duplicate items that could be used jointly. They made sure Mary's pack was the lightest. George took along fishing line and hooks so the group could enjoy the catch of the day. When everyone was packed to go, the four started off for the river in George's Jeep.

George said, "The first place I want to take you is the spot where the bones were found." He drove as far as he could in the Jeep and parked near the trail leading to the river's edge. They locked their gear in the Jeep and proceeded on foot.

The group followed the trail along the winding Black River. The river flowed from the mountains downstream past the reservation, in the direction the four were walking. The mountains on both sides of the river formed a river valley. The leaves on the trees were beginning to change color, allowing Mother Nature to show off her wonderful new coat. The river seemed to flow slowly and dark in the deep areas and more swiftly in the shallow areas where the river bottom was visible.

They passed a man-made dam and Frank explained, "That's one of the dams that Lloyd Kramer of The Army Corps of Engineers adjusted for us when the skull was first found. Right, George?"

"That's right. Lloyd raised the level of this dam and lowered the level of the dam downstream of the site where the bones were found. That way the level of the river was lowered enough for the searchers to find most of the bones."

Paul scratched his head. "You know it really seems strange for us to be talking about the bones of my friend, Jack Spencer, when I plan to bring him back next week."

Frank looked at Paul. "If it bothers you, we won't mention the bones again."

"No, it doesn't bother me. It just seems strange."

"I know what you mean," said George.

Their hike took them twenty minutes to get to the spot where George's son, Tommy, and Ricky Johnson found the skull. The site was still marked off by yellow tape, making it easy to find.

Paul looked around in all directions. "I wonder how much of this area I'll be able to recognize when I go back?"

George said, "This area has never been developed. Look off in all directions from this site and try and memorize the shape of the mountains. In particular, notice that large peek on the mountain back the way we just came. From that mountaintop, you can see this entire river valley. We call that peak Lookout Point. There are caves in these mountains, and one cave in particular is located at Lookout Point. I plan to take you there. You could use this cave, Paul, for sheltered until Jack arrives."

Paul took a long look in all directions. He pulled out a small camera from his pocket and took panoramic pictures, making sure he included the mountain peak that George had singled out. Paul also took out his global positioning device and recorded the exact coordinates of his current location.

Paul smiled at George and said, "I don't want to just rely on my memory."

George asked, "Won't the global positioning system be useless to you when you go back in time?"

"Yeah, but I need to select a destination spot for the time travel device to send me."

"Good idea, but I would suggest Lookout Point. You'll see the advantages of the Point when we get there."

Having seen the site where the bones were found, the four started back the way they came. Mary and Frank were walking hand in hand behind George and Paul. For them this camping trip was another opportunity to get better acquainted.

Mary smiled and asked, "Would you ever consider having another family, Frank?"

He smiled back and said, "Sure, if the right girl came along."

Mary punched him gently in the shoulder, "Seriously, would you?"

"I don't see why not. I know what to expect. Have you considered it yourself?"

"Sure, I want a brown-haired boy who looks just like you."

"Or maybe a pretty little dark-haired girl like yourself?"

"That would be nice, too."

Frank looked directly at her, "So who do you plan to marry?"

Mary kicked some dirt in his direction and blushed.

When the campers reached the Jeep, it was time for lunch. George pulled out some turkey sandwiches his wife had packed for the occasion, and sodas from his cooler. "Enjoy these because once we get going on the trail, we can only eat the food we carry or what we catch."

The morning walk had made them hungry. The group devoured the sandwiches in short order and thanked their host.

After lunch, George drove the group along a trail back towards the mountain where he had pointed out the one particular peak. They parked the Jeep at the base of the mountain and put on their backpacks.

George pointed to the trail, "It's about a five-hour walk up the mountain to Lookout Point and the cave I want us to stay in tonight. If we don't make it all the way, there's another cave about three quarters of the way that will do as well. Are you people game?"

Frank looked at Mary and Paul, and then to George, "Sure, lead the way."

The first hour of climbing didn't seem too bad. The narrow trail wound from side to side up the mountain, gradually getting steeper as the trail ascended. By the time the second hour had elapsed, all four climbers were winded. They stopped to rest at a point where the trail was wide enough to sit comfortably.

Paul asked, "George, what kind of wildlife might I encounter next week?"

"It's a little hard to say really. There are deer, rabbits, raccoons, opossum, wild turkeys, foxes, black bears, and some snakes that inhabit this area now."

"Snakes?"

"You probably won't have any trouble with snakes because it will be too cold for them to be out at the time of year you're planning to go back to."

"That's good. What about prehistoric animals?"

"Not likely. Woolly mammoths and saber tooth tigers were pretty much extinct nine thousand years ago. You'll probably see deer. They ran in large herds back then."

"How about mountain lions and bears?"

"Mountain lions are mostly found out west, as are grizzly bears. However, I really can't speak for the time you are going to. You might see black bears because we have them around here now. The black bears are not nearly as dangerous as the brown grizzly, but they can kill you just the same."

"What if I do come across a grizzly bear?"

"Grizzly bears can be very dangerous. They're meat-eaters. The male in particular is extremely dangerous. They've been known to even eat young grizzly bears. They can smell you for miles if you are upwind of them. If you happen to see any, and they don't appear to have seen you, give them plenty of room and try and stay downwind of them."

"What about black bears?"

"Black bears are generally not interested in fighting with humans unless they feel cornered, are protecting their young, or starving to death. Just the same, I would stay downwind of them as well."

"What should I do if I encounter a bear?"

"First of all, don't act frightened and run away. He can out run you."

"Well, what do I do?"

"Take the upper hand. Be aggressive. Throw rocks in his direction. Beat a stick on the ground. And all the time you are doing this, gradually move backward while looking at him. By giving the bear more space, most of the time he will go his own way."

"What if the bear attacks?"

"If the bear approaches with his head lowered and his ears back, take out your gun and put a bullet between his eyes. Your gun will be your only real protection."

Paul digested this information and asked, "Do you think I might encounter any people, George?"

"It's possible. The history of my people goes back that far."

"Should I fear them?"

"Not if you're armed with that Glock automatic I saw you put in your back pack. Besides, any people you might encounter will likely be trying to survive the winter in some kind of shelter."

"Would I find people in the caves you are taking us to?"

"Maybe, but from what I know of our ancient history, most of my ancestors lived in huts or tepees for shelter from the cold winters."

"Why not in the caves?"

"Mostly for practical reasons, I guess. They'd likely want to be within a short distance of the river for water and fish."

"If I stay in the cave as you suggest, how will I get water?"

"You can go down to the river and fill your canteen. You can also catch fresh fish."

"It's a long walk to the river to go down there daily, George."

"You're right. You'll be here during the winter. You can melt snow anytime you don't want to go to the river."

"That's a good idea. What if I meet up with some of your ancient relatives? What about the fact my skin is dark brown?"

"I don't know. My ancient relatives probably wouldn't have seen a dark brown-skinned person before. They likely wouldn't have ever seen a white person either."

"That's not a comforting thought."

"I wouldn't worry about it, Paul. After all, I took a liking to you right away."

"Well, then I hope these people are like you, George."

After their break, the four continued up the trail. Paul spoke up. "Something is bothering me about this cave you're taking us to."

"What's that?"

"What makes you think this trail we're following will be here when I go back in time?"

George paused, looked back at Paul and smiled. "This trail is a very old animal trail, but, I'll give you my reason for thinking the path will be here when we arrive at the cave."

Paul gave him a curious look as George continued up the mountain.

Frank reminisced as they climbed. "The last time I did this was when George and I were in the Boy Scouts."

"You mean you've been up here before?"

"Yes. The chief, I mean George's father, Chief Joseph, led our troop up here for our hiking merit badge. I remember it like it was yesterday. About twenty of us climbed this trail. There was a lot of griping by some of my friends over one overweight boy who was slowing us down. We were continually stopping and waiting for him to catch up. Some of the guys called him Fat Al."

"Did you call him Fat Al, also?"

"Maybe, but I did feel sorry for him. I moved to the back of the line and asked him what the problem was. Fat Al told me his pack was too heavy."

"What'd you do?"

"I traded packs with him and took out the rocks when he wasn't looking."

"Rocks? That was thoughtful of you. Who put the rocks in his pack?"

George had been listening and looked back at Mary and Frank with a smile. Frank smirked, indicating that the two had likely conspired in this together.

Mary laughed at them and asked, "Do you remember his last name?"

"Sure. Al Hastings."

"You mean the mayor?"

"Yes. Lucky for me, we're still friends."

The climbers arrived at the first cave and decided to have a look. They removed their backpacks and left them near the cave entrance. George led the way. He stopped and picked up a lantern that was on a niche in the wall of the cave, just inside the entrance, shook it to make sure there was enough kerosene, took out a lighter and lit the lamp. The light from the lamp gradually illuminated the walls of the cave. The four adventurers walked crouched over for about ten feet and then were able to stand erect. There was not enough light from the lantern to overcome the bright sunlight from which the group had just come.

George stopped and said, "We need to wait here for a few minutes for our eyes to get adjusted to the dark."

Frank took the opportunity to pull Mary into his arms and gave her a kiss. She responded eagerly. When their lips parted, he whispered, "I love you."

Mary whispered, "I love you, too."

Gradually, their eyes began to allow them to see more of the cave. The walls appeared to have been widened to about a twenty-foot circle in this area of the cave.

George commented, "This part of the cave has been used by my ancestors and more recently by campers."

They walked into the center and looked around. There were Indian paintings on the wall depicting men with bows pointed at deer. There were also signs of more recent inhabitants. There was a heart shape with the initials V. S. + G. L. inscribed within the heart.

George pointed to the heart shape on the wall and said, "My wife Virginia and I camped here when we were dating."

Frank smiled at George, "I didn't know you were so romantic."

He looked back at Frank, who was still holding Mary in his arms, and said, "I think I'm not the only one."

There were other writings on the walls depicting dates and some graffiti. At the back of this room, there was a small opening where the cave continued deeper into the mountain.

Paul pointed to the opening. "How far into the mountain does this cave go?"

"I've explored deep into this cave because we played here as boys. That opening leads to several passages that continue deeper into the mountain. However, the openings are narrow and break off into other tunnels. Unless you are familiar with them, it's not really a good idea to go deeper without using string to retrace the way out."

Frank asked, "How deep into the mountain do they go?"

"There are places where it gets too small for most people to get through. So I don't know just how deep they go. The main ones that I'm familiar with probably go in about an eighth of a mile."

Paul raised an eyebrow, "That far? Can you show us a little more of the cave?"

They followed George through the small opening at the back of the first chamber. The narrow tunnel led slightly upward as the adventurers worked their way deeper into the cave. They had to crouch down in several places where the ceiling was only about four feet high. They came to a second chamber where the cavern widened. There were five tunnels leading in different directions deeper into the mountain from this room.

George raised the lantern to better illuminate the choices. "The second one to the right goes the farthest, but it has several other branches that can confuse anyone who hasn't studied this cave. The two on the left eventually meet and become one again, but that one passage also branches out into others. The other two tunnels are dead ends after only about fifty yards. I suggest we don't try to go any deeper today because I'd like to continue our hike to the other cave."

The others agreed. The four adventurers retraced their way back to the cave entrance and came out into the bright light of day. They squinted as their eyes adjusted to the light. Frank helped Mary with her backpack and put on his own. George put on his pack and continued to lead the way with Paul right behind him. Mary and Frank again brought up the rear.

The trail became a little steeper slowing down their progress. In a few narrower places, George had them take each other's hands to make sure no one fell. As they climbed the upper portion of the mountain, the trees lining the trail became sparse. They reached a flat area of about twenty yards where the entire river valley, including the reservation, was visible. Just behind this flat area, the mountain continued to rise about another one hundred feet.

George said, "Welcome to Lookout Point."

All four removed their packs and sat down on the ground for a rest. The view was breathtaking. They were in the shade of the top of the mountain, but the sun was still shinning on the eastern side of the adjoining mountains tops. The colors of the trees were resplendent in various shades of brown, green, yellow and red.

Mary took a deep breath. "The view is worth the climb. You can see the entire river valley from here."

George smiled. "That's exactly why I suggest this is the best place for Paul to be transported to next week."

Paul took out his global positioning device. He walked to the center of the flattened area and recorded the coordinates of the location. After doing this, he turned to George and asked, "Where is the cave you told us about?"

"Right behind you."

Paul and the others turned to see an obscured outline of an upside down "V" shape in the side of the cliff. The entrance wasn't obvious from the trail because it was partially covered by a bush. They left their packs on the ground and got up to follow George to the entrance.

George pointed to the bush. "My father planted this years ago to hide the entrance so this special place wouldn't be entered by just anyone."

George pushed the branches of the bush to one side revealing an entrance just big enough for one large person to enter. He went through the entrance and stopped to pick up a lantern that was on a niche in the wall, just like in the first cave. He checked out the lantern and lit it. The light gradually illuminated the cave.

The others followed George into the cave. They stopped after going only a few yards and waited for their eyes to adjust to the dark. When their eyes had adjusted, they beheld a large room about fifty feet in diameter with a ceiling that rose up about twenty feet. There was a large fire pit surrounded by rocks in the approximate center of the room. Above the fire pit, there was a natural hole in the ceiling where the roots of an ancient tree appeared to have been struck by lightning and burned out, leaving a chimney to the sky.

There were several places in the walls where torches stood ready to be lit. George walked over to the torches and lit them one at a time until the entire room was filled with light.

As the others looked around the room, it became obvious why this cave was a special place to the Indians. The walls of the room were covered with the skins of bear and deer. There were wall paintings depicting scenes from the lives of the early Indians. The floor around the fire pit was covered with animal skins. At the far back corner of this room, there was a passage leading into another smaller room. Unlike the first cave, there was no visible graffiti on the walls.

"Once a year, the elders of my tribe have a special meeting in this place," George said. "Stories that have been handed down by mouth for centuries are repeated here so that our history may be retained. I am the youngest of my tribe to know these stories. Some day my son also will be told the stories and hopefully his descendants after him."

Mary looked around in awe. "We're honored that you would bring us here."

"I'm honored to have you special friends here. Let's get our packs and make camp for the night."

A half-hour later, they had a campfire going in the center fire pit and had picked out places for each of them to sleep. The campers pulled out their rations and had their dinner.

After dinner, all four people walked outside the cave and observed the stars, millions of them twinkling brightly. It was a clear cool night. Mary said, "I've never seen so many stars."

George responded. "That's because there are no city lights. We're looking at the night sky the way the people did centuries ago."

Paul added. "It's a little like it was when I was in the desert during the Gulf War in '91. That is until all hell broke loose."

Mary looked at Paul. "The war must have been terrible. Were you injured?"

"No, I was lucky. We mostly kicked the hell out of the Iraqis. During the Gulf War, I worked for Norman Schwarzkopf. In January of '91, when Saddam Hussein's Iraqi Army invaded Kuwait, the

General and I were called on short notice. I was just an aide, but I got to see the great man's mind at work. I wouldn't have wanted to be with any other General."

Frank asked, "Did you see the fires from the Kuwait oil wells?"

"Yes. There were over six hundred oil wells, storage tanks, and refineries ignited by the Iraqi army as they fled Kuwait in February of '91. The smoke seemed to turn day into night at some locations. I hope I never see anything like that again. It took the better part of a year to put out the fires."

George commented, "I hope none of us see anything like that again."

Paul continued, "The damage to the earth's environment has helped deplete the ozone layer and cause global warming."

"It wasn't just the Kuwait Oil fires that caused the trouble."

"You're right, Mary. It was twentieth century industrial smoke stacks, and automobile exhaust that was the real cause, but the Kuwait oil fires tipped the scale."

"If we assume you rescue Jack Spencer, and Jack eventually completes his mission to stop the Kuwait oil fires, isn't there still a problem with industrial pollution?"

"Sure there is, Mary. There are other plans being considered by my 'REPEAT' group. We may need to go back and very subtly give today's pollution control technologies to some past generation. But before we do this, we need to review the other things that would possibly change as a result. It'll be some time before we're ready to take that step in our program. You understand, you cannot speak about any of this."

Frank responded, "We understand. Tell us about Jack Spencer. What kind of man is he?"

"Jack's a great guy. He's full of life. He can play the piano and sing along with the best of them. Whenever the guys needed cheering up, Jack was there to do it. We met years ago in the Army Ranger's boot camp. He and I became friends when we both struggled to get through the rigorous training. After boot camp, the Army put us in a special covert unit that took care of situations around the world.

You know, the kind of operation that nobody back home ever hears about. I think that was one of the hardest things about it. When we did get to visit home, we couldn't talk about anything we had done. Eventually, you just learn to live with it."

Frank asked, "Are you telling us you were one of those guys who jump out of airplanes at night and go in and kill the bad guys or rescue somebody?"

"Something like that. Both Jack and I moved up in the ranks over the years. After a while, someone in the Army took notice of us. They sent Jack and me to West Point where we learned the strategies and logistics of war. We became officers. I met the General there, and later became a strategist assigned to him during the Gulf War."

"What about Jack?"

"Jack didn't reenlist after he finished his tour of duty. Instead, he went to work for the NSA. From what he told me, he had a number of assignments that took advantage of his Army Ranger experience. Mark Denver recruited me at the same time Jack was reassigned to Mark. I retained my commission because somebody high up wanted someone from the Army involved with the program."

"Who do you think that person is?" Frank asked.

"I couldn't say, but I figure I'll be contacted some day. I'm sure Mark knows, but he hasn't told me."

"So I guess you and Jack are the key time travelers for the program?" Mary asked.

"That's right. We also plan everything out before hand in the way of strategies and logistics."

"Don't you get frightened of the idea of going back in time?"

"Sure, but not any more than doing some of the other things I've been assigned to do in my life."

"I think we're in the presence of a true patriot," George commented.

"I'm just one of many, but I do consider myself a true patriot, thank you."

George shivered. "It's getting colder. I think I'll go inside."

With that said, they all turned towards the glow coming from the side of the mountain and went inside. Frank sat down and leaned against his rolled up sleeping bag in front of the fire.

Mary came over and said, "Is there room for me?"

Frank moved away from the heat just enough for Mary to sit between his outstretched legs with her back against Frank's chest. George and Paul rolled out their sleeping bags and got comfortable on the other side of the fire.

George asked, "Would anyone like a beer?"

"You lugged beer all the way up here?" Frank asked with a raised voice.

"No, you did. I put a six pack into your bag before we started up the mountain."

Frank looked at George with a smirk, and felt around in his bag until he found the beer. The beer had been wrapped in a plastic cooler bag and was still cool. Frank passed the beers around so all could enjoy them.

After a while, Mary asked, "Where might the ladies room be?"

George pointed to the entrance. "Outside the cave, there's a bushy area about fifty feet to the right. Just past that, there's an outcropping of rock that forms a somewhat sheltered area. Stay next to the mountain wall and go past the bushes until you come to the outcropping of rocks. There, you'll find the latrine. There's even a natural rock basin where rain water catches, so you can wash. Take the lantern when you go, so you don't fall off the mountain."

George pulled a roll of toilet paper from his pack. "Here, all the comforts of home."

Frank asked, "Do you want me to come with you?"

"No, I'll manage."

When Mary went outside, George said, "You've got quite a woman, Frank."

"I know. I plan to ask her to marry me. I brought along a ring to give her when the moment is just right."

When Mary came back five minutes later, she looked at their faces and said, "Did I miss something?"

"No, just man talk."

Mary handed George the roll of paper and resumed her former position in front of the fire. When the beer was consumed and they were talked out, George put out the torches, leaving the room in the subdued light of the central fire. George and Paul curled up in their sleeping bags and went to sleep. Mary and Frank put Mary's sleeping bag on top of Franks for extra padding and both slipped into Mary's bag. Exhausted from the day's events, they talked for only a few minutes and fell asleep in each other's arms.

Frank awoke to the small amount of light that was coming from the cave entrance. He was cozy in the sleeping bag with Mary, but as soon as he got out of the bag he realized how cold it was in the cave. Still dressed in yesterday's clothes, he got his lighter and started a fire in the central fire pit. He put on a jacket and lit some of the torches in the cave. Frank then grabbed his shaving kit and a clean shirt and went outside. He found the outcropping of rocks and prepared himself for the day.

When he came back inside the cave, Mary was up and making coffee. She smiled at him and said, "Good morning. How did you sleep?"

"Like a rock. I was really tired from the climb."

"Me, too. I put on some coffee. Would you watch the pot doesn't fall into the fire while I make a visit around the corner?"

"Sure."

She put on her jacket and went out of the cave with a small bundle under her arm. When Mary came back, she had freshened up and had on clean clothes. Her black hair was combed back revealing her beautiful face. She walked over to Frank and gave him a kiss.

Frank hugged her and said, "You're so beautiful Mary. I love you."

Mary smiled at him and Frank said, "I have something for you." He reached into his pocket and produced a diamond ring. Frank got down on one knee. "I know this isn't the most romantic spot, Mary, but I want you to be my wife. Will you marry me?"

She took the ring and said, "This is a perfect spot," with tears in her eyes. "Yes, I'll marry you. You know I will." They fell into each other's arms and kissed.

George awoke and said, "What's going on?"

"Frank just asked me to marry him and I said yes."

"Congratulations!" George mumbled, and rolled over and went back to sleep.

Mary put the ring on her finger and went closer to the fire to get a better look at it. "I love the ring, Frank."

"I hoped you would. I searched all over town for just the right one."

When Paul and George awoke to the smell of coffee, they found their breakfast prepared for them.

After breakfast, all four sat around the fire talking. George said, "This is great news. Have you decided on a date?"

Frank and Mary started talking at the same time and Frank said, "Go ahead, Mary."

"Frank and I were discussing it this morning while you were still sleeping. We'd like to get married right away. We want to keep our wedding small with just our immediate family and friends."

George asked, "Am I invited?"

"Of course you are."

Paul asked, "How about me?"

"Sure, if the timeline hasn't been changed by then."

Paul and George looked at Mary and Frank. Nobody talked as they pondered Frank's words.

Mary finally said, "Frank and I have talked about this at some length. That's why we want to get married right away. The events surrounding the bones won't happen if Paul rescues Jack Spencer. But my coming to work with the Black River Sheriff's Office shouldn't change. Therefore, Frank and I will still meet and hopefully fall in love again."

George smiled. "Sure you will. It's meant to be."

"I wish we could be sure."

George said, "Paul, I assume when you go back in time and complete your mission, you'll be the only one who remembers this timeline."

"I guess that's theoretically correct. Jack will remember what happened to him. Where are you going with this line of thinking?"

"You could play match maker to make sure Mary and Frank get together."

"Wait a minute. That's not my line of work."

"Just make sure Frank and I meet, please!"

"I guess I can do that much."

Mary said, "Thank you," and got up and gave Paul a hug.

Paul then said, "You know there is no guarantee that I will be successful in going back nine thousand years into the past."

George said, "You want to bet!"

With that George got up and walked to one of the walls of the cave. He grabbed a torch from the wall and said, "Come over and see what I'm about to show you."

The others got up with all curiosity and walked over to the wall were George stood next to an animal skin.

George said, "According to my people's history, this has been here for thousands of years. When my people first saw this, they didn't know what to make of it. In fact, neither did I until just recently."

With that said, George pulled up the animal skin and brought the torch closer. On the wall they saw the words:

> I made it
> Paul Andrews
> 7000 BC

CHAPTER 25

The words were carved into the hard rock wall and looked like they had been there for a very long time. Paul said, "That sure looks like the way I make my letters. I guess I'm really going back."

"It gives me an odd feeling to think I'm standing next to the man who wrote that," Mary commented.

"Me, too," said Frank. "This is fantastic. This proves that everything we heard at the underground facility is true."

Paul pondered. "The writing proves I'm going to get successfully transported to this spot and to seven-thousand BC, but it doesn't prove I make it back with Jack Spencer."

"That's right," answered George. "Only time will tell."

All four stared at the words.

Frank broke the silence. "Do you have any other surprises for us, George?"

"I'm afraid not. There're no other markings on the walls of any of the caves around here to provide additional information about your trip back in time."

"How about from the history handed down from your people?"

"The only thing mentioned is what I already told you, Frank. In our ancient history, there's a story of a pale-faced stranger who visited our ancestors. He wore unusual clothes and spoke with a strange tongue. Our people didn't befriend him at first. One day during a hunt, the stranger jumped out of nowhere and killed a large bear with a fire-stick in his hand that sounded like thunder. He lived with our people for one moon. One night this man and my people observed a strange fire coming from the mountain. The next morning the man thanked my people and left. The stranger was never seen again."

Paul said, "This is wonderful news for me. This could mean Jack arrived before me and lived with your ancestors until I arrived. I was planning on taking flares with me. I could set them off each night from Lookout Point, hoping to attract Jack's attention. What do you think?"

Frank looked at Paul. "Sounds like a good idea to me, but if I were you, I'd take along some climbing gear. There's no telling what the conditions of the mountain will be when you go back."

"Good idea. I'll do just that."

Everyone smiled and Paul said, "I'm getting excited about going back now that I know I'll actually make it alive. Thanks, George, for bringing me here and telling me your part of the story."

"It has been my pleasure to share this with you."

George and Paul spent the rest of the day exploring the area around the top of the mountain where the cave was. They went up to the top of the mountain and found the chimney hole that was above the fire pit in the cave. They found the hole easily because there was smoke trickling out from the ashes of their morning fire. The chimney was about three feet in diameter and angled slightly downward to the cave.

Mary and Frank chose to remain at the camp. They were very much in love and enjoyed the time alone. They brought their sleeping bags outside and stretched them out in the afternoon sun in a secluded spot where they could look out over the entire river valley. Mary and Frank both had concerns about how a new timeline might affect their relationship. They decided to exchange vows to each other right there overlooking the beautiful river valley. After professing their love, they held each other closely.

After awhile, Mary said, "I can't remember when I've been happier."

"I feel the same way. I think we should come up here again."

"Oh, yes. I hope we can."

They talked for a couple of hours and fell asleep in the afternoon sun. They were awakened when they heard their names being called out by George. They grabbed the sleeping bags and walked back to the area just outside the cave entrance where George and Paul were standing.

George said with a smile, "Oh, there you are. We thought you might have fallen off the mountain. Are you ready for dinner?"

"Sure, what do we have tonight?"

"We're having an Italian dinner tonight. We have 'Chef Boyardee Ravioli', Italian bread, and red wine. How does that sound?"

"Sounds great. What can we do to help?"

"Just bring yourselves inside. Dinner is ready."

The group went inside the cave where George had a good fire going and everything laid out as nicely as he could with the camping utensils. He handed each a towel wrapped, open can of heated Ravioli. They passed around a loaf of Italian Bread and drank the wine from their metal cups.

Mary said, "This is delightful, George. Thanks for setting up our dinner."

After dinner, the four sat around the fire talking and sipping the remainder of the wine. George and Frank reminisced about their football days and recounted the game they won by one point in the last seconds over their high school rivals. As the wine took effect, they curled up in their sleeping bags and went to sleep.

The next morning, the campers had breakfast and packed up their things to return down the mountain. They cleaned up after themselves, leaving the cave the way they found it.

George led the way down the mountain trail. While the going was easier than climbing up, they could feel the use of new muscles. The group stopped outside the lower cave. They rested for a short while and continued down the mountain. By the time they reached the base of the mountain, they were glad to see George's Jeep.

After packing their things in the Jeep, George drove them to one of his favorite spots by the river. George pulled two bags out of his Jeep and handed them to Frank. Before long they had the two small tents ready for the night. Mary and Frank stayed at the campsite and made a campfire between the tents. George and Paul fished along the river, and after a couple of hours, they brought some fish back to the campsite.

When eating the fish, Mary said, "I've never tasted fish this good before."

George replied, "There is nothing that compares to eating a fresh catch, but I'm sure being as hungry as we are has something to do with it."

The campers finished their dinner and sat around the fire talking until it started getting dark. They decided to call it a day. Mary and Frank took one tent and Paul and George the other.

The next morning, the four had their breakfast, and packed up their things to return to the more civilized world. They drove to George's home and thanked him for the wonderful experience.

George said, "Just a minute, Paul. I have something for your trip." George went into his home and reappeared a minute later with a plastic container. He handed it to Paul and said, "It contains a mixture of tar and lighter fluid that you can use to make torches. Just dip the end of a stick into the mixture and light it."

"Wonderful! Thanks again, George, for everything."

They wished Paul success and parted for their regular lives.

Each had their own deep feelings about this camping trip and what it meant to them, but for Paul Andrews, it was about to be an adventure in time he would never forget.

CHAPTER 26

Paul Andrews said his good-byes to Mark Denver and the other team members who came to see him off. Paul entered the chamber and buckled himself into one of the two specially fitted chairs for his journey into the past.

Hours earlier, Denver and some of the team had looked on as Paul carefully packed his backpack for his trip through time. Along with a sleeping bag, food rations, and survival gear, he packed a Browning automatic of the same caliber as Jack Spencer's gun. He also packed a flare gun and flares, and an extra form fitting winter outfit for Jack. He put a lighter, a small penlight, and extra clips of ammunition in his armored vest pockets. Paul looked like an astronaut in his black, form-fitting outfit. He was fully equipped from his helmet to his hiking boots.

The camping trip with George had helped him determine what to bring on the trip. He brought along climbing gear and the plastic container of tar and lighter fluid that George had given him.

Denver looked at Paul strapped into his chair in the bubble chamber and said, "Remember, you must get out of the chamber within five minutes after you arrive because the chamber will return here."

"Right. And I press this button on my wrist band to signal I'm ready to return." Paul's retrieval-signaling device was attached to his wrist with a velcro strap, like an oversized watch.

"That's right, but it could take us several minutes to get the chamber to you."

Paul smiled. "Don't worry, I'll be waiting, and hopefully, Jack will be with me."

Denver said, "Good luck, Paul!" as the opening to the chamber closed.

Denver and the others moved away to the control room. The coordinates were set to deliver Paul to the designated spot at Lookout Point. The time circuits were set to seven thousand BC. The lights dimmed for a few seconds as the power for the laser and electromagnet generators powering the device came on-line. The control room was filled with Denver's team leaders and their top people watching their respective areas of responsibility. Sam Magnum called out the checklist to the others. One by one each answered, "We're green to go."

When Sam completed the checklist, he said, "Thirty seconds and counting. You hit the power button on zero, Paul."

"Here goes," Paul hit the power button as the countdown reached zero. The chamber hummed in resonance with the magnetic fields surrounding it, but inside Paul could only feel the motion of the chamber being pulled up into the laser tube. As soon as the chamber entered the tube, it accelerated at tremendous speed. It traveled in seconds to Lookout Point, landing precisely outside the cave, as planned. The chamber then took on an eerie glow as it resonated to allow the chamber to travel into the past. Paul sat motionless until the time circuits told him he had arrived at seven thousand BC.

The chamber door opened automatically. Paul unbuckled himself from his special chair and stepped out. One look around told him he was indeed atop Lookout Point as planned. Reaching back into the chamber, he unbuckled his backpack from the floor, and carried it about twenty feet away. The door automatically closed two minutes later. Then the chamber took-on an eerie glow and vanish right before his eyes.

As he raised the faceplate of his helmet and took a deep breath of the fresh cold air, he could see his breath. Judging by the position of the sun in the western sky he guessed it was mid-afternoon. The ground was lightly covered with wet snow. There was a dry brown colored circle in the ground where the chamber had been. Paul walked over to the circle and felt an electrostatic charge that made his hair tingle.

He moved away from the circle and looked out over the river valley. He went back to his backpack and rummaged around for his compact, high-powered, Bausch and Lomb binoculars. Paul found them and gazed out over the valley, looking carefully for any signs of life.

The river valley looked much the same as it had on the camping trip except the trees were bare. There where larger clumps of melting snow on the ground surrounded by bare spots. He figured it must be late winter. Most of the low lands were forest as far as Paul could see, with only a few open spaces. In a clearing beside the river, in the distance, he could see a herd of deer. He said to himself, 'At least I won't go hungry if I have to be here for some time.'

Paul turned around and walked over to the cave entrance. It looked the same except there was no bush covering the entrance. As he started into the cave, Paul noted, as expected, there was no provision for light. He took out his penlight from his vest pocket and shined it into the dark. Paul walked in about ten feet, turned off his light while his eyes adjusted to the dark, and several minutes later, turned his light back on and looked around the cave. The basic dimensions were the same, but there was little sign of life. Shining the light upward, he noted there was the same hole in the ceiling. The hole seemed smaller, but it did appear to go to the sky, as he could see a little light through it. There was no sign of a campfire below the hole.

Paul went back outside and rummaged around for something to burn. He found dry branches, leaves, and pine needles under cliff overhangs and under trees. He started a fire in the cave where the fire pit had been located. Paul then brought in his backpack and rolled out his sleeping bag beside the fire. He took his hunting knife from his utility belt and carved several of the branches into three-foot-long sections. Paul pulled out the plastic container filled with the mixture of tar and lighter fluid and dipped the ends of the torches into the mixture. He lit one and placed it into a crack in the wall, angling the torch upward so that it would burn slowly. He located the next torch on the opposite wall and a third near the cave entrance.

Paul sat down by the fire and took out two large ham sandwiches. He knew he needed to eat the sandwiches this night before they spoiled. He pulled out his canteen of water and took a drink. He ate all but a half sandwich and put the remaining half back into the backpack figuring he'd eat it later that night.

Paul went outside and found that it had gotten dark. He went back inside, got the flare gun, three flares, and went back outside. He loaded the gun and fired it into the sky, in the general direction of the river. He waited a few minutes and fired the second, and a few minutes later, the third. Paul watched for half an hour for any sign of life and went back into the cave. The fire had warmed the cave to the point that it seemed comfortable.

Paul took off the retrieval-signaling device that was velcro attached to his wrist and placed the device in the opened end of his backpack. He put out the torches on the walls and got into his sleeping bag. He removed his utility belt from his waist and put it alongside the sleeping bag. As Paul lay there, he thought about the day's events. It was still very hard for him to believe he was nine thousand years in the past. After a while, he dosed off to sleep.

In the smaller room at the back of the cave, there were two black bears hibernating. It was near the end of the hibernation period and the larger male bear was awakened in the middle of the night from the heat of the cave. As the bear started to come awake, it sniffed the air. The bear smelled the ham sandwich and followed the scent. The bear sniffed Paul, and then found the open backpack. The bear stuck its head in the backpack and rummaged around. It grabbed the entire backpack and dragged it back to the smaller room where the other bear was. After eating the remains of the ham sandwich and peanut butter from a plastic jar that it crushed open, the male bear went back to sleep.

CHAPTER 27

By the time Paul arrived, Jack Spencer had been living with the Indian people for a month. He had already learned enough words of their limited language to be able to converse with these people. Spending their days hunting and fishing, the men would leave the camp shortly after sun-up each morning and usually return with a deer or sometimes a bear.

The women stayed in the camp and took care of most everything else. They prepared food, cared for the children, made clothing, and even constructed new tepees when required. Jack had shared a tepee with a family of four until he came back from a hunt one day and was presented with his own tepee.

He had made himself a coat and hat from bearskin. He sewed them together with strips of deer hide. Jack also covered his shoes with deer hide, wrapping his lower legs to just below the knees. Between his blue dress suit and the fur coat, Jack wore his homemade armor. It consisted of the top and bottom sides of his Samsonite brief case. After removing the special computer, and cutting up the brief case, Jack fastened together a chest and back plate with deer hide at the sides and over the shoulders.

Not knowing if he would ever be rescued to his own time again, Jack had fully resolved to live as full a life as he could with the Indian people.

Late one night, as Jack was preparing to go to bed, he heard a commotion outside his tepee. He rushed out to see several people talking and pointing to the top of the mountain to the west. He looked in this direction and saw the most beautiful sight he had ever seen. Only he recognized the flare for was it was. Sighting on the flare in the dark, Jack bent down to the ground and scratched an arrow into the snow and ice. He then gathered some twigs and filled them in the arrow.

The next morning, Jack was up at first light. He located his arrow in the snow from the night before and sighted off into the distance. The arrow pointed almost one hundred and eighty degrees opposite the rising sun. Jack figured, 'Great! All I have to do is follow the setting sun.'

Jack told some of his new friends that he was going to the mountains. He put some smoked fish and deer meat into a deer hide bag for the trip, and packed up the rest of his things. He waved goodbye to those who watched him leave.

An hour later, Paul Andrews woke up in the cave. It took him a few moments to remember where he was. Except for a small amount of light coming from the entrance, it was dark in the cave. Paul took out his lighter and restarted the fire with dry branches and leaves set aside the night before. He reached over to get some water from his backpack and was shocked to see it wasn't there. He frantically pulled his penlight from his vest and looked around in all directions. He noticed a drag impression left in the dirt floor, and followed the trail with his penlight to the back of the cave, which led to the smaller room. He had completely forgotten to check out this room the night before. Carefully, he turned the corner to the entrance of the smaller room and shined his penlight inside.

There, he saw the two black bears sprawled out with his backpack located between them. The pack had been torn and some of his things were spread out nearby. Paul went back and put on his helmet. He then remembered his gun was in the backpack. He felt his wrist and remembered he left the retrieval device in the backpack, also. He thought to himself, 'Okay now, Paul, don't panic. Stop and plan your next move.'

Paul went back to the smaller room and carefully shined his penlight to get a better look at the situation. Careful not to shine the light into the bear's eyes, he concluded the position of the bears was such that he would have to step on one of the bears to get the backpack. He walked back to the main room and stood between the fire and the cave entrance looking in the direction of the smaller room. As Paul thought about his situation, it dawned on him that the warmer the cave was, the more likely the bears would wake up. He pondered this for a minute and thought: 'Do I want these bears to come awake?' Paul decided he didn't want them awake until he had a plan, so he put out the fire. Not wanting to be alone in the dark with the bears, he went outside.

Outside the cave, it was a clear day and the sun was shining brightly, a direct contrast to his inner turmoil. It took him a few minutes to get used to the light of day. Paul stayed just outside the cave entrance to one side figuring his next move. It dawned on him, that without his gun, he couldn't stay where he was. If the bears came out, he was dead meat.

Paul thought for a while and decided he better make camp in the lower cave until he figured a way to retrieve his backpack. He went back into the cave and got his sleeping bag and the plastic container of tar and lighter fluid. He quietly went back outside and started down the mountain trail, which seemed almost nonexistent in places. The trail was no more than a footpath, likely used by the bears and other animals. Just the same, he made his way down to the lower cave in about an hour. He found a dead tree limb and made a torch.

Paul left his sleeping bag and plastic container of tar and lighter fluid just outside the cave entrance and ventured inside. He let his eyes adjust to the dark, and then looked around the cave cautiously, knowing there might be more bears hibernating in this cave. He didn't see any sign of life in the main room, so he proceeded to the next chamber. Paul got to the next chamber where the cave started to branch out into five more tunnels. He looked for signs of animal tracks, but didn't see any.

Paul tried to remember what George had said. 'Lets see, I think George said the second on the right goes the farthest and the two on the left eventually meet and become one passage. The other two George said were dead ends.'

He decided to go a short way into each passage to check for hibernating bears. Armed only with his hunting knife, he slowly followed the passage on the far left until it became two passages. He took the one that seemed to double back to the entrance of the five passages, and felt relieved when he arrived back at the entrance of the second passage to the left. He then followed the third passage on the left until it dead-ended. Paul retraced his way back and followed the second passage on the right until he came to more branches. He retraced his way back and took the passage on the far right until it also dead-ended. He was happy he didn't see any signs of life.

Paul went back to the main room of the cave and then outside where he had left his things. He spent the next hour gathering kindling for a fire. He was planning to spend the night in the main room of the cave, but while gathering branches, he came up with a scheme to retrieve his backpack from the bears. He gathered more than enough branches for one night's campfire.

Paul sat down outside the lower cave entrance and leaned against the rock wall. One stick at a time, he made two dozen torches. He sharpened the end opposite the fire end of each torch so the torches could be stuck into the ground. He then took out a full clip of ammunition from his vest pocket, took the bullets from the clip, and wrapped them in a mixture of tar and lighter fluid. He then wrapped the bullets in three bird's nests he had gathered, and fastened the nest material and bullet mixture to the end of one torch with dry grass.

Paul looked at the level of the sun in the sky to guess how much daylight he had left. He figured about two hours, just enough time to go back up the mountain and carry out his plan. He wrapped the bundle of torches and his plastic container of tar in his sleeping bag so that the tarred ends stuck out from the bag. He picked up the bag and started back up the mountain.

A little over an hour later, he arrived back at Lookout Point. It was getting dark, so he needed to work fast. Paul put the sleeping bag down adjacent to the entrance and went inside the cave. He stopped to let his eyes adjust and to listen for the slightest sound. Not hearing anything, he proceeded cautiously to the back of the cave with his penlight. He peered around the entrance of the back room just long enough to surmise that the bears were still resting in the same position. Retracing his way back outside, he went to work.

Paul placed the torches in the ground one by one making a direct path from the entrance of the cave to the cliff. He kept the last two torches fifteen feet back from the cliff so not to illuminate the edge. Paul then went inside the cave and placed the remaining torches in a way to make a direct pathway from the back room where the bears slept to the cave entrance. He had two torches left: one to light the others and the special torch with the bullets.

Paul went back outside and found it was almost dark. He waited until it was completely dark and said a little prayer. He lit all the torches outside the cave and proceeded inside, carrying the lit torch in one hand and the torch with the bullets in the other. He lit the torches inside the cave and quickly went to the back room where the bears were.

Paul looked over the situation once more and made a quick decision. He placed the lit torch in the ground next to himself, and then took the torch with the bullets, and very carefully stepped over the head of the nearest bear. His body was now straddling the bear's head. Paul stuck the sharpened end of the torch with the bullets in the ground between the bears. The backpack with most of its contents was now within reach. He grabbed the strap of the backpack in one hand and slowly slid it to himself until it was at his foot. As he bent over to pick up the backpack, the bear started to come awake.

Paul quickly picked up the pack and stepped back across to the other side of the bear where the lit torch was stuck in the ground. He could see the bears were starting to wake up. He had to act fast.

Paul grabbed the torch, and reaching across the bear, lit the torch with the bullets in it. He quickly carried the pack into a darkest corner of the main room of the cave. He stuck the lit end of the torch into the dirt, and fumbled for his gun in the backpack, while focusing on the back room. After a few moments that seemed like an hour, he found the gun and pulled it out. He checked the clip and made sure he had a bullet in the chamber. Paul removed the safety and waited in the shadows.

CHAPTER 28

A few minutes later, the bullets started firing. All at once, Paul saw the first bear come running out of the back room followed by the second bear. The bears followed the path lit by the torches, through the cave and out the entrance.

Paul waited about fifteen minutes and cautiously moved to the entrance with his gun at the ready. He peeked outside the cave. So far his plan had worked. Not knowing where the bears were, he continued to follow his plan.

He picked up one of the torches, keeping his gun ready in his other hand. He slowly walked to the edge of the cliff, crouched down, and looked over the edge, but couldn't make out anything in the dark below. He listened for a while for any sign of life, but didn't hear anything. He gathered up the torches that had been used to light the way to the cliff, and stuck them into the ground in a circle blocking the outside cave entrance. He took one last look around and went back inside the cave.

Paul set his gun on safety, holstered it on his utility belt, and lit the three torches he had placed in the walls the night before. He gathered up the torches inside the cave that had been used to light the exit path for the bears, and stuck them in the ground just inside the entrance.

He took a deep breath, feeling some relief from the tension. His stomach growled reminding him he hadn't eaten anything all day. He built a campfire with the remaining wood, and brought his backpack over by the fire for inspection. His rations had been broken into and the ham sandwich was gone, but everything else seemed intact. Paul found a can of beef stew, opened it, and set it carefully on the fire to warm it up. He watched the stew until it started bubbling and then consumed it.

As he finished eating, Paul became alarmed, 'Where's my retrieval device?' He hadn't remembered seeing it in the backpack.

Paul grabbed the pack and furiously went through it again. Not finding the device, he spread out his sleeping bag by the fire, and dumped the entire contents of the pack onto the bag. The device wasn't there.

He took a torch and looked in the corner where he had hidden from the bears, and then went to the back room where the bears had been. Paul found the remains of a peanut butter jar and the paper the ham sandwich had been rapped in, but no sign of the signaling device. He went back and looked all over the entire cave, and then went outside with a torch. After ten minutes, he decided it was too cold and dark to keep looking outside. Exhausted, he returned to the cave.

Paul repacked his backpack and took off his utility belt. He removed his gun from its holster, and crawled into his sleeping bag, keeping his gun beside him. As Paul lay there, he continued to wonder where the signaling device might be, but was so tired, he fell asleep.

Earlier the same day, Jack Spencer walked to within a mile of the base of the mountain. He found a small clearing where the mountaintop could be seen and made a campfire. He hoped to see another flare after sunset.

Jack prepared a place to sleep in a hollow between the bases of four pine trees grouped together adjacent to the clearing. He piled pine branches to make walls between the trees, leaving some pine branches and pine needles as a mattress, and to cover himself during the cold night.

Jack went back to his campfire and warmed up some of his smoked fish and deer meat. After dinner, he sat cross-legged with his back to the fire watching the sun set behind the mountain. About forty-five minutes later, Jack thought he saw a glow of light on the mountaintop. He sighted on the spot as best he could and made another arrow in the ground. He stared at the glow of light. All at once, he saw a single light moving about. His heart raced. 'Could this be someone who came back for me or have I just found the existence of more people. But surely the light I saw the night before was a flare, or was it?'

Jack watched until he started to dose, let the campfire die down, and climbed into his pine bed for the night.

The early morning sun warmed the male bear and it awoke to find itself on a ledge some twenty feet below the cliff. The bear followed the ledge as it wound around the mountainside towards the trail.

Meanwhile, Paul woke up in the cave having slept restlessly all night wondering if the bears were going to attack him. Except for a little light coming in through the entrance, the cave was dark. His torches and campfire had burned out during the night.

He listened for any sign of life, climbed out of his sleeping bag, and put his automatic into its holster on his utility belt. He put on his utility belt and helmet, and ventured out of the cave. After answering a call to nature, he went directly to the spot where the bears would have gone over the cliff. He looked over the edge and saw one of the bears lying far below. He went back for his binoculars, returned to the edge of the cliff, and laid down on the edge to get a steady view. He looked for any signs of life in the bear. The bear was lying on its back and its head was cocked off to one side suggesting the neck might be broken. Paul continued to view the area around the bear to determine if he could make his way to the site. It had occurred to him during a sleepless part of the night that the bear might have eaten the retrieval device.

Paul went back into the cave and replenished the tar and lighter fluid mixture on some of the torches. He took another grand tour of the cave. Not finding the device, he scoured the area outside the cave. He then went back inside and made himself some breakfast. As he ate, he kept a constant watch on the entrance. He had mixed feelings about a confrontation with the remaining bear. Paul figured he had the upper hand with his Browning automatic, but he knew he would need to hit the bear between the eyes or in the heart to bring it down.

A mile away from the base of the mountain, Jack Spencer woke up. He quickly lit a fire and warmed himself. He heated some smoked venison over the fire. As he ate his breakfast, he looked towards the mountain, and picked out a small clearing on the mountainside above the tree line that was in the same direction his arrow was pointing. He finished his meal and packed his things.

A half-hour later, Jack was at the base of the mountain. He started going directly up the mountain with some difficulty. Eventually, he came upon the main animal trail and followed it up the mountain. The trail was easier going because it wound its way up the mountain on a more gradual slope. About four hours later he came upon the lower cave.

As Jack approached the entrance to the cave, he took out his gun and chambered a bullet. It was then that Jack saw it.

CHAPTER 29

While eating his breakfast in the Lookout Point cave, Paul decided to try to reach the bear lying below the cliff, to find out if it had eaten his retrieval device. He separated the things he would need for the day from his backpack. Looking around the inside the cave, he thought to himself, 'How can I keep the rest of my things in my pack safe from bears or other wild animals?' He looked up and remembered the natural hole in the ceiling where an ancient tree appeared to have been struck by lightning and burned out, leaving a chimney to the sky. Roots from the tree looped out from the bottom of the hole. He took out his climbing gear, cut off about twenty feet of rope, tied one end of the rope to an iron-climbing spike and threw it over a tree root. He recovered the spike and hammered it into a crack in the cave wall. He then tied his backpack to the other end of the rope and hoisted until the pack was just below the chimney. He tied the rope to the spike in the wall, hoping this would outwit the bear if it returned to the cave.

Paul proceeded down the mountain trail with the remaining rope and other climbing gear over his shoulder, looking for any trace of the bear along the way. He went only a short way before spotting fresh bear-tracks in the wet snow. Paul pulled out his gun and looked in all directions, but didn't see the bear. The tracks led down the trail. He followed them until they veered off into the woods.

Paul thought about it for a few moments and decided he didn't want to confront the bear until he had a better plan. He holstered the gun, took out his hunting knife, and put markings on a tree where the tracks veered off the path. He then continued down the winding trail until he was about fifty feet directly above the bear. The bear was lying on an area where the mountain leveled off before continuing downward. He tied the end of the rope to a large tree and threw the other end over the cliff to where the bear lay.

Using Ranger skills, he rapidly rappelled down the cliff, pushing his feet off the mountain wall as he went. He reached the bear in a matter of seconds. He took out his automatic and kicked the bear as he approached it. When he was sure it was dead, he put away the gun and took out his knife. He sliced the bear down the belly and pulled out its intestines. Twenty minutes later, Paul was satisfied this bear had not eaten his retrieval device. He then removed about ten pounds of meat, pulled out a plastic bag he kept folded in a pocket on his utility belt, and put the meat in the bag. Paul figured he would at least have a good bear steak later in the day.

He washed his hands in some wet snow, and took a few mouthfuls of snow to quench his thirst. He looked at the bear and said, "Sorry to take your life. Rest in peace."

Paul climbed back up the mountain with the extra ten pounds of bear meat. He was huffing and puffing by the time he reached the top of the rope.

Jack Spencer couldn't believe his eyes as he looked down at the ground in front of the entrance to the lower cave. They were not just footprints, but boot prints. They were modern hiking boot prints. Jack hollered into the cave, "Halloo!" He listened and then hollered again, then fired his gun into the air.

Paul had just reached the trail after climbing up the rope and was trying to get his breath when he heard the shot come from below. He took out his gun and fired a shot into the air.

Relief washed over Jack when he heard Paul's shot. Jack fired another shot and started up the trail. About twenty minutes later, they came upon one another.

Paul took off his helmet as he saw his best friend. He grabbed Jack by the shoulders and exclaimed, "You're a sorry sight for sore eyes," as he looked at Jack covered in his homemade bearskin coat and hat.

Jack smiled and said, "I thought no one would ever find me. What year is it, anyway?"

"Would you believe seven thousand BC?"

"Seven thousand BC! You've got to be kidding?"

"No, I'm not, Jack. Sam's control that was supposed to send you back nine years, actually sent you back nine thousand."

"Nine thousand?"

"Yes, it took Sam's team seven months to figure out what went wrong."

"Seven months! I've only been here about six weeks."

"Right, on your timeline, but on my timeline you've been gone for almost eight months. We didn't know how far back in time you went until someone found your bones."

"My bones! What are you talking about?"

"It's a long story. I'll fill you in when we get back to my home away from home. Right now, we both need to watch out for a black bear. I'm sort of hunting it and it may be hunting us for all I know. So keep your gun ready as we go up to the top of the mountain."

Together they started up the trail to Lookout Point. Paul took the lead.

Paul said, "I'll keep an eye out for the bear, while you watch the trail for any sign of bear tracks."

"Sure. Is this black bear that dangerous?"

"You might say our lives depend on us finding the bear. The night before last, while I was sleeping in a cave near the top of the mountain, a bear stole my backpack. In the pack, I had a new retrieval device that allows us to alert our people back home that we want to return to our time. Without it we're stuck here."

"So if we find the bear, we might find your pack and the device?"

"It's not as simple as that. When I woke up yesterday morning and found the pack missing, I followed drag marks in the ground to another room at the back of the cave. There, I saw two large sleeping bears and my pack lying between them. The way the bears were positioned, I didn't think I could get to my pack without stepping on one of them."

"What'd you do?"

"I grabbed my sleeping bag and a container of a mixture of tar and lighter fluid and went down the mountain to the lower cave."

"Why didn't you just shoot the bears as they lay sleeping?"

"I couldn't. My gun was also in my pack. I just arrived here the day before yesterday."

"Did you set off a flare the night before last?"

"Yes. Then you saw my flare?"

"Sure did. That's how I was able to find you. I've been living with a group of Indians for the past month. One of them saw the flare, and the commotion outside my tepee brought me out in time to see it before the light burned out. I started coming here yesterday morning. I think I was at the lower cave you're talking about when I fired my gun. I saw your footprints outside the cave entrance and fired a shot in the hopes you would hear it."

"Did you see any bear-tracks outside the entrance to the lower cave?"

"No. I only saw hiking boot tracks like you're making now. So I guess you went down to the lower cave yesterday morning?"

"That's right. I'd planned to stay there until I came up with a good way to retrieve my backpack."

Paul told Jack about his plan and how he scared the bears out of the cave the night before.

When Paul finished telling his story, Jack said, "I spent last night in a small clearing about a mile from the base of the mountain. I saw the glow of your torches last night, probably while you were moving about on top of the mountain."

"You must've. After the bears ran out of the cave, I went to the spot where the bears would've gone over the cliff. I didn't see anything of them, so I blocked both sides of the cave entrance with torches. I went inside and looked through my backpack. I ate dinner and was going to sleep, when it dawned on me that I hadn't found the retrieval device. I looked all over, inside and outside the cave, but couldn't find it."

"Then what'd you do?"

"I went to sleep, but I didn't sleep very much last night. I kept thinking about the missing device and what might happen if the bears came back to the cave while I was sleeping. This morning I looked for it again. I looked over the ledge where the bears might've fallen off the mountain as I had planned. One of the bears lay dead about a hundred feet below, but I didn't see the other one."

They came upon the spot where Paul's rope was still tied to the tree. Paul went over and started retrieving the rope. As he wound the rope around his elbow and hand, he said, "Take a look down there."

Jack looked over the edge and saw the remains of the bear.

"That's the one that went over the ledge. I cut him open and inspected his stomach to see if he had swallowed the retrieval device."

"And you didn't find it?"

Paul pointed to the plastic sack and said, "No, but I did get some bear meat so we can dine on bear steaks tonight."

Jack smiled at his friend, "Well, that's good. You don't know how glad I am to see you, Paul."

"Yeah. Good to see you, too."

They proceeded up the trail until they came to the spot where Paul had marked the tree. He stopped and showed Jack the bear tracks leading away from the trail at this point. Jack commented, "I didn't see any other tracks while coming up the trail."

"Now that there are two of us, it might be a good idea to follow the tracks before they get cold."

The tracks wandered through the trees at the same elevation and then started going downward. They followed them until the hard rock surface made it difficult to determine the bear's direction.

Jack looked between the trees at the sky. "We've only got about two hours before the sun goes down behind the mountain."

"You're right. We better start back to the upper cave."

The time travelers followed markings they had made on the trees back to the trail and proceeded up to the cave. They figured they would continue the search the next day. Both men gathered dry branches as they made their way.

They entered the cave with guns drawn, and Paul said, "Wait here while I light some torches."

Using his penlight in the dark, Paul located the torches on the walls and lit them. He showed Jack around the cave pointing out the natural chimney in the ceiling. He then lowered his backpack to the ground and opened it. Paul rummaged through the pack and pulled out the extra form-fitting winter outfit he brought along for Jack. "Here, hope they got your size correct."

"Thanks, Paul." Jack took off his bearskin hat and coat.

Paul pointed to Jack's homemade armor and said, "What's this?"

"It's my Samsonite body armor. I made it by cutting out the top and bottom of the case that held my computer."

"Well, that explains the Samsonite they found with your bones. What happened to your computer?"

"My computer was completely useless to me after the batteries died, so I smashed it and threw the pieces into a deep spot in the river. Again you mentioned my bones. Are you ever going to tell me what happened?"

"Yes, but let's get dinner going first."

Paul made a fire while Jack changed clothes. Jack's new outfit was a perfect fit. It even included a pair of clean sox and hiking boots.

Jack showed off the new suit. "This sure feels good after wearing my other clothes for six weeks. Thanks for bringing it along."

"No problem. Here, I've got a job for you." Paul grabbed one of the used torches and said, "Round up the other torches that aren't lit and stick the ends in this mixture of tar and lighter fluid."

"Okay. How'd you know to bring along tar and lighter fluid?"

"George Littlefield suggested it. I'll tell you about him along with the rest of the story after we eat."

Paul sliced off two large portions of bear meat and put them on sharpened sticks. Both men sat down around the fire. While the meat cooked over the open fire, Paul started telling Jack the story of how they found him.

"Last July, two boys were fishing along the Black River and found the bones of a man about your size. The river at the bottom of this mountain is the Black River. The local Black River Sheriff's Office investigated what they thought might be a homicide because the skull of the man was cracked. It turned out the sheriff's office had a smart detective by the name of Frank McDermott who, with the help of a sketch artist, and a former FBI agent, connected your missing person picture to the bones."

"You told the police I was a missing person?"

"What else could we do? We had to come up with a story for your wife and the police."

"My gosh, with all the excitement, I forgot to ask, How is my wife?"

"She's fine. She now has a top-secret clearance. Mark kept her in the dark for as long as he could and finally broke down and told her what happened. She'll be happy to see you."

"I'll be happy to see her, too. How did these people from Black River ever match the bones to me?"

"Their sketch artist made a drawing from your skull. The former FBI agent, named Mary Webber, ran the sketch through missing persons and your picture came up. They traced you to Mark. When your bones were carbon-dated to be nine-thousand-years old, they kept investigating. She was a computer programmer and expert hacker for the Bureau. She hacked into our computers and they eventually figured out what we were doing. One thing really tipped them off. They found some plastic along with the bones. They didn't think anything of the plastic at first, but eventually they carbon-dated the plastic as nine-thousand-years old, also. This really helped them figure out what we were doing."

"Let me guess, the plastic was Samsonite."

"You guessed it."

"How did Mark handle the security breach?"

"When he found out these people were investigating, he got Ray Blackwell appointed a U.S. Marshal. Mark sent Ray to Black River to keep tabs on how close these people were to the truth.

"By the way, most of this river valley is now an Indian reservation. When your bones were carbon-dated as nine thousand years old, it started a small war between the local Indians and archeologists who came here from all over. The Indians claimed the bones were their ancestors and wanted them reburied. The archeologists wanted the rights to look for more bones on the reservation."

"Where did they find my bones?"

"In the shallow water at the edge of the river several miles east of here."

"Did they estimate how old I was when I died?"

"Yes. Not much older than you are right now. That's why Mark had our entire team working overtime to retrieve you. We wanted to save you before anything happened to you on this timeline."

"You know, I'm not back yet. There isn't anything that says I'll get back."

"Eliminate those negative thoughts, Jack. We'll get back."

Jack smiled. "Even if we don't get back, I'm sure glad you came after me. How did you know to come to this cave?"

"When the people from Black River figured out what we were doing, Mark brought them into our facility and got them top-secret clearances. I made friends with these people, including George Littlefield, the Indian Chief's son. It was George who helped McDermott come up with the time travel theory. Last week, George, McDermott, Mary Webber, the former FBI agent, and I spent three days on a camping trip in this area. George is quite knowledgeable about this region and how to live off nature. He taught me a lot, and brought us to this cave. It really hasn't changed that much in nine thousand years. The cave seemed like a good base camp for me. I planned to set off flares every night hoping you would see one and come to this spot."

"How did you know exactly when to come?"

"For a long time, we didn't. When they carbon-dated your bones to nine thousand years, this helped Sam and his team figure out that the control was off by a factor of a thousand. They worked overtime on the control until they figured out they needed to reduce the power. Bedford and Kirkpatrick ran reliability tests on Sam's new control. They determined the error, in going back nine thousand years, could be a month in either direction. We set the time circuits for the time you left based on their estimate."

"So I guess you could say we're pretty lucky to be sitting here together."

"You could say that, but unless we find the retrieval device, our luck may have run out."

Both men sat there thinking for a few minutes and Jack said, "How about going over with me exactly where you last saw the device."

"Okay. It was my first night here. I was by the campfire getting ready to go to sleep. I removed the retrieval device from my wrist and put it into the open end of my backpack, which was right next to my sleeping bag. The next morning, the entire pack was gone."

"How big is the device?"

"Like an oversized watch."

"Okay. You said you removed the device from your wrist. Was it buckled to your wrist?"

"No, the device is held on by velcro."

"What did the bear steal from your pack?"

"I think, only the remains of a ham sandwich and a jar of peanut butter."

"Where was the sandwich in relation to the device in your bag?"

"I put it in the open bag before I put the device in, so the device must have been on top of the sandwich."

"Was the velcro band on the device open or closed?"

"Open!"

They both looked at each other like a light came on, and Jack said, "Maybe the device is stuck to one of the bears."

"You could be right. Good logic, Jack."

"Yeah, but I don't know if this is good news or bad news. If the device was only lightly stuck to one of the bears, it could have fallen off anywhere. Did you look all over the dead bear's body today and the ground around the bear?"

"No. It landed on its back and its head was cocked off to one side. The neck looked broken. I didn't think of looking underneath the bear or the ground around it for the device. We better go back to that spot tomorrow."

"Yeah, and after that, we better follow the other bear's tracks again."

"Sounds like a plan."

While finishing their steaks, Paul said, "You know the other bear is probably getting pretty hungry by now unless it went back to sleep somewhere. We've got some meat left over we could use for a trap. It sure would be easier to lure the bear to us than to try and hunt it all over this mountain. It could jump out as us at any turn."

"Paul, I've got some smoked venison and fish left over, also. What have you got in mind for a trap, and how much food do you have for us to eat?"

"I've got rations in my pack for at least two days. After that, we'll have to hunt or fish. I figure we better leave the meat outside the cave in the snow. That'll not only keep the meat cold, but we might get lucky and lure the bear to the cave. We can take turns standing guard.

"I like that idea, Paul. I've been hunting or fishing every day since I got here. It's exhilarating. You track a beast you know can kill you with one swipe of its massive paw, corner the animal, and put your life at risk to bring home dinner. It's actually gotten to be routine. My

Indian buddies come and wake me at daybreak to go on the hunt, sort of like having a carpool pick you up. The difference is, knowing you might wind up as dinner for the creature you're hunting. If we get back to our time, supermarkets will take on a whole new meaning for me. Having said all that, I feel good about our chances getting the upper hand with any bear knowing you're with me."

"Good. Let's plan this out. I figure, since the bear had been hibernating in this cave, it might come back. Let's put some bait outside."

The time travelers went outside with torches and kept their guns at the ready. Paul led the way around to the right of the cave entrance where the outside latrine was located in modern day. He found the rock formation that collected water into a natural basin, and said, "This is where George Littlefield had the latrine. We can use this natural water basin to wash."

"Very convenient."

They found snow farther around the top of the mountain on the western side and put three-quarters of the remains of the bear-meat in the snow. They took the other quarter of the meat and cut it into small pieces. The two men traced their way back to the cave and continued past the entrance to the trail leading downward. As the two friends went along, they dropped pieces of meat about every ten feet until they were out of meat. They went inside the cave and put three torches across the entrance.

Paul said, "Let's not light these unless we're both too tired to stand guard."

They piled more dead branches on their campfire and prepared for the night. Paul repacked his backpack except for a climbing hammer and spike. He hoisted the pack up to the chimney for the night.

Jack put his deerskin bag with the remains of his smoked venison and fish just inside the cave entrance. "I figure if the bear comes in during the night, this food might give it something other than us to start munching on, and a few extra seconds to take aim."

"Good idea."

Paul prepared his sleeping bag for the night by the fire. He then took the climbing hammer and spike over to the wall of the cave.

Jack soon heard him hammering something into the wall and came over to see what he was doing. Jack watched him chisel out the words: "I made it" and then under that, "Paul Andrews."

As Paul was spelling out "7000 BC" under the other words, Jack smiled and said, "I'm curious. What suddenly prompted you to put that on the wall of the cave?"

Paul looked at Jack with a serious look on his face. "You won't believe it. George Littlefield took me over to this wall last week and showed me this exact writing on the wall. He told me that according to his people, the writing had been here for thousands of years."

"You're kidding?"

"No, I'm just fulfilling history."

Jack could see Paul was telling the truth and said, "Well, I'll be dammed."

Both men prepared for the night. Jack didn't have a sleeping bag, so he spread out his bear skin coat on the ground, on the other side of the fire from Paul. Jack walked over to the entrance. "I'll take the first watch."

Light from the three torches in the walls kept the men warm and the cave in a glow, as did the fire in the central fire pit. As he was getting comfortable, Paul said, "George Littlefield told me another story last week. It seems George's people have handed down their history for centuries by word of mouth. He's one of the persons chosen to hear and pass down their history. George told me there is an ancient story, handed down by his people, telling of a pale faced stranger who visited his ancestors. The man wore strange clothes and spoke with a strange tongue. His ancestors didn't befriend him at first. One day, during a hunt, the stranger jumped out of nowhere and killed a large bear with a fire-stick in his hand that sounded like thunder. The stranger lived with the Indian people for one moon. One night this man and George's people observed a strange fire coming from the mountain. The next morning the stranger thanked the Indian people and left. The stranger was never seen again."

Jack said, "Son of a gun, that was me! I had a hard time getting those people to trust me. I even gave them fresh fish. But, it wasn't until I saved some lives one day that they started to accept me. I followed their hunting party early one morning staying out of sight. They reached the mouth of a cave in the mountains north of here. Two men went into the cave while the others waited outside with their bows and spears at the ready. After a little while, the two men came running out of the cave, one holding a torch and the other a spear. A large bear was coming out right behind them. The bear tripped the second man coming out of cave and was on him in a second. I already had my Browning out and put a bullet between the bear's eyes."

"Lucky shot."

"I suppose you could say that, but I did take dead aim."

"So they accepted you after that?"

"Yes. I think the Indians were a little frightened of me at first, but they eventually warmed up to me. The women even built me a tepee."

"That's good. If we don't find the device, we have another place to live."

"Did this George say anything more about me?"

"No, that was it. The Indian people never saw you again. I guess that means we don't live with the Indians in the future. Hopefully, that's because we get back to our own time."

"Yeah, sure hope so."

Paul said, "hear, catch," as he tossed a couple of ammo clips to Jack, one at a time.

"I've got a Browning automatic just like yours."

"Good man." Jack put the clips in his pocket and chambered a bullet. "Get some sleep. I'll wake you when I get tired."

They took turns all night long watching the entrance until three hours before daybreak. Seeing Paul sleeping soundly, Jack decided not to wake him. He lit the torches just inside the cave entrance hoping this would keep them safe, and laid down on the other side of the dying fire. He thought, 'I'll just take a cat nap.' Two minutes later he was fast asleep.

CHAPTER 30

A hulking form prowled quietly in the dark mist. Hunger kept him moving and his steps quickened at the scent of fresh meet. He followed the scent until it brought him to the first piece of meat, and continued to follow his nose, eating the small pieces as he went. When the bear got closer to the cave entrance, the new scent of smoked venison and fish lured him to the opening. His mouth was watering for the meat, but the fire from two of the three torches frightened him away. He moved around the outside of the cave, following his nose until he found the next piece of meat. He continued following the trail, eating as he went along, and was rewarded with the large piece.

After eating the raw meat, the creature followed the scent back to the smoked meat. It was dawn by this time and all of the torches at the cave entrance had burned out. The bear entered the cave and quickly found Jack's deerskin bag with the smoked meat and tore into it. Minutes later, this meat was gone.

He sniffed the air inside the cave and picked up the scent of the two men. Both men were still sleeping on opposite sides of the remains of the campfire. The bear sniffed its way, in the dark, over to where Paul was sleeping. He was about to take a bite out of Paul's right leg when he put his back feet onto the coals of the fire. As the hot coals burned his feet, the bear let out a roar of pain waking both men.

Paul could only see a dark outline of the monster from the little light that was coming from the cave entrance. His first reaction was to kick his feet at the dark object. The bear stood up on his hind legs and backed away from Paul's feet, putting him right on the hot coals of the fire. The bear continued moving backward until he tripped over Jack. The bear scrambled to his feet and headed for the light of the exit. Paul fired a shot at the creature as it ran out of the cave. Both men found their way to the exit and went out after him.

They stood outside the entrance with their guns in their hands.

Paul said, "Which way did he go?"

"I'm not sure, but look at this. You must have hit him."

There was a drop of fresh blood on the ground by Jack's feet. The trail led downward. The two men pursued a short way and stopped.

Paul said, "We better go back to the cave and get everything we'll need to follow the bear."

"Good idea."

As they ran back to the cave, Jack said, "I think I saw it, Paul."

"Saw what?"

"Your device. I only got a quick glimpse of it in the dark, so I'm not sure. When the bear walked backwards and fell over me, I think I saw something silvery stuck to the back of its neck."

"The velcro strap is black, but the device itself is metallic silver in color. This is great news!"

They went back inside the cave and lit some torches, and then looked all over the area where the bear had been in case the device had fallen off. They didn't find it.

They packed up things they planned to take with them on the hunt, grabbed a quick bite to eat from Paul's backpack, and hoisted the things they planned to leave behind up to the chimney.

Jack looked at Paul. "You ready?"

"I was born ready. Here's an extra ammo clip. Let's go!"

The two hunters started down the mountain following the trail of blood. As they went, they were careful to look all around the trail for the device. The bear seemed to stay on the main trail as if it had a destination in mind.

About an hour later, they had followed the trail right to the entrance of the lower cave. There were bear tracks leading in, but none leading out.

Jack smiled, "I think we've got him cornered."

"Yes, but it's not as easy as that. George Littlefield brought me to this cave last week. I also explored it myself after the bear stole my backpack."

Keeping an eye on the cave entrance, Paul pulled Jack about fifteen feet away and said, "Keep the entrance covered while I tell you about this cave."

Jack pulled out his gun and chambered a bullet. Paul grabbed a stick, knelt down on one knee, and started drawing in the dirt. Jack looked over Paul's shoulder while pointing his gun at the cave entrance.

Paul drew an oval circle. "Here's the entrance. This is the main room." He drew a passage opposite the entrance leading to another circle. "This tunnel goes to another chamber." He then drew five passages leading away from the back chamber and said, "The second on the right goes the farthest into the mountain, and the two on the left eventually meet and become one tunnel. The other two are dead ends after only about twenty yards. If the bear gets into one of the passages that goes deep into the mountain, we'll have a devil of a time finding him."

Jack replied, "We can follow the blood."

"Right. Keep the entrance covered while I make a couple of torches."

Paul found some dead branches, quickly cut them to size with his hunting knife, and applied his mixture of tar and lighter fluid. He handed the two torches to Jack. "Hold these."

While Jack held the torches, Paul pulled out his gun and chambered a bullet.

Jack handed a torch to him and said, "Let's use our hand signals."

"Yeah. We'll go ten steps inside without lighting the torches. Then we'll stop until our eyes adjust to the dark. Let me go first and stay close behind. I'll keep my gun pointed ahead of us. When your eyes adjust to the dark, light your torch. I'll light mine from yours."

"Okay."

They entered the cave and stopped just short of the main room, listening anxiously for any sound as their eyes adjusted to the dark. They heard nothing. Several anxious minutes went by and then Jack lit his torch. Both men strained their eyes to see what was in front of them. Paul held his torch back in Jack's direction and Jack lit it.

Paul cautiously moved forward letting his torch illuminate the main room of the cave. Jack touched Paul's arm and pointed to a trail of blood that led to the back of the chamber. They followed the trail of bear prints and blood into the tunnel leading to the back chamber. As the hunters came into the back room, they heard a sound coming from one of the five passages that led deeper into the mountain, and followed the trail to the passage on the far-left.

Paul pulled Jack back from the entrance to the far-left passage, planted the end of his torch in the dirt, and pulled out his knife. He quickly drew the passage the way he remembered it, as an upside down "Y."

Paul then whispered, "The passage on the left intersects the passage to the right of it and doubles back to where we're standing. Both passages go deeper into the mountain at the point where they intersect. I'll follow the trail and you wait here. If the bear doubles back, it will come out the second passage on the left. Be ready to shoot."

Jack gave Paul the thumbs-up, staked his torch in the center of the back chamber, and positioned himself at the entrance to this room. This way he could cover all five passages from one spot. The bear would have to get past him to leave the cave.

Paul returned the thumbs-up and proceeded into the passage on the far left, following the trail until he came to the place where the passages intersected.

As Paul was trying to figure out which way the blood trail went, he turned to see the bear standing on its hind legs right in front of him. He pushed the torch in the direction of the creature's face and dropped down. The bear knocked the torch to the ground and the flame went out. Paul instinctively ducked under the blows of the bear and fired two quick shots, and then backed himself to the wall of the cave. The animal let out a roar.

Severely wounded, the beast turned and limped deeper into the cave.

Paul listened to the receding moaning, pulled out a penlight from his vest pocket, and looked around. He retrieved the torch on the other side of the passage, lit it, and quickly found the bear's trail. The trail led deeper into the cave.

Paul knew Jack would have heard the shots and would be wondering what happened. He retraced his way back to where he had left Jack.

As he approached the chamber where Jack was positioned, Paul called out, "Hey Jack, don't shoot! It's me!"

Paul quickly filled him in. They decided to each take a passage and meet at the intersection in case the bear tried to exit the cave. Each followed a tunnel until they met where Paul had encountered the bear.

Paul said, "Let's do this Army style."

"Right."

Paul let his torch illuminate the next three paces deeper into the cave. Jack covered him as Paul took three quick steps and pushed his back against the right wall of the tunnel. Paul covered Jack as Jack went past him by three steps and pushed his back against the left wall. The two former Army Rangers continued advancing deeper into the tunnel this way until they came to another intersection where the passage divided into two more tunnels. The trail of blood led to the one on the left. Paul started to advance and Jack grabbed his arm.

Jack whispered, "What if this passage connects to the other passage? The bear could double back and get behind us and leave the cave."

"You're right. What do you want to do?"

"One of us better stay here and guard this intersection."

"Okay, you stay and I'll go flush him out. Be careful not to hit the device."

"Right."

Paul continued into the passage following the blood trail.

Jack put his torch in the ground so that it illuminated the intersecting passages, and then positioned himself in the main passage giving him a clear view of both tunnels.

Paul advanced until he came to still another intersection. This time the tunnel divided three ways. He figured there was nothing he could do but follow the bear's trail down the center passage. As he advanced slowly, he picked up the sound of the bear moaning in the distance. The sound grew louder and Paul figured he was getting closer. Then the sound receded, and Paul realized it was moving away. He cautiously quickened his movement in the direction of the sound.

Paul came to a place where the passage curved around and seemed to head back toward the main cave. Then he found a spot where the bear must have been lying. There was more blood. Paul continued to follow the trail until he heard the bear again. He turned a corner and saw it moving away from him. Paul chased after it trying to keep the bear in sight.

He passed an intersection and realized the bear had doubled back and was going in Jack's direction. He hollered, "He's coming your way!"

Jack heard his cry just as the bear came running out of the passage to his left. He was sitting on the ground in the middle of the passage supporting his gun in both hands with his elbows on his knees. The bear came out of the passage and continued running straight for him. Jack shot the bear twice: in the heart and right between the eyes. The forward momentum of the bear carried its body right on top of him.

Paul came out of the passage a moment later and saw the bear lying in the passage on top of him. "Jack! Jack! Are you alive?"

"I think so, but I can't move. Get this thing off me!"

Paul staked his torch in the ground and rolled the bear off of Jack. Covered with blood, he raised one hand and extended something in Paul's direction. Paul moved his torch over so he could see what he was holding.

Jack smiled and said, "Here."

Paul reached out and took the device from his hand.

Ten minutes later, the two men left the cave. As soon as their eyes adjusted to the light, they inspected the device. It was dirty and scratched up, but appeared intact.

Jack said, "Do you think it's okay?"

"It looks okay, but we won't know until we try it."

"How does it work?"

"Well, I'm not Jane Kirkpatrick, but as I understand it, when I push this button, the device gives out a unique frequency that is unlike anything in this time. Our folks back home have a device that is constantly monitoring the frequencies for this time. When they pick up the frequency from this signal, they send the chamber for us."

"Can we go home right now?"

"No. We need to go back to Lookout Point. The chamber will return to those coordinates."

"Let's go!"

The time travelers hiked back up the mountain encouraged by the prospect of going home.

When the two men reached Lookout Point, Paul said, "We need to clean our things out of the cave and pack them up. We can't leave anything of ours in this time, not even junk."

Forty-five minutes later, they stood just outside the cave entrance with all their possessions packed up and ready to go.

Jack took one last look out over the river valley. "What a beautiful view."

Paul responded, "Maybe I can get George Littlefield to bring us here after we get our lives back to normal."

"That would be nice."

Paul then said, "Okay, when the chamber arrives, we only have five minutes to get inside before the door shuts and we leave. There's a seat for each of us. Are you ready?"

"Yeah, push the button."

Paul pushed the button. They waited for something to happen. Five minutes went by and then ten. Jack sat down on the ground and said, "Do you think the device is broken?"

A low hum cut through the air. Jack stood up as the chamber materialized. When the chamber was completely visible, the door opened automatically. The two men scrambled for the open door. Paul stepped in and Jack handed him their belongings before he entered. They buckled themselves into their seats and waited. Two minutes later, the door automatically closed. The chamber hummed and the time travelers were on their way home.

Epilogue

At this point, our story takes us back to July 15th, 2000 on the Indian reservation near the little town of Black River. Ricky Johnson and Tommy Littlefield are fishing along a portion of the Black River where they have never fished before. Ricky hooks into a big fish and is struggling to land it. Tommy puts down his rod and comes over to lend a hand if needed. Ricky wades out into the shallow water, grabs his fish and holds it up for his friend to see.

Later the same day, at the Black River Sheriff's Office, Mary Webber is introduced to Frank McDermott. They take an instant liking to each other. Mary and Frank fall in love and eventually get married. They continue to live in Black River and work for the sheriff's department. From time to time Mary is recruited by a special agency of the government to help out with top secret projects that on occasion require her to do some very unusual traveling.

Mary recommends Harry Packard for a special job in Washington. Harry impresses top officials in the FBI and is given a permanent position that takes full advantage of his drawing skills.

Jack Spencer is happily reunited with his wife and friends. After taking three weeks for a well-deserved vacation, he goes back to his job where he and Paul Andrews prepare for an adventure. They are equipped for a special trip back to the time just preceding the Gulf War.

Several months later, George Littlefield receives a letter from Paul Andrews asking if he and a friend might be allowed to visit the cave at Lookout Point.

ABOUT THE AUTHOR

Richard Tiernan was born in Rochester, N.Y. in 1946. He received a Bachelor degree in Mechanical Engineering in 1969 from the University of Detroit. After working most of his career in the design and development of jet engines, obtaining five U.S. patents, he retired from Engineering in March of 2000, and began a new career by writing his first novel, Bones. In 2011, After 10 years of working with and later leading a local writers group, he republished an improved version of Bones, with the new title, The Dawn of Time Travel so that an improved version would be available as a book or E-Book for future generations.

BIBLIOGRAPHY

Harter, Richard. "The Piltdown Man Home Page." Richard Harter's World web site.<http://www.tiac.net/users/cri/piltdown.html>. 15 May 1999.

John, David. "The Strange Case of the Piltdown Man." Richard Harter's World web site.<http://www.autopen.com/piltdown.shtml>. 15 May 1999.

Lee, Mike. Andy Perdue. "The Latest News: The Story." Kennewick Man Virtual Interpretive Center. Tri-City Herald. 23 October 1998 <http://www.tri-cityherald.com/bones/news/102398.html>. 23 October 1998.

Lee, Mike. "Scientist Make Exciting Finds During Kennewick Man Site Study." Kennewick Man Virtual Interpretive Center. Tri-City Herald. 16 December 1997 <http://www.tri-cityherald.com/bones/news/121697.html>. 23 October 1998.

Lee, Mike. "Kennewick Man Poised for '60 Minutes' Role" Kennewick Man Virtual Interpretive Center. Tri-City Herald. 23 October 1998 <http://www.tri-cityherad...nes/news/102398.html>. 23 October 1998.

Lee, Mike. "Tribes, Asatru Pay Respect to Old Bones Before Move to Seattle Museum." Kennewick Virtual Interpretive Center. Tri-

City Herald. 30 October 1998 <http://www.tir-cityherald.com/bones/news/103098.html>. 15 November 1998.

Perdue, Andy. Mike Lee. "The Story" Kennewick Virtual Interpretive Center Tri-City Herald <http://www.kennewick-man.com> 27 March 2001.

Schafer, David. John Stagg. "Anthropologists Fight to Study Kennewick Bones." Kennewick Man Virtual Interpretive Center. Tri-City Herald. 18 October 1996 <http://www.tricityherad.com/bones/news/1018.html>. 15 December 1997.

Stagg, John. "Skull Found on Shore of Columbia." Kennewick Man Virtual Interpretive Center. Tri-City Herald. 29 July 1996 <http://www.tri-cityherad.com/bones/news/0729.html>. 15 December 1997.

Stagg, John. "Tri-City Skeleton Dated at 9,000 Years Old." Kennewick Man Virtual Interpretive Center. Tri-City Herald. 28 August 1996 <http://www.tri-cityherad.com/bones/news/0828.html>. 15 December 1997.